# THE SECRETS OF A VISCOUNT

LINDA RAE SANDE

The Secrets of a Viscount



V1.7

Cover photograph © PeriodImages.com

Background photograph ©123RF.com

Cover art by Twisted Teacup Publishing.



https://www.lindaraesande.com

ISBN: 978-1-946271-04-4

Library of Congress Control Number: 2017910789

Twisted Teacup Publishing, Cody, Wyoming

PRINTED IN THE UNITED STATES OF AMERICA

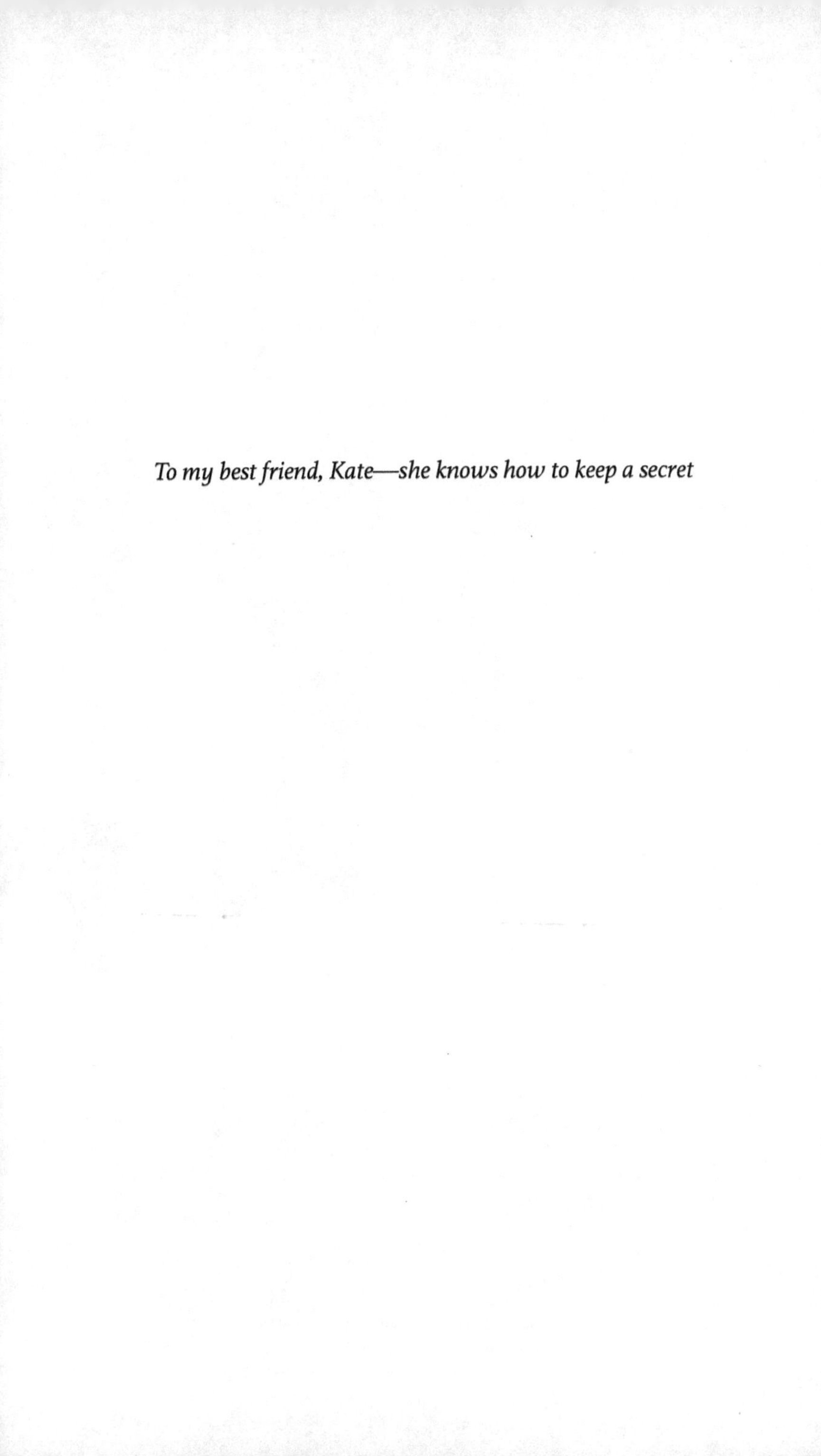

*To my best friend, Kate—she knows how to keep a secret*

# ALSO BY LINDA RAE SANDE

*The Daughters of the Aristocracy*

The Kiss of a Viscount

The Grace of a Duke

The Seduction of an Earl

*The Sons of the Aristocracy*

Tuesday Nights

The Widowed Countess

My Fair Groom

*The Sisters of the Aristocracy*

The Story of a Baron

The Passion of a Marquess

The Desire of a Lady

*The Brothers of the Aristocracy*

The Love of a Rake

The Caress of a Commander

The Epiphany of an Explorer

*The Widows of the Aristocracy*

The Gossip of an Earl

The Enigma of a Widow

The Secrets of a Viscount

*The Widowers of the Aristocracy*

The Dream of a Duchess

The Vision of a Viscountess

The Conundrum of a Clerk

The Charity of a Viscount

# CHAPTER 1
# TALK OF A MARRIAGE IN A
# LIBRARY

*Late May 6, 1818, during Lord Weatherstone's annual ball*

"Good God, man!" David, Marquess of Morganfield, shouted when he discovered he wasn't alone in Lord Weatherstone's library. "You nearly frightened me to death."

He hadn't expected to be alone—he had arranged a liaison with his wife, after all—but he didn't count on finding Godfrey Thorncastle seemingly deep in his cups and ensconced in the middle of the long divan David had planned to use as the basis for his liaison.

The fellow aristocrat acknowledged the marquess' entrance but didn't get to his feet. "I suppose I should have put the 'Occupied' sign out on the door handle," Godfrey replied, his voice devoid of the humor the comment deserved. The library at Weatherstone's mansion in Park Lane may as well have been a brothel seeing as how many couples used it for assignations during the annual early Season ball. One of its frequent occupants had fashioned a rather elaborate shingle and carved the word 'Occupied' into its face. Hung by a drapery rope from the door handle, it prevented couples from inadvertently interrupting others who might already be busy with their dalliances.

"Since you didn't, and since my marchioness is probably still in the retiring room, tell me what has you looking so glum," Morganfield encouraged as he moved to the sideboard and helped himself to the brandy. Lord Weatherstone had his servants restock the stuff several times during the ball, although they had to time their visit to coincide with when a couple took their leave of the room, usually between dance sets.

Godfrey took a breath and let it out. "I have to get married," he claimed.

Morganfield took an experimental sip of his brandy just as the proclamation sounded. Frowning, he regarded the viscount for a moment. "Whom did you ruin?" he asked in shock, for Godfrey Thorncastle wasn't known to have engaged in anything scandalous in his entire life.

The man wasn't a rake. He wasn't a rogue. He probably hadn't even set foot in a brothel in... well, Morganfield wasn't sure when the viscount might have last visited such an establishment since it had been a very long time since he had frequented any of them. He was a happily married man with a marchioness who suited his carnal needs far better than any courtesan or high-flyer could do. Hearing Godfrey Thorncastle *had* to marry was completely unexpected.

"Oh, no one, I assure you," the viscount replied with a quick shake of his head. "But, I have been reminded that it is my duty to sire an heir, and I am on the cusp of yet another birthday. One of those *milestone* birthdays, no less."

Morganfield took another sip of the brandy, deciding it was rather good. He didn't know Godfrey's age, but he figured the man had to be verging on forty. At the moment, given his glum expression and eyes befitting a hound dog, the man could actually pass for fifty. "Have you a candidate for your viscountess?"

Looking as if he were about to cry, Godfrey nodded. "Lady

Burroughs."

Having just taken another sip of his brandy, David nearly choked. "Ariley's daughter?" he clarified. Elise Burroughs hadn't been identified by that name in a very long time. Ever since she had married Viscount Lancaster and, upon the death of his father, become his countess when he inherited an earldom.

And been left a widow upon his death.

*That had to have been at least a year ago*, Morganfield reckoned. *Probably two.* She wasn't exactly a young woman anymore, either. Why, the duke's youngest daughter had to be at least...

"She's two-and-thirty," Godfrey stated, as if he already knew the marquess was doing the arithmetic in his head. "And I dearly love her."

Deciding he didn't want to take another chance at being surprised, Morganfield set his brandy balloon on a side table and took a seat in a large winged-back chair adjacent to the divan. He was remembering more of what he knew of the former Elise Burroughs. The lady was a vivacious creature, ash blonde and blue-eyed and every bit as comely as her older sisters, Jane, Lady Reardon, and the late Lady Margaret.

She looked, in fact, much like her mother, Margaret Merriweather, had looked when she was in her early thirties—probably an easy task given Margaret had given birth to five children by that time and Elise was still childless.

The daughter of the Duke of Whyte, and said to have had a dowry of one-hundred thousand pounds, Margaret enjoyed a steady stream of suitors until Henry, Sixth Duke of Ariley, appeared at her family's country estate in Derbyshire and announced he would be making her his duchess. He didn't even ask permission, but Margaret's brother, John, agreed to the union since the man had his own fortune. As such, John was assured the duke wasn't after his sister for her dowry.

After only fifteen years of marriage, two sons and three

daughters, the Duke of Ariley had died. His eldest son, James, was now the seventh duke. The younger son, Andrew, was a banker and a widower with three children (although given his disappearance earlier that evening with the widow, Jane Fitzpatrick, Morganfield thought perhaps another wedding was in his future). With Margaret having died in childbirth and middle daughter Jane having married nearly twenty years ago, that left Elise as the only currently unmarried Burroughs daughter.

"Does Lady Lancaster know of your... affections?" Morganfield asked, his brows furrowing when he realized Godfrey Thorncastle hadn't yet proposed to Elise. If he had, David was sure it would have been the *on-dit* at that night's ball.

Godfrey allowed a sigh. "She won't agree to a union if she doesn't think I hold her in high esteem," he said at first, but then added, "No. I have written her with my proposal, but I didn't include all that..." He waved a hand in the air. "Flowery language of love."

Morganfield frowned, tempted to ask, *Why not?* "Have you posted said proposal?" he asked instead.

"Aye. Sent it this morning."

Before he asked the next obvious question, Morganfield allowed some time to pass. After he counted to ten with no input from Godfrey, he asked the obvious question. "And did the countess send a response?"

Godfrey allowed a shrug. "Not yet, or if she has, I haven't received it, which is why you find me in this pitiable state this evening." He was about to say more. He was about to lament that he had expected to find the woman at the ball. He had hoped to at least *dance* with the lady. And he was about to confide in the marquess but realized Morganfield might not be the best person in which to tell his deepest, darkest secret.

The rather personal situation in which he managed to find himself despite his age. Despite expectations. Despite his rank as a viscount.

Rolling his eyes, the marquess finished off his brandy. He gave a quick glance in the direction of the fireplace and the clock on the mantel. "Do let me know how it goes, won't you?" he ventured. "If I can be of any assistance, I'll certainly do what I can," he offered just as his marchioness breezed into the library.

"So sorry to keep you and little David..." Adeline, Marchioness of Morganfield, stopped short when she realized there was another man in the library besides her husband. "Oh, hullo, Lord Thorncastle. Keeping my husband company for me, are you?" she asked as she moved to allow the marquess to kiss the back of her hand. Despite having lived in England for more than twenty years, she still spoke with the hint of her native Italian accent.

Godfrey was up and out of the divan in an instant, as if the very presence of the Marchioness of Morganfield was akin to having the queen pay a visit. Her red satin ball gown displayed her rather generous bosom as a pair of rising moons. Godfrey figured the marquess looked forward to the evenings when they were full moons and unencumbered by any satin at all.

It was at that point he realized *he* was the one who shouldn't have been in the library. The Morganfields were no doubt there for an assignation. An opportunity to continue what they had begun behind one of the potted palms in the back of the ballroom. Godfrey realized that if those potted palms could talk, why the gossip would be more than the space available in a weekly edition of *The Tattler!*

"I was, my lady, but now that you are here, I shall say 'good evening' and take my leave." He gave the deepest bow he could safely perform without pitching forward, turned to the marquess and, with a nod, hurried out of the library.

Morganfield turned his attention to his wife, giving her a half-shrug. "Have I told you how positively gorgeous you look this evening?" he asked with an arched brow, openly admiring her red satin gown. And her rising moons. No self-respecting

English lady would wear such a scandalous gown to a ball, which was exactly why Morganfield was so happy to see that she did.

"At least twice this evening, but I don't mind hearing it again," Adeline replied. She turned her attention to the library's only door. "I do hope Thorncastle is well," she commented, noting how the viscount had quietly shut the door behind him. She rather hoped he made sure the 'Occupied' shingle was left hanging from the doorknob. "He seemed out-of-sorts this evening. He didn't even ask me for a dance, which is rather unusual for him when he's in town," she murmured. She turned her attention back to her husband. "I apologize for my tardiness. Lady Lancaster caught me in the hall and asked for a moment of my time."

David had already moved to take her into his arms, though, and her last words were nearly swallowed by his kiss. He pulled away, his head angling to one side. "Is she contemplating Thorncastle's proposal?"

Adeline blinked, rather surprised by the query. "She is contemplating *a* proposal, but she didn't say from whom," she answered, her bright eyes widening with the realization of just *who* had the other woman so discombobulated.

Morganfield thought his wife's expression so beautiful, he kissed her again, rather heartened when Adeline wrapped one arm around his shoulder and speared her fingers into his graying hair. His entire body shivered at the sensation her fingernails created beneath his scalp.

When he finally pulled away, it was to whisper, "He says he has to get married," at the same time he lifted the skirts of her gown to her hips and lowered her to the divan.

"She knows. Which is why she..." The rest of her words were lost to a gasp.

Morganfield rather liked her look of shock when he impaled her. Adored how her eyes darkened as she met his thrusts with her own. Thrilled at how pleasurable their mutual release felt, how exquisite oblivion could be in each other's arms.

But he really loved landing on her full moons the most, her breasts cushioning one of his cheeks as he settled in for a quick nap.

When the last vestiges of her release had passed and the stars had finished dancing before her eyes, Lady Morganfield was left to wonder just why Elise hadn't given Godfrey Thorncastle an answer right away. Didn't the woman miss the pleasures of the marriage bed—and where ever else a couple could manage a quick tumble?

Another thought struck her. Perhaps the widow had already lined up a lover. Perhaps she wasn't missing anything at all.

Or perhaps her late husband had been a poor lover and the poor woman had no idea of what she was missing! The thought had Adeline frowning despite what her husband's tongue was doing to one of her moons, which was no longer eclipsed by the satin of her gown.

"You will share what you know of that particular *on-dit* when you're able, won't you?" she whispered as she again speared her long fingers through her husband's salt-and-pepper hair and scraped her fingers along his scalp. She allowed a mischievous grin when she felt his entire body shiver again.

"Of course, my lady," the marquess replied in a whisper that suggested he might just remain right where he was for the rest of the night. One thing he knew he would be doing was placing a bet in the betting books at White's. Who else would know Thorncastle was getting married? And soon? *Because he had to?*

Adeline Morganfield smiled, rather liking just how agreeable her satiated husband could be. Knowing the latest gossip was power, after all.

That, and being able to render a husband speechless.

## CHAPTER 2
## THE REMINDER OF A PROMISE

*M*eanwhile, in the Weatherstone ballroom

"You look as if you're playing host this evening, rather than Lord Weatherstone," a familiar voice said from behind Felix, Earl of Fennington. The tall man stood with his hands clasped behind his back, his steady gaze on a couple dancing the waltz. Or many couples. The ball was a crush, and the floor was filled with whirling, colorfully gowned women and their partners.

"And you had better greet your mother on this evening or risk my wrath," Fennington replied, turning to find his best friend perusing the ballroom for familiar faces. "Did you just now get back to London?"

Adam Comber, Viscount Breckenridge and heir to the Aimsley earldom, gave a slight shrug. "Oh, I've been in town a week at least, but your sage advice will be heeded at this very ball. I would have paid a call on Aimsley House earlier this week, but I've been told the countess has been engaged in something that required her full attention. Thought I might find her here."

Fennington gave a nod to his left, and Adam's gaze followed until he spotted his mother dancing with... He blinked. "Is she dancing with my *father?*" he asked in surprise.

"Waltzing, yes," the earl replied with a nod. "Something I hoped to see you doing with your betrothed on this fine evening."

The words were said with a hint of disdain, their meaning at first not quite clear to the viscount. The man's words dislodged a memory Adam had tucked away a long time ago, though. The memory of a bet made years ago, at White's, and recorded in the betting book. *Damnation!* "I am not yet thirty, but I take your meaning, Fenn. I will not allow you to lose a sum of money you cannot afford. I promise I will find a suitable young lady and marry her before I turn thirty," Adam said in a solemn voice.

*Dear God!* He hadn't thought of that damned bet in years! Not since Fenn had inherited an earldom beset with almost insurmountable debt. The man's father had gambled away all the unentailed Fennington lands and left markers scattered all over the east end of London. Even as Felix Turnbridge attempted to pay off the debts as best he could, new markers appeared in the hands of burly men who demanded they be paid immediately. Broke and aware his life might be in danger, Fenn had approached Mark Comber, Earl of Aimsley, and requested a loan to cover the remaining markers.

Felix and Adam had been friends since Eton. Given Fenn's ability to keep Adam out of scrapes at school—or help get him *out* of them—Patience Comber, Countess of Aimsley, convinced her husband to provide the funds necessary for Felix to pay off his bills. Little did she know just how the man thought he might reimburse the Aimsley earldom.

For it took a rather unusual gamble to do so, a gamble Felix decided was a sure bet.

And it was.

Felix bought a struggling newspaper business, turned it into the gossip rag, *The Tattler*, and took on the duty of editor—

never letting anyone know he was the one who penned most of the gossip found in the weekly paper. Within three years, Fennington had paid off the Earl of Aimsley and was seeing to improving his earldom. No one knew he was the secret editor of *The Tattler*. Not even Adam.

But the Countess of Aimsley knew. At least, now she knew. And as a condition of his bid to marry Emelia Comber, Adam's younger—and only—sister, Felix had to divest himself of his gossip rag. Patience Comber was about to become the secret editor of *The Tattler*.

Felix decided a bet was a bet, though, and he wasn't about to tell Adam he needn't live up to his end of the bargain. "I think you should know I have decided on whom I wish to marry," he stated in a lowered voice.

Adam's eyes widened. "You? Married?" he whispered, his head leaning in. "Do I know the poor chit?"

Felix cleared his throat and lifted his chin. "Indeed, although it's probably been so long since you've seen her, you will have forgotten her," he stated with an arched brow.

More than a bit stunned, Adam stared at his best friend for several seconds before asking, "She's that young, is she?"

Felix allowed a one-shouldered shrug, managing to hide a wince at his friend's words. It was true Emelia Comber was much younger than him, but he'd known her since she was in leading strings. "She's out of the schoolroom, of course. Looks rather resplendent this evening. Perhaps you won't even recognize her. God knows, I didn't at first, when she attended a garden party with her mother," Felix said, his voice betraying his affection for the young woman.

"Have you sought her father's permission?" Adam asked, still rather surprised by the news—why, his best friend was about to be leg-shackled!

"Of course. Immediately after the garden party, in fact. I was given eight weeks to court her, and although the time has come when I can propose, I find I cannot. I lack the funds, you see. I could use the money from the bet for a wedding trip. You *do* want my bride to be happy, I hope."

The viscount thought to make a joke refuting the earl's claim of his future wife's happiness, but thought better of it. He didn't wish to begrudge his best friend anything.

"I will marry. Soon," Adam replied with a nod. *I have no idea whom I'll marry*, he thought with a hint of panic, his gaze once again taking in the guests at the ball. *But I will.*

"I'm relieved to hear it," Felix replied with a nod. He had to withhold a chuckle when he realized Adam Comber had no idea who he planned to make his bride.

Or that they would soon be brothers.

# CHAPTER 3
# A BROTHER FINDS A SISTER
# IN THE GARDENS

*eanwhile, out in the gardens*
James, Duke of Ariley, strode through the Weatherstone gardens, his manner far too serious for the mood that had settled over the storied surroundings. He had a passing thought as to how many couples might have shared their first kiss beneath the statue of Cupid or behind any one of the hedgerows that were perfectly planted to hide such scandalous acts.

Or there was the fountain, the bottom of which was always scattered with any number of coins. One of his old sovereigns was in there somewhere. The one he had tossed in the day he had proposed to his current wife. His duchess.

Helen Harrington had agreed to marry him in these very gardens, although his proposal had been made under a midday sun in full view of Lord Weatherstone. He had thought to propose in Kew Gardens, but one of the princesses was hosting a party that day, and he preferred a more private place in which to pledge his devotion.

Although James loved Helen, she hadn't been his first love in life. Lily Albright had filled that role. Bore him two daughters and devoted her life to seeing to it that he, a future duke, would one day understand the importance of family despite the need to perform his duty. She had died...

James blinked as tears pricked the corners of his eyes. *Dammit.* He had promised he wouldn't allow the environs of the gardens to bring on the melancholy. He had a wife now. Two small children in addition to the two grown daughters who were making their way in the world without him.

Finding his youngest sister, Elise, brought him back to the matter at hand. She was seated on the stone bench in front of the statue of Cupid, her gaze resting on the marble of the naked boy. Until he cleared his throat, he realized she was unaware of his presence. When she turned to regard him, he took note of how she rolled her eyes and how her shoulders seemed to slump.

*Well, this isn't going to be a pleasant conversation*, he realized.

The prettiest of his three sisters, Elise was also a widow only a year out of mourning. From her reaction to his appearance, he realized she already knew why he had sought her out.

James took a seat on the bench next to her and followed her gaze. Cupid was regarding her with what he thought was a rather impertinent stare. "Did he hit his mark? Or miss it?" the duke asked.

Elise inhaled a breath and seemed to hold it a moment before letting it out in a huff. "Depends, I suppose. He got me good a long time ago. Mortally wounded me. I'm trying to decide if he's going to renew his lease on that arrow or leave me be."

Frowning, James angled himself on the bench and gave his sister a quelling glance. "Do share your preference," he implored.

Tearing her gaze from the marble, Elise gave her brother a wan smile. "I thought I would sit here until I sorted it. Or he did on my behalf."

James blinked. "How long have you been out here?"

Elise shrugged. "What time is it?"

The duke gave a long sigh. "He still loves you, Elise," he said, knowing she had to be considering a marriage proposal. He knew because Godfrey Thorncastle had renewed his request for permission to marry Elise, despite the fact that she was two-and-thirty and could make her own decision on the matter. That she hadn't been allowed to do so eighteen years ago was why she wasn't married to the man right now. Why she was instead the Dowager Countess of Lancaster. *At least I won't be called a dowager countess*, she thought for at least the tenth time. She wasn't the mother to the heir, after all.

"So he says in his letter," she replied with a sigh.

Frowning again, James put his arm around his sister's shoulders and pulled her against his side. "Have your feelings changed? I know you once loved him—"

"So why did you allow Father to force Lancaster on me?" she countered, her sudden anger apparent in the set of her shoulders and the ire in her voice.

James pulled his arm back as if she had burned him. "As I recall, I had little say in the matter," he replied quickly. "And even if I had, circumstances required a... " He stopped when he realized she was staring at him.

"Circumstances?" she repeated.

Rolling his eyes—a trait all the Burroughs children had learned from their mother—James sighed. "Father couldn't afford a dowry for you." When he saw the look of puzzlement slowly develop on her face, he added, "He had just finished paying dowries for Margaret and Jane—far more than he should have, if you ask me. Lancaster wanted a duke's daughter for a wife and agreed to forego a dowry to have you. He had more clout. And Father owed him a gambling debt—"

"This was about... *money?*" Elise replied, her ire increasing with each breath. *I should have run away with Thorncastle*, she thought then, an option she and Godfrey had briefly considered all those years ago. But Godfrey had little in the way of funds back then, his father's viscountcy always on the brink of receivership.

"It's always about money, Elise," James replied in hushed tones, hoping her outburst hadn't been overheard by any of the others who were strolling the gardens. Or hiding behind the hedgerows. "Although... " He allowed the thought to go unspoken. Godfrey Thorncastle had managed to build up a small fortune over the years. And the Ariley dukedom could certainly afford to give Elise her inheritance. His careful management and the employment of a secretary who was actually an accomplished estate manager helped in that regard.

"Although?" Elise prompted.

"It's not anymore. Thorncastle's fortunes have changed. He can afford to take a wife," he explained. "He never did, you know. Stayed in the country except when he had to be in London for Parliament. Has a rather fashionable townhouse here in the city. Doesn't gamble, although he plays a decent hand of whist. There's not been a hint of scandal regarding the man."

Elise listened to the list of the viscount's virtues, still wishing she had known of her father's reason for making her marry Charles Batey in the first place. "I'm well aware of his virtues," she replied with a sigh. Well, at least she had known them all those years ago. She hadn't seen him in the intervening years, at least not up close. Nor had she exchanged any correspondence with him.

"Then consider this. I'll settle your inheritance on you in the morning. You can do with it as you wish. Thorncastle doesn't require it to marry you, so you can hide it or give it to him or—"

"Inheritance?" she interrupted. "Now?"

James sighed. "It's only fair you receive what Lancaster never took," he reasoned.

"Because you feel guilty," she accused.

"Yes," he agreed with a nod, deciding he didn't want to

argue the point. "Besides, I'm already arranging my younger daughter's dowry, so I can see to yours at the same time," he reasoned.

Allowing a wan smile, Elise regarded her brother with an appreciative gaze. "Has Daisy already passed that age?" she asked. Although she probably shouldn't have even known of his illegitimate children, she had been close to his youngest, Diana, for several years. She was Diana's godmother, after all. Too old to have been like a daughter to her, Diana was more like the younger sister Elise never had.

"Well past. And from her comments on the topic of marriage, I rather doubt Daisy will ever wed." He paused a moment. "Diana might, though, although I cannot imagine how she might come to meet an eligible bachelor given she's teaching spoiled rotten girls at a finishing school all day," he complained.

Elise grinned as she considered thoughts of her younger niece. "She's not adverse to the idea of marriage," she offered carefully. "She just doesn't want to marry unless she feels affection for the man."

"Probably because you've made your thoughts on the matter quite clear," James accused lightly.

Giving him a guilty grin, Elise ducked her head a bit. "She has a good head on her shoulders, that one," she said. "She's bright, and smart, and is good with numbers. You and Lily did well with both of them."

James swallowed the sob he felt nearly choke him as tears once again threatened. "I love Helen. I truly do. But there are times I miss Lily so—"

"Of course, you do," Elise said softly. *But not enough to force her to marry you.* But then, marriage to a woman known to have been a courtesan wouldn't have been acceptable. Especially an illegitimate daughter of a baronet. Despite the protection Lily would have had as a duchess, she would have suffered the cut indirect for the rest of her life.

Elise allowed another sigh as her attention returned to the statue of Cupid. "I don't yet know how I'll respond to Godfrey's note," she commented.

Sighing, James leaned forward and allowed his elbows to rest on his knees. "He loves you, Elise. He always has. He needs an heir. You want children... " He allowed the sentence to trail off, as if he had run out of reasons she should marry the only man she had ever loved.

"I thought about going to Italy... "

"You'd hate it. Too hot. Everyone speaks Italian. And those counts are horny bastards," James stated, a lopsided grin giving away his attempt at humor.

"James Burroughs!" Elise admonished, her shock changing to a grin when she saw how a smile split his face.

"I apologize," he replied, his seriousness returning. "Marry him, Elise. Have some babies, and make me an uncle."

"You already are," she countered.

"I'll like your children better than your sisters'," he replied, annoyance evident in his features.

Elise blinked. "So will I," she murmured.

They sat in companionable silence for a few minutes before the beginning strains of a waltz sounded from the ballroom. "I promised my duchess this dance," James said as he suddenly stood up. "Don't stay out here all night, Elise, or there will be a note about you in the next issue of *The Tattler*," he warned. Then he turned and disappeared on the flags leading back to the ballroom.

*The Tattler*, Elise thought with a sigh, not bothering to watch her brother's retreat. What could the gossip rag claim about her other than she had never appeared in the Weatherstone ballroom the entire night?

She may as well have stayed home. But then, if she had, Cupid wouldn't have made the shot that seemed to help make up her mind regarding a certain marriage proposal.

Damn the little cherub.

## CHAPTER 4
## A DAUGHTER
## CONTEMPLATES A DANCE

*A few minutes later, on the mezzanine above the ballroom*

"One, two, three, one, two, three," Diana Albright murmured as she watched the swirling couples on the ballroom floor below where she stood. Three of her students were keeping up with their partners just fine, their steps sure and their posture perfect. The fourth, not so much, but then that particular girl was the youngest of those in attendance. And she suffered from having partnered with a poor lead. Lord Graham's youngest son had been born with little in the way of brains and two left feet.

Diana gave a start when she spotted an older couple join the circle of dancers. *Father*, she realized, her attention going to the man's partner. His countess.

She had never been formally introduced to Helen Harrington, and rather doubted the day would come when she would have that honor. At least her father seemed happy with the woman. The duchess had born him two children in the three years they had been married.

And she was gazing at her husband as if she adored him.

"They're not embarrassing you, I hope."

The voice from her left had Diana stepping away from the

balcony's edge. She turned to find Elise Burroughs regarding her with a grin. "They are not. At least, most of them seem to be doing fine," Diana replied as she moved to give her aunt a kiss on the cheek. She stepped back to regard Elise with wide eyes. "You look... radiant. As if you should be down there dancing, too," she murmured.

"And what of you?" Elise countered.

"I don't have an invitation," Diana whispered. "The butler let me come up here so I could watch my students."

Elise frowned at this bit of information. Her niece was dressed in a coral confection of silk and tulle, the gown far more elegant than most in the ballroom below. "Your gown is gorgeous. No one would know—"

"*I* would know," Diana countered. "And I only wore the gown because..." She paused, chiding herself for the bit of whimsy she had felt at deciding to spy on her charges this night. Lord Weatherstone's balls were always a crush and always the harbinger of how a new Season's pairings might play out with respect to marriages. "I didn't wish to stand out."

Elise arched an elegant eyebrow. "Then you should have worn a grain sack," she countered with a grin. "Someday, Diana, you will be swept off your feet by a handsome gentleman, and you will be forced to realize that you, too, can be like any of these other women," she said with a wave of her hand over the colorful circle of couples below. "You deserve nothing less."

Diana regarded her aunt for a moment, rather wishing her words had merit. "And what about you? Don't *you* deserve a happy marriage?"

Elise inhaled sharply, rather surprised her niece would ask such a question. Especially now. Especially when she was considering marriage. Or remarriage, rather. "Perhaps," she allowed when she noticed how Diana's attention was directed to one of the couples on the floor below. At her hiss and pained facial expression, Elise followed her gaze and allowed a hiss of her own. "Oh, dear," she managed between hisses.

"I'm quite sure it's Mr. Graham and not Lady Theodora who is to blame," Diana whispered. "She performs flawlessly during dance class at Warwick's," she added when she noted how Elise gave her a quelling glance. "She has a voucher from one of the patronesses at Almack's."

Not bothering to mention that a voucher wasn't necessarily a ticket of ability to waltz, Elise merely grinned.

"Who were you off to see?" Diana asked, realizing her aunt hadn't expected to find her at the ball.

Elise gave a shrug. "I thought to locate Lady Morganfield somewhere up here," she admitted. "I find talking with her rather refreshing. She tends to have a different perspective on matters." The daughters of the *ton* hadn't exactly welcomed the Italian daughter of a count when David, Marquess of Morganfield, had returned from his Grand Tour with the woman on his arm. She could barely speak English. But after a few years, she proved adept at gossip and at entertaining, her experience as a daughter of European aristocracy her secret weapon in the parlors in Mayfair. She was also adept at listening and providing advice when asked to do so.

"I saw her head toward the library only a moment ago," Diana said as she turned in that direction. There, in a bright red satin gown, the marchioness was just leaving the company of another woman to make her way farther down the hall.

Elise followed her niece's gaze and gasped. "Forgive me," she managed as she took her leave and hurried off to join Lady Morganfield.

"Of course," Diana managed, despite her aunt's hasty departure.

Hoping her aunt would find the answers she sought from the marchioness, Diana returned her attention to the couples below and breathed a sigh of relief when the strains of the waltz came to a blessed end for her youngest student. At least the poor girl could still walk. God knew how many times Lord Graham's son had trod upon her silk dance slippers.

Deciding she wouldn't stay to watch anymore of the dancing, Diana took her leave of Weatherstone's mansion, hailed a hackney, and made her way back to Warwick's Grammar and Finishing School.

She had classes to teach the next day.

# CHAPTER 5
# AN UNMARRIED WOMAN
# CONTEMPLATES CUPID

*L*ater *that night*

The youngest sister of the current Duke of Ariley watched in the looking glass as her maid took the pins from her elaborate coiffure and combed out sections of her honey blonde hair. She winced when she caught sight of an errant gray hair at her temple. *What a waste of a perfectly good styling*, Elise thought, now regretting her decision to avoid making an appearance in the ballroom of Lord Weatherstone's mansion.

At least she had made it to the gardens by way of a side gate, deciding since her driver had gone to the trouble of getting her town coach through the crush of traffic in Park Lane, she could at least pay a visit to the grounds. Better to simply spend some time amongst the early spring foliage and statuary before the couples made their way from the French doors for their assignations in the gardens.

She had stared at the statue of Cupid—uninterrupted— for nearly an hour, trying to decide if she should curse the cur or kiss him on his chubby cheeks—the round ones just above his chubby thighs.

She rather doubted she could reach the others.

In the end, she had done neither, her reverie interrupted by her oldest brother's appearance. At least he had known of her quandary, although she didn't know how much help his words provided. His promise of her inheritance was a surprise, though she didn't want it to color her decision to marry or not.

When James had taken his leave of her, she was left to once again contemplate the chubby cheeked marble. At least until she was once again interrupted by a giggling chit straight out of the schoolroom. That particular girl was led by some young buck intent on teaching her how to kiss. Elise had managed to make it into the house by way of another back door.

Finding first her niece and then Lady Morganfield had been a pair of pleasant surprises. She could chide her niece on her lack of a husband and then turn around and hope for an excuse to avoid taking another for herself. The few minutes she had of the countess' attention afforded her the opportunity to put voice to her concern without mentioning exactly who had her so concerned.

*If I loved a man a long time ago, and he still wants to marry me, should I? Marry him, that is?*

The marchioness had angled her head to one side and allowed a brilliant smile. *Why, of course,* she replied as she leaned in. *Love is enduring. And it can help keep you young even after the blush of youth has faded.*

Faith! Had the blush of youth taken its leave of her already? Or was Lady Morganfield referring to the future?

"You're awfully quiet this evening, my lady," her lady's maid, Merry, commented. "Did something happen at the ball?"

The younger woman regarded her own image for another moment before returning her attention to the maid's reflection. "I wouldn't know. I never actually made it *into* Lord Weather-stone's ballroom."

Merry stopped combing and stared at her mistress in the

mirror, her eyes widening as she did so. "Were you accosted by footpads?" she asked in alarm. Despite nothing nefarious ever having happened to either her or Elise, Merry seemed to think the worst was about to happen whenever one of them went out.

"Worse," Elise commented with an elegantly arched eyebrow. "Cupid shot me."

*Again.*

Or could it really be considered a second shot if the effects of the first had never actually worn off?

It had been so long, she realized the poor boy had probably forgotten he had already struck her, straight in the heart, back when she was only thirteen.

Damn the archer. Damn him and his chubby cheeks.

The object of her not-so-sudden affection had put voice to a similar claim about her at the time. He had kissed her. She had kissed him. Promises had been made. And then the realities of life in the aristocracy had intervened—or death, rather—and their worlds had been turned topsy-turvy.

Merry stared at Elise for several seconds, her attention fixed on her mistress' reflection until she shook herself out of her apparent shock. "But, you're an independent woman, my lady," she said in a hoarse whisper, the words 'independent woman' said as if they were some sort of armor that would prevent such an attack by the archer. "I thought Cupid knew enough to stay away from the likes of you."

Elise couldn't help the giggle that bubbled up despite the sense of despair she had felt since her time in Lord Weatherstone's gardens. "I, too, thought I was immune to those pesky arrows. Seems time and..." *Him.* "Well, let's just say I have given the thought of having children another think through, and I certainly can't be having any of them unless I marry..." *Him.* "So, I suppose I shall have to accept an offer of marriage on the morrow."

Blinking rapidly, the maid moved to the side of the dressing table so she could regard Lady Lancaster directly. "Where is my mistress? What have you done with her?"

A tear escaped the corner of one of Elise's eyes before she allowed a shrug and a watery grin. "She's grown old and feels rather alone." She squeezed her eyes shut. After such a disastrous marriage, widowhood promised respite. Independence. A happy life. But after a year of mourning and nearly another of the independence so many widows welcomed, life was anything but happy.

Something was missing.

"Perhaps it's time I marry again. Have a child or two. Become a mistress of a mansion in town and an estate in the country. Be in charge of a phalanx of servants and host a ball every year." *Mother had five children by the time she was my age,* she didn't bother to add.

Merry waved a hand in front of Elise's face. "I'll ask you one more time, my lady. What have you done with my mistress?"

Elise allowed a look of contrition before she gave a shrug. "Surprise!" she said with a noticeable lack of enthusiasm.

Truth be told, the trappings of an aristocrat's life had never appealed to her. She had grown up in such homes, one in London and one in Derbyshire. Oh, and the one in Brighton, even if the family was only there for one month every summer.

She had watched her older brother, James, and two sisters marry into exceptional families. Although Margaret had died giving birth to her son, her husband had hired an experienced nurse and to this day remained a widower. Her younger brother, Andrew, was following in his uncle's steps as a banker at the Bank of England. Even though he claimed he would never marry, he had done so at a young age and then been left widowed when his wife, Bess, died in 1807.

As for how she felt about her siblings, Elise had cried for three days when Margaret had died giving birth to her second baby and laughed for nearly as long when James, a supposedly confirmed bachelor who knew damned well he was going to have to marry and sire an heir, did just that in the course of nine months after falling heels over head in love with Helen Harrington.

A younger sister of the Earl of Mayfield, Helen was proving to be the perfect duchess. Her firstborn, a son, was now the heir-apparent to the Ariley dukedom. The second, a girl, had her father happily wrapped about her pinky.

Elise hoped the boy wouldn't still be drooling when he inherited. Drooling and saying, "No!" to everything he was told to do.

*It's the only word he seems to know,* her sister-in-law claimed one afternoon whilst they had tea in her parlor. Having met the nursemaid, Elise could certainly understand why. The woman said the word at least a thousand times a day!

*I shall never employ such a strict nurse,* Elise thought. *If I were to be blessed with a boy, I would allow him some latitude at such a young age. Then, when he was older, I would start to say "no."*

She blinked. She had never given thought to such an edict before!

*A boy!*

"I should have been sent to a convent," Elise claimed before blinking away the odd thought and shaking her head.

*Now where the devil had that idea come from?*

From the expression on her maid's face, Merry apparently agreed.

"I'm not that bad," Elise countered, her chin coming up in an effort to examine her neck in the looking glass.

"I cannot believe you are considering matrimony again when you aren't even being courted," Merry said, moving to continue the ritual of removing all the pins from Elise's hair before braiding it for bed.

Elise gave her maid a quelling glance in the mirror. "Why, I'll have you know, I *was* courted by this rather handsome gentleman," she said with a firm nod. When Merry stopped braiding her hair to stare at her in the mirror, Elise sighed. "A long time ago, of course, before I married Lancaster. But... true love is... timeless, it seems." What else could explain why she had received an offer of marriage after...

*Faith!* Had it really been nearly twenty years?

Despite her maid's look of disbelief, or maybe because of it, Elise sighed and angled her head, braiding be damned. "He sent me a letter this morning. A rather sweet note, actually. Asking for my hand. I plan to pay a visit to render my answer in person in the morning," she said, her manner meant to prevent Merry from rendering any protests. "I'll wear my royal blue carriage gown and pelisse, and you shall do my hair in the same style you did for tonight's ball," she ordered, almost tempted to have her maid redo it right that very moment so she could pay a call on the man tonight and give him her answer in person.

Before she could change her mind.

Before he could change his.

Although, if his words were to be believed, he had held a candle for her ever since their first—and only—kiss. She supposed it was rather unlikely he would change his mind now.

A quick glance at the mantel clock had her changing her mind just as quickly—it was nearly two o'clock in the morning. *How long was I sitting in Lord Weatherstone's garden?*

Had she actually entered Lord Weatherstone's ballroom that evening, she could have danced with the man. He would have been there, she was sure, which was why she had instead spent the evening in the gardens. Unseen but surrounded by the amorous activities of at least a dozen couples over the course of a few hours, she had enjoyed two glasses of champagne—a footman had the good sense to make the rounds with a tray of flutes filled with bubbly—whilst she pondered her future as a remarried woman.

Apparently her maid was doing the same pondering, given the expression on her face.

"Oh, really, Merry. You needn't think the worst," Elise said with a wan smile. "It will just be another adventure for us."

Merry allowed a nod, realizing there was nothing she could say to change her mistress' mind.

Apparently, Lady Lancaster was getting married again.

To whom, Merry had no idea.

# CHAPTER 6
# ABOUT A BOW WINDOW

*May 7, 1818 in St. James Street*

The moment she realized she was walking in St. James Street, Miss Diana Albright wondered if she could turn back. Wondered if she could simply stop, turn around, and begin walking in the opposite direction. For in her few moments of introspection, or what most would refer to as daydreaming, she had made the turn onto St. James Street, completely unaware she had done so.

She wanted to go in the direction the street would take her, of course. She just didn't want to pass by the window.

The bow window.

The one that had been added onto the front of the building that housed one of London's most notorious men's clubs.

White's.

As much as she supposed the men therein didn't know their secret was out, it was. Even her students at Warwick's Grammar and Finishing School knew what went on in the bow window at White's. Apparently, before his departure to the Continent the year before, Beau Brummel occupied the table in front of the window, his status as a socially influential gentleman his ticket to watch the world go by.

Or rather, the women of London. The women of the world.

The ones that dared walk down St. James Street did so either because they didn't know any better or because they did and were curious as to how they would be rated by him—or those in his company who watched.

Diana knew there was some discussion as to what constituted a rating of a 'one' versus a 'ten'. Were 'ones' given to those young ladies deemed most beautiful? Or were those 'tens'? For unless one knew which was considered the better end of the rating spectrum, only the women deemed a 'five' knew exactly where they stood in the rankings.

That is, if they actually overheard the numbers being called out by the young bucks who ruled the roost of the bow window.

She rather imagined there were times when no one was in the window, or when older gentlemen managed to claim the seats closest to the window simply because whoever was deemed most socially influential wasn't present in the club at the time. Certainly an older gentleman would be more discreet if he bothered with the practice at all.

Given it was entirely too late to simply turn around and walk the other direction, Diana held up her head and continued her walk toward Jermyn Street. If her hips swayed any more than usual, she wasn't conscious of it. If a slight smile played at her lips, it was only because her daydreams were rather pleasant. Anything was better than thinking about the never-ending days spent attempting to teach spoiled rotten girls basic arithmetic and dancing.

Well, the dancing she didn't mind so much—at least the young ladies *wanted* to learn to dance. That was part of their ticket to an advantageous marriage, after all.

The fact that Diana wasn't married and probably never would be was the only reason she was teaching arithmetic and dancing at Warwick's Grammar and Finishing School.

When the hairs on the back of her neck suddenly tickled,

Diana nearly paused in mid-step. Something skittered down her spine, and she was quite sure it wasn't an insect.

And then she did pause. Her head turned at an angle and her attention immediately went to the bow window.

A man was watching her. A rather handsome man, in fact, was openly gazing at her. He didn't even try to hide the fact, nor look away when he realized he'd been caught staring at her.

Diana was suddenly conscious of every piece of clothing she wore. A peach muslin gown, sprigged with tiny embroidered flowers over which she wore a darker peach spencer. Not a fan of poke bonnets—she was quite sure a gust of wind would send an especially light young lady sailing away down the streets of London—she preferred hats with silk flowers. Not the large, overpowering silk flowers which festooned some lady's hats, but rather small, delicate flowers that merely lined the edges of where a brim met its crown. And none that featured feathers. Goodness! Some of those hats sported ostrich plumes that nearly grazed a ceiling and required their wearer to duck down when passing through a doorway.

The one she wore today was a rather simple hat, peach with darker peach and green flowers. A shade of peach that showed off her charcoal black hair to its best advantage. Her half-boots were well-hidden beneath her skirts, a reticule that matched her hat hung from one wrist, and white kid leather gloves hugged her fingers almost too tightly.

*I'm at least a five*, she found herself hoping as she stared at the gentleman. And then, quite before she realized what she was doing, she approached the front door of White's and rang the bell. Reason arrived far too late to have her stepping away. Stepping away and running down the street in an effort to escape before anyone could answer the door, for an older, liveried man did indeed open the black-painted door. He regarded her with a set of gray eyebrows that were rather high on his forehead and combed into elaborately shaped fans.

"My lady?" he ventured, as if he were seeing a woman for

the very first time in his entire life. Well, he probably was seeing a woman at this particular door for the very first time, Diana realized. White's was a men's club, after all. Women were not allowed.

Diana bobbed a curtsy, the action so automatic she didn't realize she needn't have done so given a servant answered the door. "Could you please provide me the name of the distinguished-looking gentleman who is currently presiding in the bow window?"

The butler's eyebrows seemed to go even higher and fan out wider, if that were possible. "I... cannot," he replied carefully. He seemed to reconsider his answer and then said, "One moment," as he held up an index finger. The door closed, and Diana was left on the stoop feeling ever so much a fool.

*What the hell am I doing?* she wondered, not bothering to chide herself over the curse she used in the process. Why, if the daughters of the *ton* she was responsible to teach five days a week had any idea of her inner thoughts just then, they would certainly swoon from shock.

She was about to step away, turn around, and begin running toward Jermyn Street when the black door suddenly reopened. The same butler, his voice kept low, said, "I'm to tell you to wait one moment as the gentleman retrieves his coat and hat."

Diana's eyes widened. "But," she started to protest, realizing just then it was entirely too late to make her escape. If the man was retrieving his coat and hat, then what did he intend to do? Before she could even consider the possibilities, he was standing in front of her.

If she thought him handsome through the bow window, she didn't know what word to use to describe him without a pane of glass and the reflections of the buildings lining St. James Street in front of him. He wore his nearly black hair cut quite short, a hint of gray highlighting his temples. His sapphire eyes were lined with black lashes and tiny crinkles, a testament to a life filled with amusement and perhaps a bit too much drink. The straight nose suggested he had never been punched at Gentleman Jackson's boxing saloon. His square jaw held a mouth with lips she could imagine saying any number of words and doing rather wicked things to a woman's lips.

And other body parts.

A frisson shot through her and nearly had her allowing an audible gasp. Instead, she managed a curtsy.

Realizing she was staring, she blinked. Before she could get a word out, though—she thought to simply apologize and claim she thought him to be someone else—the man said, "Oh, my sweeting, I apologize profusely. Do forgive me. I completely lost track of the time." He turned and gave the butler a quick nod before placing his top hat upon his head.

He offered her his left arm, and Diana placed her right hand on it without even thinking—it's what she taught her students to do, after all—and shook her head. "Uh... nonsense, darling. I just thought I had misunderstood the plans," she managed before she heard the door click shut behind them. *Faith!* He obviously had her confused with someone else! She was quite sure she had never seen the man before in her entire life, and yet he was acting as if they were married!

The man led her in the same direction she'd been walking before she became aware of his perusal. His attention occasionally darted her way before he returned it to the pavement. They were nearly to Jermyn Street when they both attempted to speak at the same time.

"I apologize, sir, I merely—"

"Thank you for saving me..."

The two stopped and blinked at one another. The gentleman allowed a slight grin. "You go first, my lady," he said, the crinkles on either sides of his eyes deepening with amusement.

Diana regarded him a moment and wondered how she would explain herself. Honesty, although not always the best policy, seemed so in this case. Especially since she truly wished to know. However, she was curious as to what he meant when he claimed she had saved him. "However did I save you?" she countered.

The gentleman took a look around, as if he realized they were relatively alone on the corner. "Where is your lady's maid?" he asked. "Or your companion?" he added after another quick glance behind them.

Diana swallowed, a hint of color touching her cheeks. "I... I didn't bring her along today," she answered, her chin lifting a bit. "I am quite capable of looking after myself."

"And who provides protection for you?" he countered, deciding he had better discover her marital status before continuing his flirtation.

Inhaling as if she were about to answer but not about to admit *exactly* who held that responsibility, Diana was relieved when another gentleman called out, "Good morning." The man before her redirected his attention briefly, and lifted a hand to wave to Lord Weatherstone as the older gentleman made his way in the direction of the men's club. "So sorry I couldn't stay long at your ball. Congratulations on the usual crush," he called out.

Lord Weatherstone tipped his hat and gave him a shrug before continuing on his way.

When the viscount returned his attention to her, he asked, "Now, where were we?"

Not about to say who provided protection on her behalf, Diana decided to go with her original question. "I merely wondered, sir, when I saw you in the bow window, what your... that is to say... the number... of how you found me? In appearance?"

The gentleman regarded her for a moment, the expression on his face turning to one of bewilderment. "I'm quite sure I don't know what you mean," he replied. "The number?"

Her shoulders slumping with his words, Diana could feel a

blush coloring her face. "I thought... I was under the impression that those who stood in the bow window did so because they liked to watch... and rank women as they walked by," she managed to get out. Only after she'd said the words did she realize just how ridiculous the whole idea sounded. Why, didn't the men at White's have better entertainments available to them than watching women walk by? She was quite sure they played cards and placed bets. Smoked cheroots and drank scotch. Read *The Times* or *The Morning Chronicle*.

*Perhaps watching women walk by really was more entertaining,* she realized.

His brows furrowing, the gentleman seemed to deflate before her very eyes. "Is that why you walked by White's today?" he asked, disappointment evident in his voice.

"Oh, no!" Diana replied quickly, her head shaking from side to side. "In fact, I was about to turn around and go back in the other direction the very moment I realized I was in St. James Street. I make it a point never to walk in front of White's and Brooks' for that very reason, I assure you," she claimed.

The words seemed to appease the gentleman somewhat. "And this... *number* you referred to?"

Diana sighed, the blush still pinking up her face to match the gown and spencer she wore. "I saw you watching me, and I decided I wished to know what you thought."

His brows furrowing so a fold of skin formed between them, the man responded with, "Truly?"

She gasped at his response, her anticipation gone. "Well, I did at that moment," she admitted sheepishly. "It's silly, I suppose, but I figured, what do I have to lose?" *Besides my self-respect.*

The gentleman sighed. "I find I must ask from whence you learned of such a practice?"

The young woman gave a slight shrug. "From an article in *The Tattler*, I suppose it was," she said before allowing a sigh of frustration. When she realized to what she had admitted, she rolled her eyes. "I rarely read the rag, but sometimes my students leave a copy behind—"

"You're a teacher?" he interrupted, this time only one brow furrowing as if he were disappointed at hearing she had an occupation.

Well, far better than being a seamstress, or a milliner, or a governess, or... well, she couldn't put thought to that *other* occupation in which nearly ten percent of her sex had to engage.

Diana swallowed, realizing the man might have thought her a lady. Her manner of speech would suggest so, as would her clothes. "I am an instructor. At Warwick's Grammar and Finishing School," she admitted.

"You probably knew my new sister, then," he murmured, the comment made in almost a whisper, his eyes darting off to the side as if he were considering options.

"Your sister?" Diana repeated, hoping he might divulge her name. He certainly hadn't divulged his. In fact, they hadn't yet been properly introduced!

The man shook his head. "Just acquired, actually."

Diana blinked, rather surprised by his terminology. How did one simply *acquire* a sister? Certainly his mother was too old to give birth to one—the man had to be around thirty years of age!

"My brother recently took a wife," he went on, his hint of a grin betraying his awareness of how she was attempting to reconcile his comment and probably doing the arithmetic in her head. "Lady Julia. The Earl of Mayfield's daughter."

Suppressing her gasp of surprise at learning the man on whose arm she rested her hand was the brother of Alistair Comber, Diana stopped in her tracks. "You're Adam Comber," she stated in awe.

And since she had no idea of what Adam Comber, Viscount Breckinridge, had just promised to do whilst at White's only moments ago, she was completely unprepared for what he did next. In fact, she was left quite speechless as his lips descended onto hers—they were still quite open with her expression of awe—and kissed her at the corner of St. James and Jermyn Streets. Never mind that there were all manner of witnesses to his scandalous act. Never mind that several even paused in mid-step to gawk at them. The man simply kissed her as if it were his right to do so.

When he finally pulled away and straightened, Diana was forced to open her eyes and stare up at him. Aware they were being watched, she was about to admonish him. She was even considering raising a hand to slap the man across the face. But he glanced around, a huge grin on his face, and announced, "She said 'yes'!"

Those that paid them any mind either grinned and went on their way or broke out into cheers and applause.

Diana did neither, for if there was ever a time she thought it appropriate for a young lady to faint, she realized this might be the perfect moment. And she might have done so, except the viscount returned his attention to her and gave her a huge smile as one of his arms moved to her back to offer the support he probably realized she required just then.

"I do think you'll make the perfect viscountess."

At which point, the heavens seemed to open up, and rain began to fall.

# CHAPTER 7
# A DESPERATE MAN'S REASONING

*O*ne hour earlier

Adam Comber, Viscount Breckinridge, regarded his friend for a moment, trying to decide if he should punch the man in his aristocratic nose, or burst into laughter. Felix Turnbridge, now the Earl of Fennington, had been his best friend at Eton and, later, at Oxford University. He had managed to extract Adam from a number of scrapes—a daunting task in that Adam seemed to get into trouble all the time—and he had done so without so much as a pence in recompense. Adam just knew his mother, Patience, Countess of Aimsley, thought of Fenn as her eldest son's savior and was always thanking him for his selfless acts on his behalf. So he couldn't quite believe what the man had just said.

"What the hell did you just say?"

It wasn't the first time he had cursed at the man. Wouldn't be the last, he knew. Although Felix had managed to get him out of all manner of scrapes back when they were in school, he had sometimes helped Adam get into them. Felix was the more responsible one, though, and, given his father's age back then, Felix knew he would be inheriting an earldom devoid of funds and a future of hardship. Even though he could carouse with the best of them, Felix was usually far more serious than his schoolmates. When he made a joke or found humor in a situation, it was rare. Adam knew all of this, so he knew the comment Felix had just put voice to hadn't been made in jest.

"I said I rather doubt there is a gently bred woman in this town who will deign to marry you," the earl repeated, tossing a card onto the green felt. "One, please."

The dealer set a card in front of him as all the eyes at the table turned to regard the viscount. Then they exchanged curious glances with one another. Either this was a ploy to distract them from what could be a winning hand in the hands of Adam Comber, Viscount Breckinridge, or the two former best friends were about to come to blows.

Adam couldn't help the sudden anger he felt just then. Ever since their days at Oxford, Felix had become even more sober, if that were possible. More serious. Perhaps the strain of trying to prop up a financially destitute earldom had him lashing out. Or perhaps Felix was looking to start trouble, a rather unlikely scenario. He was usually the one to help rein it in. He had been the one who was left to clean up after Adam back in the day. "Why, in the name of everything that is holy, would you make such an asinine comment? And *now* of all times?" Adam countered. His eyes suddenly widened. His mouth followed suit. He gasped in shock. "It's because *you're* getting married!" he accused, a grin replacing his grim expression.

Despite having told Adam just the night before that he would be marrying, Felix's eyes rounded. Did Adam know Felix had asked his father's permission to marry his sister, Emelia? Mark, Earl of Aimsley, apparently hadn't even told his wife, for the gossip in Mayfair parlors certainly didn't suggest a proposal was forthcoming. Perhaps in a week, if he could manage it. "I want to," he agreed. "But you, more than anyone, know I cannot truly afford a wife," Felix claimed.

The words were a bald-faced lie, but he wanted Adam to believe them as much as possible. Between his burgeoning business—he was the publisher of a gossip rag that was doing quite well financially—and his decision to marry the man's younger sister, Emelia—Felix didn't want to lose track of what might cause him additional financial hardship.

Gambling did that.

Bad bets.

Losing bets.

Even if they were supposed to be sure things.

Felix allowed a sigh as he rearranged his cards. "I'll open," he added as he tossed a coin into the kitty.

The other players took their turns before Adam could form a response. He did so after he placed a coin onto the modest pile of bets. "I am not yet thirty. I'm in no hurry to be leg-shackled."

"Which means I stand to lose a good deal of money I cannot afford to lose," Felix reminded him, his voice kept so low the other two card players couldn't hear him. They exchanged glances, indicating their uncertainty as to whether or not the conversation was supposed to distract them from the card game.

"Jesus," Adam whispered to no one in particular. His best friend really did expect him to get married. And right away!

"I'll call," he said aloud. He placed his cards on the table, sure they were good enough to win what little there was to win. He ignored the curses of the other players, and then joined them when Felix slowly fanned out his cards to reveal he had beaten all of them that round with a straight.

"Christ! You're hiding cards up those ruffled and lace-edged sleeves of yours," Adam accused with a bit too much annoyance.

"You, more than anyone, know I do not *cheat*," Felix countered, his glare a warning sign.

Adam swallowed. "I apologize. I was just... I was sure I had that hand," he replied as he pushed himself away from the table. It's not as if he couldn't afford to lose a hand or two of cards—he had a rather generous allowance, and apparently Felix could use the money more than him—but Adam found he no longer wished to play. The earl's comment had him rather bothered.

Rather incensed.

Feeling rather... challenged.

Not quite thirty meant he was almost thirty. At one time, way back when, he had expected to be married by thirty. He had even allowed his best friend to make a bet of it. Well, time had caught up to him. "Excuse me, gentleman. I do believe a look at the betting books is called for," he said by way of apology. With that, the viscount took his leave of the card room.

But Adam didn't make his way to where the bets were recorded for any member of White's to review. Instead he made his way to the bow window, deciding a rare bit of sunshine was in order just then.

Until last night's ball, he had completely forgotten about the bet he had agreed to all those years ago. A bet designed to make it possible for Felix to win some much-needed blunt while ensuring the future Earl of Aimsley was married and settled with his future countess by the time he had been on the earth thirty years.

Trouble was, there was no future countess.

There wasn't even a candidate for the position.

And his thirty year mark on the planet was fast approaching.

Adam hadn't courted a woman his entire time as a viscount. He hadn't even *looked* at a woman with the thought she might one day be his wife.

It's not that he was particularly adverse to the idea of marrying—he always knew he would one day have to marry—duty required it. His mother and father had a rather congenial marriage, although he was quite sure it was because the Countess of Aimsley had her husband wrapped about her petite pinky. A rather powerful pinky, it seemed, since Mark,

Earl of Aimsley, seemed to do whatever he must to see to it Patience Waterford Aimsley was happy. But then, she seemed rather willing to put up with a man who was usually rather grumpy. Sour-faced and insolent. A complainer. A man who was never satisfied with what happened in Parliament.

That is, until his mother had worked her wiles on the man and left him in a rather good mood, if only for a day or two.

Adam frowned, wondering if his parents were happy with one another because they were happy in bed together. He quickly shook the thought from his mind, unwilling to even imagine his mother sharing a bed with his father. His entire body seemed to give an involuntary shudder at the thought.

He concentrated on the problem at hand. A new crop of debutantes was being introduced at this Season's balls, but the idea of marriage to someone almost half his age held little appeal.

Adam gave his head a shake. *No appeal*, he amended.

But whom did he know that might make a suitable wife? Someone he could at least get along with until such time as they might grow to love one another? Until such time as she had him wrapped about her proverbial pinky?

Thoughts of every sister of every peer in the realm he personally knew flashed before his eyes.

Good God!

*They're all married!* he realized.

Well, not *all*, of course.

Some were merely betrothed. Or about to be betrothed. There were obvious matches, of course, and he dared not seek a young lady when he knew she was destined to be claimed by someone else.

As for the ones he didn't know personally...

He shook his head. The very last thing he wanted to do was buy a subscription to the Wednesday night dances at Almack's. The thought of the tepid lemonade and lobster cakes had him as disgusted as the thought of having to deal with the mothers of the available chits in attendance.

He could accept an invitation or two for the soirées and balls this Season. Why, his sister-in-law's mother, the Countess of Mayfield, always hosted a crush for her ball.

Then there was last night's ball at the Weatherstone mansion. As famous for its fabulous lobster cakes as for its always-flowing champagne, it was best known for what happened in the gardens behind the ballroom. Rather wishing he'd taken advantage of the last opportunity he'd had to impress the statue of Cupid in those particular gardens, Adam sighed. Perhaps the archer might have shot him—and the young woman he was kissing at the time. She was married now, though, and living in the country. Last he'd heard, she had three children and another was on the way.

Faith! Eight years had gone by since university! He almost banged his head against one of the glass panes that made up the bow window of White's, a move he thought might put him out of his misery by putting him out for a time, but a vision in peach had him suddenly straightening.

A young lady walked as if she owned St. James Street and every building on it. Her steps had her hips swaying gently from side to side, her reticule following suit from her wrist. Her almost-black hair, simply coiffed but elegant, was apparent because she didn't wear a ridiculous bonnet favored by so many of the young women. Instead, she sported a rather tasteful hat. And not one of those hats that featured plumage too tall for doorways. No, this woman's hat was adorned with small flowers.

No sooner had he taken note of the flowers when he was taking note of her large eyes. And doing so because she was suddenly staring at him.

He didn't look away. He couldn't. She had him mesmerized. Her heart-shaped face looked as if it were made of porcelain with just the slightest hint of pink atop her high cheekbones.

Her lips formed a perfect rosebud, plump and ripe and a shade of pink that somehow managed not to clash with the colors of her gown and spencer.

The woman obviously wasn't fresh from the schoolroom. Not with the pleasing figure promised by the gown and spencer she wore, and certainly not given how she held her head and shoulders. The way his mother did. As if she ruled the country rather than Prinny. *Mother would probably do a better job of it,* he thought just before he decided the young woman must be in her mid-twenties.

But her most beautiful features were her eyes.

Why, she had the largest eyes! Doe eyes, although hers weren't brown, but an arresting shade of blue-gray, and they were topped by dark eyebrows that gave her an air of elegance one found in only the purest of English misses.

*I should know her*, Adam thought. *But I don't.*

She held herself as if to the manor born. She appeared a bit older than a typical unmarried daughter of an aristocrat, but she certainly wasn't a spinster. She certainly wasn't on the shelf.

*Who the hell is she?* he wondered as he stared at her.

Adam had half a mind to fetch his hat and coat and go after her. And he almost did except she stopped in her tracks, gave him another glance that included a slight arch to one of those gorgeous eyebrows, and made her way up the walkway to the front door of the club.

*What the hell?*

Adam blinked, and he had to quell the urge to rap his knuckles on the window to regain her attention.

Women weren't allowed at White's!

*What is she doing?*

Panic gripped him just then. This was his chance, though. Perhaps he could meet her at the front door. Save her from certain embarrassment when she realized what she was doing —or worse, should the snob of a butler be the one to inform her of just where she was. He could feign being an acquaintance. Escort her to wherever she was going.

Marry her.

Explain himself later.

For Viscount Breckinridge's best friend was due to lose a lot of money if Adam wasn't married soon.

Very soon.

# CHAPTER 8
# AN ANSWER TO A PROPOSAL

*An hour later*

An unmarried woman never paid a call on a man at his residence, unless of course she was his sister or his daughter. Or his mother, perhaps, but whoever heard of a bachelor informing his mother as to his whereabouts?

So it was with a bit of trepidation that Elise, Dowager Countess Lancaster, approached the townhouse of one Godfrey Thorncastle, Viscount Thorncastle, on the gloomy morning following Lord Weatherstone's ball, rain threatening at any moment. She supposed her royal blue umbrella would shield her from the curious eyes of those who might have noticed her as she made her way up to the front door. In the dim light, her royal blue carriage gown and pelisse probably looked black.

Perhaps mourning clothes were more appropriate for just such an occasion.

Elise sighed. What had such a sense of melancholy settling over her? It wasn't as if Godfrey Thorncastle was a poor choice for a husband. If she'd known back then what she knew now, she might have refused to marry Charles Batey. Proposed to Godfrey and suggested they head to Scotland for a quick wedding. Her father would have disowned her, of course.

Refused to pay her dowry. Made it difficult for Godfrey—politically as well as socially. Why, he probably would have blackballed his membership application to White's!

But then she could have avoided the disastrous marriage in which she had played the suffering wife to an impossible beast for sixteen years.

Elise shook her head as if to clear the 'what-ifs' from her thoughts. She needed to look to the future. *Their* future. Just because they hadn't ended up married as Godfrey claimed he wished them to be way back when didn't mean they couldn't start now.

As long as he agreed to her conditions.

She dared another quick glance down Bruton Street, rather impressed with the townhouses lining the lane. No one could deduce her identity from the equipage in which she arrived. Her town coach was unmarked, but only because Tilbury had just finished building the glossy black coach with royal blue squabs the month before. The gold crest of the Duke of Ariley would eventually be painted onto the doors. Since the Lancaster coach was now in the possession of her brother-in-law, the current Viscount Lancaster, her brother, James, insisted she have at least that much protection. Elise wasn't always in the company of a footman or a companion, after all, one of the benefits of being an independent woman.

Perhaps a different crest might be painted on the doors. She was pondering how the Thorncastle crest might appear in bright gold paint when she reached the house.

The front door opened before she could lift the brass lion-head knocker, a stout butler giving her a quick bow before stepping aside. In true staid form for his profession, he allowed no hint of surprise or recognition at her appearance.

"Good morning, Nigel. Is Lord Thorncastle in residence?" she asked as she collapsed the umbrella and stepped into the vestibule. Her white pasteboard calling card was out of her pocket and into the butler's hand before he could answer her query.

Nigel, rather surprised the woman knew his name when he couldn't immediately place her identity, was quick to take the umbrella and drop it into a nearby urn. Without giving the pasteboard a glance, the butler took it and said, "I'll be but a moment. Would you prefer to wait in the parlor, my lady?"

Elise didn't bother to hide her surprise at hearing the bachelor house possessed a parlor. "That won't be necessary."

"As you wish, my lady." The butler turned and made his way into the grand hall but only managed to make it halfway to the study before Godfrey Thorncastle stepped out of it, his attention directed to the vestibule.

To her.

Elise inhaled and held her breath. She hadn't seen Godfrey Thorncastle in an age, but the years had not been unkind to him. He looked exactly like his father had looked just before he died, his light brown hair ruffled a bit, his hazel eyes suggesting mischief, the line of his jaw matching that of nearly every aristocrat in the *ton*. *Common ancestors*, she thought before allowing a brilliant smile.

But then her attention was forced to his mouth, to lips that had once smiled easily and that had kissed with a tenderness that made her weep.

She let out the breath she'd been holding, realizing from his expression that he at least recognized her.

What if time hadn't been as kind to her as it had been to him?

Bobbing a quick curtsy before stutter stepping in his direction—Elise wasn't sure if she should make her way to him, or if he would close the short distance between them—she was suddenly in front of him, staring up at him. She couldn't help it if her hand went up to the side of his clean-shaven face, if the tips of her gloved fingers pulled it down so their lips met, couldn't help that her lips met his for a brief kiss of greeting.

When she pulled away, it was because she wasn't sure how much longer she could stand up on her tip-toes. She was afraid she might pitch forward and end up pressed against him, and, oh, dear, the butler was right there staring at them, his staid professionalism taking its leave of him for a moment before he blinked and resumed his normal air of boredom.

"I do believe that's where we left off when last we were in each other's company," she said brightly—and with enough volume for the butler to overhear.

Stunned at what had just happened—no woman had ever simply walked up to him and planted a kiss on his lips— Godfrey was left speechless.

Even his mother hadn't done such a thing.

Thank the gods.

But Godfrey certainly wasn't about to complain.

He stared at the vision before him. Dressed in a royal blue carriage gown with a matching petite feathered hat, Elise looked as if she could have been part of Queen Caroline's contingent. Her ash blonde hair, caught up in a series of perfectly placed curls, was piled atop her head. Age had not only been kind, but had left a quiet confidence and an elegance few other ladies of the *ton* possessed. A complexion he thought of as peaches and cream set off her blue eyes and pink lips. *Make that red lips*, he thought with a hint of satisfaction, realizing they were red because of his kiss.

Or rather, her kiss.

It had been far too long since their first kiss. The thought reminded him that it was his turn to speak.

"You received my letter," he stated, immediately regretting the comment. Of course she had received his letter. She wouldn't have come to his residence out of the blue—wearing royal blue—for any other reason, especially on a gloomy, rainy day such as this.

"I did, indeed," Elise replied, giving a sideways nod toward what she realized was his study. "Perhaps we can discuss it over a cup of tea?" she hinted, well aware the butler finally had his eyes back in his head.

"Yes. Yes, of course," Godfrey replied, tearing his gaze from Elise to give a wave in the direction of Nigel.

The butler gave a nod in return and hurried off while Godfrey offered his arm to Elise. "I was hoping you might attend Weatherstone's ball last night," he murmured. He led her to a divan at one end of his small but elegant study, managing to avoid a wince at thinking of the last divan he had sat in. Last night, at Lord Weatherstone's ball. The Morganfields had probably defiled said divan shortly after he took his leave of them, although perhaps it had already suffered a similar fate before he had even taken refuge in the room.

The rich leather covering of this divan, butter soft and smelling of tobacco and spirits, was surprisingly firm as Elise settled onto it. Godfrey waited a moment before taking the wingback chair across from her. Covered in a matching leather, it looked from the worn armrests as if he favored it over any of the other chairs in the small room.

Elise dared a glance at the coffered ceiling and at the phalanx of bookshelves that lined the wall behind his oak desk. Nearly every shelf was stuffed with books. "I did, in fact, although I never actually made it into the ballroom," Elise admitted when her attention returned to the viscount. "Rather, I sat in the gardens for a time," she added as she folded her hands in her lap. Her eyes were drawn down to where a tasteful patterned Turkish carpet seemed to flow over the entire floor. The dark green suited the room, setting off the furnishings to good effect.

Godfrey's eyes widened at this bit of news before he frowned. "A dalliance?" he whispered. The two words managed to sound almost strangled as he said them.

Her words obviously had him thinking the worst.

Elise showed a frown to match his. "Of course not. I merely wished to spend some time thinking, and I knew I wouldn't be able to do so inside the ballroom. The Weatherstone ball is always such a crush," she complained.

Relief at hearing she hadn't been in the company of another man must have showed on his face, for Elise angled her head to one side. "Just because I've been on my own for the past year does not mean I engage in *dalliances*," she added. There was no need to admit she hadn't had a single lover since Lancaster's death. What would Thorncastle think of her then?

Godfrey sighed. "It's heartening to hear you say it, especially after the *affaire* with Lord Reading. I take it that arrangement is... over?"

Elise blinked. And blinked again as she straightened on the divan. "I am quite sure I don't know what you're talking about," she countered. "I most certainly have never had an *affaire* with the Marquess of Reading, if that's what you're implying."

His mouth closing, partly because he had intended to state that the *affaire* didn't matter and partly because he was left speechless by her claim, Godfrey instead cleared his throat. "Oh," he finally managed.

Still stunned by his comment and not the least bit happy with his brief response, Elise huffed. "From whomever did you get the idea I had an *affaire* with the Rake of Reading?" she asked in a hoarse whisper.

Godfrey allowed a sigh. "Not a 'who,' but rather a 'what', I suppose," he replied finally. "I admit to occasionally reading *The Tattler*. I saw an entry last Season that mentioned a 'Lady E' and Reading were seen in each other's company at a number of events. I, of course, assumed 'Lady E' was you."

Elise continued to frown, the expression causing a fold of skin to develop between her eyebrows. "Godfrey, do you have any idea how many 'Lady E's' there are in the *ton*?" she asked, angling her head to one side. Besides, she was a 'Lady L'. She hadn't been a 'Lady E' in eighteen years!

The marquess considered the question for a moment. "Well, there was Lady Elizabeth, but she's Lady Bostwick now.

And Lady Eleanor, Middleton's daughter." He paused to think a bit. The sound of a *huff* had him sitting back in the chair.

"Eloisa, Edna, Eugenia, Edith, and any number of Elizabeths, and those are just the ones I can think of off the top of my head," Elise stated, her manner rather indignant. "And since you seemed to have forgotten, *I* would be referred to by *The Tattler* as 'Lady L'."

Godfrey's eyes widened more with each lady's name, apparently a testament to his ignorance of their existence. "I apologize, my lady," Godfrey replied with a sigh. "It's just, I thought the worst because, well, I was rather envious of the marquess," he managed to get out, his words sounding ever so unsure.

"Envious?" Elise repeated.

Godfrey seemed to color up a bit. "He's my age and rather popular with the ladies," he added with a shrug.

Elise settled back into the divan just as Nigel appeared on the threshold with a tea tray. She wondered if he had been just outside the door, listening to their conversation until he thought it was safe to enter.

The butler set the tray on the low table in front of the divan. When he moved to pour the tea, Elise leaned forward. "I can serve," she said as she took the handle of the teapot before Nigel could reach it.

The butler allowed a nod. "Of course, my lady." Apparently disappointed he wouldn't be able to remain in the study for what he probably thought would be interesting nuggets of information, he gave a bow and took his leave of the study.

"Do shut the door, Nigel," Godfrey called out, apparently of the same opinion as Elise as to the butler's desire to eavesdrop.

The snick of the latch had Godfrey allowing a sigh. "Now, where were we?" he asked as he turned his attention back to Elise.

"I remember you seemed to favor milk in your tea," she said as she poured a dollop into a cup and then filled it with tea.

"One lump or two?" she asked as she held the cup and saucer in one hand and the sugar tongs in another.

Godfrey swallowed, noting how she had removed her gloves to pour the tea. A vision of Elise offering the same thing every day for the rest of his life passed before his eyes.

Except she wouldn't, of course.

Once she knew his preference, she would simply add the sugar and give him the cup of tea. "I think just one this time," he finally answered.

Elise lifted an elegant eyebrow but plopped a rather large lump of sugar into his tea and stirred it before offering him the cup. "I wished to speak with you in regard to the letter you sent me," she said as she turned to prepare her own tea.

The marquess held the teacup to his lips and held his breath. "And?" he prompted.

"I have questions. And some conditions."

Godfrey continued holding his breath. "I shall do my best to answer them."

Elise didn't respond right away but rather sipped her tea. Then she finally allowed a nod. "Why now, Godfrey? Why not... why not eighteen... nineteen years ago?" *Before Lancaster made his bid and convinced my brother it was a good idea for us to marry?* She didn't put voice to the latter, but she was tempted to do so. Despite her brother's explanation the night before, she wanted to hear Godfrey's side of it.

Angling his head to one side, Godfrey considered the question. He had expected Elise would wonder at his motives, wonder why he would propose to her and not someone else. He didn't expect her to wonder at his *timing*. "I am six-and-thirty. Like Reading, I know I must marry soon. I need an heir," he replied, the words tumbling out. "As for nineteen years ago..." Here he paused and set down his tea cup. "I wasn't of a mind to marry. I had just started at university. And then, after a time, I was led to believe you and Grandby were..." He swallowed. "Were... well, *exclusive* with one another," he stammered, realizing far too late he probably shouldn't have brought up the Earl of Torrington.

Elise blinked, setting down her tea cup as she leaned forward. "Grandby?" she repeated in disbelief. "Are you referring to Lord *Torrington?*" The alarm in her voice was unmistakable. Everyone in the *ton* knew the earl had spent his unmarried years in the company of a string of widows, choosing a different one every Season until he ended up proposing to Adele Slater Worthington. The sister of the Marquess of Devonville and the wealthy widow of a man who helped design the early steamships, Adele was rather surprised when Milton, Earl of Torrington, proposed at the end of the Season of 1815. They were married shortly thereafter, and Adele gave birth to twins in September of the following year.

"Are you implying I had an *affaire* with the Earl of Torrington?" Elise asked in a hoarse whisper. About to stand up, her question was clearly a warning as to how Godfrey Thorncastle should answer the question.

Unfortunately, he didn't heed the unspoken warning.

"There is no need to deny it. I hold nothing against you for seeking a possible life with the Earl of..."

He really should have heeded the unspoken warning. He really should have understood from his original mistaken impression that mentions of 'Lady E' in *The Tattler* never referred to Lady Elise. But, alas, Godfrey Thorncastle didn't understand just how offended Lady Lancaster, daughter of a duke and sister of a duke and widow of an earl, could become. Nor did he have particularly fast reflexes, for before he could even finish his comment about the Earl of Torrington, Elise was off the divan. Her right hand, bare of a glove and no longer holding her teacup, flew through the air and soundly slapped Godfrey Thorncastle hard across the face.

For a moment, the viscount was left staring at the bookshelves of his study, wondering why there were white stars dancing in front of his books.

Or were they in front of his eyes?

In another moment, his head recoiled back to where he should have been able to look upon Lady Elise's beautiful visage. However, only the rich, dark leather of the divan came into view once he was finally able to focus. Elise was already halfway to the door, her strides as long as her gown and pelisse would allow.

"Thank you for the tea, my lord," she said before taking her leave of the study. She had to redirect her exit, however, when she nearly collided with the butler—the man was very nearly leaning against the door! "I can see myself out," she stated in a tone that suggested the man would find himself without a position should she ever be mistress of this particular house.

With that, Lady Lancaster took her leave of Viscount Thorncastle's townhouse and marched to her unmarked town coach.

Her driver, Sims, was quick to dismount the box and rushed to open the door for her.

"Home, Mr. Sims," she said as brightly as she could muster at that moment. Once inside, she settled herself into the squabs and allowed a long sigh. Before Sims had the coach moving, though, tears pricked the corners of her eyes and were falling quite freely before the coach had even reached Curzon Street. Once it had, however, Elise realized she needed a shoulder on which to cry. Lifting her arm, she rapped her knuckles on the door in the ceiling of the coach.

The driver opened the door and glanced down. "My lady?"

"I've changed my mind, Mr. Sims. Take me to Worthington House," she called up.

"Right away, my lady," the driver acknowledged.

If anyone could provide a shoulder on which to cry, Adele, Countess of Torrington, could. And would.

## CHAPTER 9
## THE AFTERMATH OF AN ANNOUNCEMENT

*M*eanwhile, back in Jermyn Street

Adam stared at the woman who stood before him, rather liking how she gazed up at him just then. As if she were hanging on his every word. As if she truly wished to hear what he had to say. As if she was expecting him to...

*Kiss her.*

The thought, more of a command than a simple desire, had him blinking at the same time he realized he was going to do just that.

So he did.

The only way out of what had turned into a public spectacle—*from where had all these people come?*—was to make everyone believe he had proposed marriage.

That didn't mean he actually had to ask for her hand, of course.

"But... but you don't even know my *name*," Diana managed to get out as Viscount Breckinridge offered his arm again. "You know nothing about me," she added as she shook her head. She wasn't about to add that she knew nothing about him. At least, nothing other than that he was Adam Comber, Viscount Breckinridge, and heir to the Aimsley earldom. She supposed that was quite enough. Quite enough to realize she had made a terrible mistake in wondering how she ranked in the eyes of the handsome man. "Truly. I apologize for having bothered you. I didn't intend for you to have to—"

"Oh, please don't," Adam said as he placed his free hand over the one that was practically gripping the top of his arm. He watched as Diana's eyes widened, sure she was about to put voice to a protest of some sort, and he nearly lost himself in their depths. "You appeared at the perfect moment. As if I conjured you out of thin air," he countered.

Faith! The man looked as if he actually believed what he was saying! "You did no such thing," Diana answered. "I was simply on my way to Jermyn Street." *Damnation*, but the man was handsome! Did he have any idea of just how he made her knees as weak as if she had drunk two glasses of champagne?

But, of course not. *I've never drunk two glasses of champagne in my entire life!*

"Miller's Hotel?" he guessed before he frowned and realized she would probably have no reason to go to that establishment. Unless she was from out of town.

Those lovely large eyes widened again. "Of course not!" she countered. She wasn't about to admit she was off to Carter's to buy a pair of shoes and then to Floris to buy a new comb. She was tempted to mention Floris just to see how he would react. Why, he probably didn't think a finishing school teacher would use a perfume. Not that she did, but she could.

"My tailor has his shop there," Adam said absently. His face screwed up a moment before he added, "In fact, so does my shirt maker. And my cordwainer, and my boot maker." He rolled his eyes and allowed an audible groan. "Oh, dear."

"What is it?" Diana asked in alarm.

"You're already married. You're off to fetch your husband's new clothes. Or shoes, or boots at Hoby's," he guessed. "Please, tell me I'm wrong," he pleaded.

Diana blinked. Well, this was easy. "You're wrong," she

assured him. "I am not married," she added, although she realized too late she could have claimed she was and then she'd be rid of him.

Not that she really *wanted* to be rid of him, but this was becoming quite a spectacle. And she certainly couldn't afford the scandal. Why, she was an instructor at a finishing school. The very last thing the headmistress would abide was a hint of impropriety associated with one of her teachers. Mrs. Streater, the ancient woman who had hired Diana three years ago, was quite clear in that regard.

His look of relief was stunning to behold. Diana was quite sure she'd never seen a man look so... beholden. So bewitched. It would be very easy to simply allow him his fantasy. What was so wrong with agreeing to be the man's wife? Except, he probably wasn't really after a wife so much as a tumble.

Which had her thoughts reeling in an entirely different direction.

Did he do this often? Accost young ladies in front of White's and propose marriage to them so that he might whisk them off to his bachelor's quarters in Bruton Street or Green Street or Golden Square and have his way with them?

She cursed the frisson that shot through her body just then.

"Have a care, my lord," she warned in a quiet voice. "Ruining young ladies may not cost you more than a six-pence, but their lives as young ladies are forever forfeit."

Adam blinked, rather startled by the instructor's words. "I assure you, my lady, I have *never* ruined a young lady," he claimed. He frowned, although his expression quickly changed to that of a wounded man. "That you would think that of me..." He shook his head. "I find myself rather offended just now." Truth be told, he felt hurt more than anything else. He had thought his days as a troublemaker long past, and such comments merely reminded him his reputation would precede him wherever he went until he had the means to change it.

And change it, he would, especially if he could marry the

woman. Why, he would show the *ton* he was a responsible man. A viscount worthy of his father's earldom. A model aristocrat. He had already accepted the writ of acceleration, offered at a time when it was determined Parliament was made up of too many older representatives and needed a bit of new blood. His fascination with politics and a willingness to discuss issues whilst at White's had helped secure the offer. As a result, he was a Member of Parliament as a viscount instead of merely a viscount in name only. He had already attended the few spring sessions that had been held, finding he rather enjoyed the process of making laws, of negotiating to win over those who hadn't yet decided how to vote.

Now he merely needed the wife to go with his new standing. What better wife to have than one who taught young ladies of the *ton?* Why, she already knew all the rules. Knew how to speak and dance. How to dress and wear her hair. How to behave.

"You kissed me in broad daylight. In front of all those people. And only a hundred feet from your men's club," she countered as one of her dainty gloved fingers pointed down the street toward the white edifice. Her ire was evident. "What, pray tell, am I supposed to think?"

The question was familiar to him, if only because his mother had asked it of him on more than one occasion. Dammit, but if this woman wasn't perfect for him. This was his chance. *Make it right*, he thought. "That I wish to marry you. That I *will* marry you," he answered simply.

Diana blinked. Then she looked down at the pavement below before raising her eyes to meet his. "Forgive me if I seem incredulous. It's merely because... I am," she said in a calmer voice.

"Allow me to escort you to wherever you wish to go," he stated.

Leery, Diana finally allowed a nod. "Carter's then. And after that, Floris."

Adam gave her a nod and a rather appreciative glance as he considered her destinations, rather surprised she didn't mention a modiste. "A pair of shoes and a fragrance, then?" he half-asked as he led them down Jermyn Street. "No... clothes? Gowns? Naughty night rails?" This last was said with eyebrows that waggled in a tease that had Diana giving him a quelling glance.

"A pair of shoes and a comb, actually," she corrected him, managing to suppress a sigh at the mention of the latter.

"You'll have to let me know if you like the scent they created for me," Adam said as they strolled.

Diana dared a glance up at the man. "Are you wearing it now?" she asked.

"I am. A bit of lavender mixed with citrus, but then I suppose I shouldn't have—"

"It's rather pleasant. So much better than the Bay Rum so many men of your persuasion prefer," she replied curtly, not about to add that her father always smelled of Bay Rum.

Adam blinked. "Most of my associates actually prefer amber with a hint of citrus, or leather, or sandalwood," he argued.

"Sandalwood is nice, but not on just any of your sex," she countered. "And amber is rather... common." This last was said as they entered Carter's. The smell of leather assaulted her nostrils as they made their way to the counter, which had her giving Adam a quick shake of her head. "I cannot imagine a gentleman wanting to smell like this all day long."

Adam took an experimental sniff and found he couldn't have agreed more.

A portly man with just a hint of hair combed over his scalp regarded her from over the tops of his spectacles. "I'll just be a moment," he said with a nod before turning his attention to the viscount. "Lord Breckinridge," he added with a half bow before he disappeared behind a curtain.

Rather surprised the man recognized his female customer

—not to mention him—Adam was about to ask just how many pairs of shoes Diana had purchased at this particular establishment when the man reappeared with what was obviously a pair of dance slippers. Although they lacked the usual ornamentation of those worn at balls, they were elegant in their simplicity.

"Would you like to try them on?" the proprietor asked, his face once again lowered so he could peer at her from over the tops of his eye glasses.

"Oh, that won't be necessary," Diana replied with a shake of her head. If she hadn't been in the company of the viscount, she most certainly would have tried them on. She wasn't about to remove her half-boots and have the man gazing at her stocking-clad ankles and feet as she tried on the dance slippers, though. Why the thought of the viscount doing so sent a shiver of excitement up her spine, she had no idea.

Diana lifted her reticule to the counter so she could dig for some coins. Adam was quicker, though, a crown appearing on the counter. He heard Diana's gasp, but ignored how she stared up at him. "Do keep the change, my good man," he stated.

"Much obliged, my lord," the shoemaker replied with a nod, his eyes widening when he realized the denomination of the coin. He hurried to place the shoes into a colorful pasteboard box, the name of the shop printed on the sides. "Will there be anything else, my lady?" His manner was more solicitous, as if he realized there might be more in it for him if he saw to her happiness.

Embarrassed and well aware of just how this purchase would appear to the shoemaker, Diana shook her head. "No, thank you." She was about to retrieve the box from the counter, but Adam beat her to it and then held out his arm for her. She managed to keep her thoughts to herself, but only until they were outside of the shop.

"Whatever do you think you're doing?" she asked in dismay, adding a, "Milord," when she realized she hadn't said it.

Adam allowed a shrug. "Buying my intended a pair of dance slippers. A rather... elegant pair of slippers, I might add," he said as one of his eyebrows waggled. "I do hope you'll be wearing them when next we dance together. Which means you'll probably need a ball gown. Do you have a ball gown?"

Shaking her head in disbelief, Diana was about to admonish him, but he already had them approaching the door to a shop of ready-made clothing. "I don't need a ball gown," she said, attempting to redirect him to the next shop. "I do own one," she claimed, not bothering to add that she had just worn it the night before. Given the comment he had made to Lord Weatherstone only moments ago, it was possible he could have seen her in it at some point during the evening.

"Of course you don't need a ball gown, my lady, but I think I should like to learn what pleases you," Adam said as he opened the door for her. "When it comes to color and style and fabrics and such," he added with a wink.

A wink!

Rolling her eyes, Diana entered the small shop, her gaze immediately going to a night rail draped over two shelves dressed to look like a bed with pillows. Although the neckline was rather chaste, the rows and rows of delicate lace repeated on the bodice hinted at something promising beneath. The same pattern of lace edged the long, full sleeves, and several rows decorated the bottom flounce.

Adam watched Diana as she gazed at the night rail, the edge of one lip turning up when he decided what he would do next. When Diana turned her attention to other racks of gowns, he waved a hand in the direction of the shopkeeper and pointed to the night rail. The woman gave a nod of acknowledgement and made her way to the garment, carefully removing it from the display when Diana's attention was on a rack of day gowns. She returned to the counter and began folding the garment, wrapping it in tissue and placing it into a pasteboard box.

"I should think you would look stunning in this," Adam suggested as he pulled a royal blue ball gown from a different rack as a means of distraction from what the shopkeeper was doing.

Diana looked over from the simple round gown she held and gave him a quelling glance. "I should think any woman would look stunning in such a gown," she agreed. She put away the gown she had been studying and moved on to a rack of carriage gowns. While she was occupied, Adam placed a coin on the counter, gave the shopkeeper a nod, and tucked the box under his arm alongside the shoebox.

"Is there anything you'd like to try on, my lady," the shopkeeper asked as she moved to join Diana.

Looking as if she'd been caught with her hand in the biscuit jar, Diana took a step back from the carriage gowns and shook her head. "Thank you, but no."

"Oh, come now, my sweeting," Adam said from where he stood regarding her. "Not even a ball gown for Lord Huntington's affair?"

Diana's eyes widened—and not just from his endearment. An invitation to Lord Huntington's annual ball was rather hard to come by, at least according to her father. "Have we received an invitation?" she countered, not feigning her surprise.

Adam blinked, remembering he didn't have such a document. At least, not yet. "I expect one will arrive in the next week or so."

Realizing she had a good excuse for denying him the pleasure of buying her a ball gown, Diana angled her head and said, "Then you may buy me one when we receive the invitation," she said brightly.

Giving the shopkeeper an apologetic shrug, Adam escorted Diana out of the modiste's shop and directly into the store next door—Floris. The bow window on this particular establishment not only displayed a colorful array of bottles of various fragrances, but also a collection of hair combs. Diana's gaze darted to several before they were suddenly inside the pleasantly scented shop. She inhaled, almost closing her eyes as she did so. *Fresh citrus*, she thought as she allowed the barest hint of a grin. "Exquisite," she whispered, not intending for anyone to hear her.

Regarding her expression from where he stood next to her, and hearing her whispered word, Adam felt a stirring in his loins. *God, but she is beautiful.* She looked as if she was in ecstasy, and he wondered if she might display that same expression when he made love to her. That same expression when she was on the verge of ultimate pleasure, brought there by his lips and tongue and manhood as he made mad, passionate love to her. On their wedding night, of course, because he already knew she wouldn't be allowing him access to what had to be a delectable body and those succulent lips anytime before that night.

They could be wed on the morrow, though. All he needed was a special license. He could acquire one in Doctors' Commons... he dared a glance at his Breguet, rather startled to find it was nearly two o'clock in the afternoon.

Dammit!

He rather doubted they could make it there before the Archbishop of Canterbury's office closed for the day.

Well, the day after tomorrow, then. He could wait until then, he supposed. Christ! He'd been waiting his entire life for this woman, and he hadn't even realized it!

"What's wrong?"

The query had him shaking his head when he realized his future wife was staring up at him with those gorgeous blue-gray eyes. "We probably cannot marry until the day after tomorrow," he replied in a quiet voice. "I'm so very sorry."

Blinking at his statement, and then blinking again at his apology, Diana shook her head. "You bounder," she whispered, her lips curling into a grin.

"I am not," he countered, just as a salesperson approached them.

"Are you in the market for a new scent?" the tall man asked as he regarded the pair. "Or something else, perhaps?" The shopkeeper closed his eyes as he surreptitiously sniffed the air around them. "Ah, Lord Breckinridge," he said with a nod to Adam. "So good of you to pay a visit this afternoon." He directed his nose to the air around Diana, and when he didn't seem to find what he was looking for in the air, he simply opened his eyes and regarded Adam with a look of expectation.

The viscount nodded before indicating Diana. "My lady wishes to peruse your combs. As you can see, her hair is of the utmost quality. Only the best will do."

Diana had to suppress the urge to giggle at hearing her escort's comment. *He is such a bounder!* Why, he knew nothing about her hair, although the thought of his fingers removing the pins that kept her chignon in place had her body shivering just then.

"Right this way," the clerk replied as he led them to a glass case filled with a variety of combs and hairbrushes.

Suppressing the urge to simply boggle at the variety, Diana took a deep breath and instead scanned the collection, one comb at a time. She pointed to one featuring a long, tapered handle and tines that ended in sharp points. The thought of that particular comb drawn over her scalp had a frisson shooting through her entire body. The viscount must have seen it—or perhaps felt it—for he pointed to the comb and said, "We'll take that one."

Diana stared up at him. "How did you know?" she whispered in awe.

Adam gave a one-shouldered shrug. "My lady, if we were ever to play cards, I should want to have your hand on my arm, for I would know exactly when to place a bet to my advantage," he replied with an arched brow.

*Damnation! Am I really that obvious?* Diana wondered as the clerk removed the comb from the case and wrapped it in tissue.

"Will there be anything else, my lady?"

"Yes. A toothbrush," she stated in a voice barely above a whisper, rather embarrassed at having to place the order in front of the viscount.

"One for me, as well," Adam stated. "And a bottle of my regular cologne if you would." He gave the clerk a quick shake of his head, indicating he wished to speak with the man away from where Diana stood.

"Very well, my lord," the clerk stated with a nod, moving away from the display case to join the viscount at a different counter while Diana continued to peruse the wares in another case.

"Include the matching hairbrush in its own box," Adam ordered, "Along with whatever that scent is that greeted us when we stepped into your shop."

The shopkeeper angled his head a moment. "That would be Limes Eau de Toilette," he murmured. "Best worn during the summer months," he added with an arched brow.

Adam frowned but decided summer was only a month away. "A bottle of it in its own bag," he whispered urgently.

"Right away, my lord," the man replied, apparently understanding the need for speed and for discretion. He hurried off to fill the orders.

Diana dared a glance in the direction of where the shopkeeper was speaking with Viscount Breckinridge. She supposed she shouldn't have been too surprised this man recognized the viscount, although she would have guessed him to be a customer at D.R. Harris & Co. His cologne reminded her of one she had smelled on a footman at her bank. She only knew its name because the man had divulged it when she sniffed the air around him and complimented him on his scent.

When the shopkeeper stepped away from Adam, she

moved to join the viscount. "How long have you been a customer here?" Diana asked as she placed a hand on his arm.

Adam considered the question for a moment before finally saying, "Eighteen years, my lady."

The number of years would have had her gasping, but it was the 'my lady' that had her jerking her attention to him. "It's really not appropriate for you to address me as such," she whispered.

"We'll be married in two day's time, so... so you really should allow me to do so," he argued.

"Two days?" she countered, surprised he was continuing his charade.

"I know, I feel *awful* about it, but given the time on the clock..." He paused to give a nod to the ornate gilt clock on one of the display cabinets. "It's too late for me to make it to Doctors' Commons today, which means I cannot procure a special license until tomorrow. I don't believe we can actually marry until the day after that," he explained with a sigh. "Please forgive me." Although he apologized for the very same reason only moments ago, Diana's reaction had been a bit unexpected. To accuse him of being a bounder had him feeling offended, but he had to give her some leeway.

She had only just met him!

Diana had to suppress the urge to laugh out loud. Why, the man still didn't know her name, and yet he was claiming he was going to marry her in two days? "No apology is necessary, I assure you, my lord," she replied, fighting with all her might to keep an impassive expression on her face. She placed her reticule on the countertop and went about capturing some coins to pay for her order.

"What are you doing?"

She finished counting before turning her attention back to him. "Paying for my order, of course," she replied.

"Put that away," he said as his gloved hand wiped the coins

to the edge of the counter. "It's on my account," he whispered, his words most urgent, as if he were embarrassed by her action.

Diana's eyes widened. "I cannot allow you to..." She was forced to hold back the rest of her response when the clerk reappeared at the end of the counter. She surreptitiously covered the coins with a gloved hand and shoved them back into her reticule.

Apparently appeased by both her action and the assurance he needn't have apologized, Adam asked, "Is there anywhere else you'd like to go on this fine day, my sweeting?"

Feeling as amused as she did embarrassed by the viscount's attentions—spending a few minutes in the company of an aristocrat was turning into an unexpected pleasure—Diana lifted a shoulder. "Why, Gunter's, of course," she replied in a teasing voice, not the least bit serious.

"What a capital idea!" Adam replied, ignoring her sudden look of shock. "Although I left my horse back at White's, I can certainly acquire the services of a hackney," he reasoned, making a move to head for the door.

Giving her head a quick shake—was nothing beyond the ability of this man and his rank?—Diana said, "I was teasing, my lord."

Adam sobered. "But I was not," he replied. "I do believe I could do with a bergamot pear ice right about now."

The clerk must have overheard him, for he approached the counter with their order, the items wrapped in tissue and tucked into elegant paper bags with handles. "Our very own equipage can you see you to your destination," the man said as he nodded to the bow window at the front of the store. "With our compliments, of course, Lord Breckinridge."

Through the bow window, Adam noticed the equipage to which the man referred. Parked at the curb was a coach-and-four. Adam gave the man two crowns and took the bag. "Much obliged," he stated before offering his arm to Diana. "My lady? Your wish is my command."

Blinking in shock, Diana dared a glance at the town coach and then at the viscount. At this point, what did she have to lose? Half the stores in Jermyn Street thought her married to the viscount. "Lead the way, my lord," she replied with a pained expression.

## CHAPTER 10
## A VISCOUNT MOURNS

*M*eanwhile, back at the Thorncastle townhouse Godfrey Thorncastle stared at the divan for several minutes before he redirected his attention to the tea tray set before him. His own teacup, still half-full with a curl of steam rising from the surface of the black and orange tea, sat in the palm of one hand as he absently rested it on one knee.

"Dammit all to hell," he murmured. "Damn *The Tattler*. Damn…" He was about to say, "The Earl of Torrington," but thought better of it. It wasn't as if Milton, Earl of Torrington, ever claimed to have bedded Elise. Indeed, the earl was always quite discreet with his *affaires* prior to his marriage. He knew better than anyone how gossip could end someone's standing in the *ton*. He knew how a woman's reputation could suffer if gossip spread through the parlors of Mayfair. Why, the earl was a paragon of propriety, a testament to what was possible for an older, single aristocrat should he simply wait to find the perfect mate. The perfect countess. Simply wait and bide his time and see to a few widows' comfort during the Season…

Godfrey blinked. And blinked again when he realized something he should have realized a long time ago.

Lady Lancaster was a widow, true. But she had been

married to Charles Batey for nearly sixteen years—the same years Milton Torrington was squiring widows to the balls and soirées of every Season. Besides, it wasn't as if Elise could have cuckolded her husband. He wouldn't have allowed it, especially given the fact that she had never born him an heir. Charles Batey, Viscount Lancaster, still expected to father an heir before his untimely death of what some said was the ague.

"Stupid, stupid, stupid," Godfrey muttered to himself as he absently swirled his tea with his finger in the dainty teacup.

*My mother's tea service*, he thought as he studied the intricate details on the silver teapot and the matching milk and sugar-pot. *Elise would have used it to serve her guests in the parlor*, he thought with some dismay.

Then he remembered Elise's question about the sugar. She had remembered his preference for milk in his tea. She had stirred in just the right amount, and then added a rather large lump of sugar instead of two small ones, as if she knew he really wanted two lumps in his tea and not just the one he requested.

*She was so beautiful sitting here in my study*, he thought with a good deal of melancholy. As if she belonged there. Perfectly poised. Perfectly ready to accept his offer of marriage.

Godfrey blinked.

*Would* she have accepted?

*I have questions*, she had said. *And conditions.*

"Dammit," he murmured again. Had he been able to answer her questions and meet her conditions—whatever they were—and had he not brought up his beliefs about her having had *affaires* in her past, they might be drinking a toast to their future marriage with champagne at this very moment!

"Dammit!" he nearly shouted, which is when he realized he wasn't alone in the study. Nigel was there, quickly seeing to the removal of the tea service. Godfrey managed to snag a Dutch biscuit before the tray was lifted from the table. "I haven't finished my tea yet," he argued, his stern expression a clear warning to the butler to leave the tray exactly where it was.

"Very good, my lord," Nigel responded as he set the tray back down onto the low table. He stood for a moment before his master dared another glance in his direction. "If I may make a suggestion, my lord?" he added with a raised eyebrow.

Godfrey regarded his servant for a moment before allowing a nod. "Be very careful in how you put voice to it," he warned.

Nigel seemed to consider the warning a moment before saying, "A heartfelt letter of apology will go a long way toward making things right with the lady."

About to argue, Godfrey realized his butler was absolutely right. He was far better with the written word than spoken ones, to be sure. The last fifteen minutes had been a testament to that!

Moving quickly to his desk, Godfrey took a seat and pulled out a blank sheet of his parchment. Loading a quill with ink, he began to write.

*My dearest Elise,*

He paused. Could he simply use her given name like this without the proper title in front of it? He certainly didn't want to address her as 'Lady Lancaster'. The reference to the rogue's name—even if he was a fellow viscount—merely brought up memories of what she must have endured being married to such a rake. Godfrey thought having kissed her before she was betrothed to the scoundrel gave him a bit of leeway when it came to how he addressed his missive.

He continued, the pen scratching the surface of the vellum as it left behind his words.

*I wish to apologize for my mistaken assumptions as to how you have been living your life these past sixteen...*

Sixteen? Goodness! It had been more like... *Twenty*, he reasoned. But he certainly didn't want her to think that he thought that she was older than she really was.

He obliterated the word 'sixteen' with a generous line of ink and continued.

*Eighteen years. I admit to having assumed a woman of your poise and beauty would be a draw for any man, as you certainly have always been for me. I admit to having believed everything I have read in print, thinking it was the truth, for otherwise, why would it be printed?*

*Thanks to your tutelage, I know better now. I have not been employing the traits of a critical thinker. I apologize and ask your forgiveness...*

Ask? Nay, beg...

He started to rewrite the sentence before he sat back and thought he might be admitting far too much with his words. It wasn't as if he had ever looked at another woman with the intention of wedding her. Of bedding her. Elise had always been his intended. His written words were merely the truth. If she didn't realize it when she read the missive, then she wasn't the one for him, which had him in a panic just then.

*Christ!*

What would he do if Elise didn't agree to marry him?

He continued to write, rather pleased with that last line about critical thinking.

*Too bad I didn't employ critical thinking eighteen... twenty years ago*, he thought as he metaphorically kicked himself in the shin. Well, twenty years was a bit on the long side. He didn't kiss her until she was what? Fifteen? Sixteen?

*You see, I have always thought you should be my wife. Always.*

He drew a single line of ink beneath the word, wanting to

be sure he made his point clear. Angling his head as he reread the sentence, he then wondered if he was being too presumptive. He crossed through the sentence, but left it readable in the hope Elise would understand his motive with his next line.

*You see, I have always believed we would one day be married.*

There. Much better.

He created a line beneath 'believed' in the hopes it would drive home the point.

*I love you.*

He swallowed. He had intended to say that line aloud, as if he thought it far too important than just written as a three-word sentence. Those words were sometimes said with such abandon, such lack of conviction. But he had overheard Lord Grandby say them about his wife—before she was even his wife—on several occasions at White's. Why, the man would sit in one of the wingback chairs near the card players and say he loved Adele Slater Worthington for anyone and everyone to hear!

*I love you,* he wrote again.

There. After a moment, he decided that if he was in for a penny, he was in for a pound.

*I want you to be my wife. I want to live the rest of my life with you. I want you to be the mother of my heir (should we be so blessed) and a daughter (who will be beautiful despite my share of her).*

He reread that last sentence, wondering if Elise was still able to have children. *Are thirty-two-year-old-women able to bear children?* Then he remembered that Queen Charlotte was still having babies, and Her Royal Highness certainly had to be older than Elise!

*Please forgive my mistaken assumptions. I thought the worst only because my fellow aristocrats can be such rakes when it comes to beautiful women such as you. Even if you had engaged in an affaire, please know this. It would not have made a difference to me. I love you, Elise. I shall always love you. Please marry me. I love you and only you, Elise.*

*Yours forever, Godfrey.*

The viscount sat up straighter and read the missive from the beginning, murmuring and groaning as he did so. When he finished, he sighed and crumbled the parchment into a ball and tossed it into the basket next to his desk.

"Dreck!" he yelled out.

Frustrated, he rose from his desk and took his leave of the study. He nearly upended his butler on the way out, his strides so large he could have parted the Red Sea as he made his way to his bedchamber.

There was a bottle of scotch in there. One he intended to finish off before the night was over.

Tomorrow was another day. Tomorrow he would have to try again to win the heart of Elise.

## CHAPTER 11
## SHOPPING WITH A
## BOUNDER

*eanwhile, back at Floris in Jermyn Street*
Diana managed a strained smile as she took
the viscount's proffered arm and allowed him to lead her to the
glossy black town coach parked in front of the shop. The store's
crest was painted on the door. "Am I going to regret this?" she
asked as they approached the equipage.

Adam took a deep breath, his first without having to inhale
the scents of every fragrance featured in Floris. "Most certainly
not," he answered firmly. "I'm rather hoping you'll thank me, in
fact. We are going to Gunter's, after all."

Considering his words as he helped her into the elegant
town coach—the interior was even scented with lavender—
Diana wondered how the man could be truly serious about his
intention to marry her. "And how do you expect me to thank
you?" she asked after he gave the driver their destination.

Adam frowned at her implication. A few years ago—probably even a few days ago—he might have been tempted to
answer with a risqué comment, but not today. "A simple 'thank
you' will suffice, of course, my lady," he replied as he took the
seat across from her and settled into the plush squabs.
Although he had been tempted to join her on the side in

which she sat, he knew he would be pressing his luck if he did so.

"And after Gunter's? Where to then?" she asked, suspicion evident in her voice. The man had both her box of shoes as well as the bag containing their order from Floris on the seat next to him. His own boxes merely added to the ruse that they had gone shopping together.

She couldn't believe what she was doing. If someone should see her in the company of the viscount—with no chaperone in sight—and report it to Mrs. Streater, why, she would lose her position!

Wondering if he had somehow offended the young woman, Adam gave a shrug and replied, "I'll escort you to Gunter's, and then to your home, of course. Safely," he added *sotto voce*.

"You don't even know where I live," she countered, her breaths coming faster as panic set in. She was in a town coach with a handsome viscount and no chaperone in sight! Her mother, God rest her soul, would probably find humor in the situation, but as an instructor at a finishing school, seeing to the education of young ladies of the *ton*, she most certainly did not.

"At Warwick's, of course. In Glasshouse Street, with the other teachers," he stated in no uncertain terms.

Diana blinked. *How on earth does he know such a thing?* she wondered, rather stunned at the curse she had imagined. But it was appropriate.

How did the man know—?

Unless... Her eyes widened with suspicion. Before she could chide him or accuse him of having accosted other teachers from the finishing school, he held up a staying hand.

"I know this only because my mother was once a pupil there," he stated. "For at least a year. As was my sister, Emelia, although a family friend wanted her companionship, so she ended up at a finishing school in Switzerland. Remember, my brother's wife attended Warwick's as well," he added when he remembered Julia Harrington's comment about the hags who taught French, elocution, needlework, painting, and drawing. Julia had never mentioned arithmetic or dancing in her complaints, though, and now he knew why. This woman definitely wasn't a hag. Why, this woman would never be a hag. Even when she was eighty years old, gray and wrinkled, those blue-gray eyes would be beautiful. "Why arithmetic?" he asked.

Diana angled her head to one side, rather surprised by the query. Thoughts of impropriety flew from her head. "A lady is frequently expected to keep the household ledgers. Especially if the housekeeper lacks an adequate education," she replied simply. "Most do, you see. And coming up with the menus for dinners sometimes requires that she make up a shopping list of all the ingredients necessary for her cook, especially when she's to host a dinner party. Simple arithmetic and a bit of multiplication makes the task much easier and less prone to disaster when the dinner is about to be served."

Adam considered the answer, not bothering to hide his surprise at hearing it. His mother did the menus, of course, and she kept a ledger. In the escritoire in her private salon. He never knew why or what it was for. "Will you do that for our household?" he asked, realizing he didn't really have a household suitable for the two of them. His bachelor quarters in Green Street were probably large enough for two, but hardly appropriate given his other neighbors. He would have to see to hiring an agent that might help him secure a townhouse, or a terrace, perhaps. Near Grosvenor Square, he thought, hoping his allowance would cover such an extravagant address. Or perhaps something on the south side of the park.

Diana blinked. "I suppose so," she hedged. Goodness, but the man seemed ever so serious about the idea of marrying her. "Do you keep a ledger now?" she asked.

Adam ducked his head a bit. "I was never very good at mathematics," he admitted sheepishly. "I was told there would be no math..." At Diana's widened eyes—those beautiful, blue-gray eyes were staring at him with what could only be described as shock—he paused. "Unfortunately, I believed them. I can do basic arithmetic, of course, but I have a... a secretary that sees to my ledgers now." He didn't add that the secretary was actually his father's man of business who basically saw to it Adam didn't overspend his monthly allowance. Beyond that, he hadn't had an occasion to remember his multiplication tables since his days at Eton.

"I see," Diana replied with a nod, hiding her disappointment. *I can do the books*, she decided. *At least I'll know if he's living beyond his means. Or gambling to excess.*

She thought of what they might look like if they were married. Of what he might look like when he was eighty, gray and wrinkled, his eyes filled with mischief.

*He'll still be handsome*, she thought, a frisson passing through her body just then. How could he not?

She dared a glance out the glass windows of the coach, surprised to see they were nearly to Berkeley Square. "Is your household very... large?" The man was the son of the Earl of Aimsley. Perhaps he didn't yet have a place of his own but merely had a room—or his own apartments—at Aimsley House. The thought of living in such splendor reminded her of the house in which she had been raised. Her mother always had the best of everything, and not just because her father saw to funding it.

Giving her question a moment of consideration, Adam struggled with how to reply. "Not at all," he finally said. He had a momentary thought of moving back into Aimsley House— there was an apartment they could share on the first floor—but he quickly shook the idea from his head. Perhaps he could find a townhouse in Curzon Street or South Audley Street. But could he do it today? Or tomorrow?

"We would of course require a few more servants," he added. "Do you have lady's maid?"

Diana blinked. She shook her head. "I do not," she replied.

Although there was a maid available to the instructors at the finishing school, she rarely required her services. The other teachers were always more in need of Mae's services, so Diana had simply learned to do without.

This seemed to surprise him. "You can dress yourself?"

Allowing a giggle that managed to bring the pink back to her cheeks, Diana nodded, deciding not to admit to the lady's maid she had once shared with her older sister. "I have almost my entire life. I pin up my own hair, as well," she added with a hint of mischief.

Adam's eyes widened. "Will you allow me to remove the pins at night?"

Diana gave a start. "What?"

Adam leaned forward, his elbows resting on his knees. "At night. Before bed. Will you allow me to remove the pins from your hair?" The words were said in a quiet voice, barely audible above the noise from the horses and the wheels on the cobblestone street. But they were said with such enthusiasm, Diana couldn't imagine denying the man his pleasure.

"I should like that responsibility," he added.

Not just one but several frissons passed beneath Diana's skin just then. They left her breathless, especially when her breasts seemed to swell beyond the confines of her stays. "I suppose. If you really must," she replied as her eyes darted to the side. He was leaning so close, he could have his hands on the tops of her thighs, his lips on hers with very little effort. She found the idea rather pleasant. Welcome, in fact. "You're going to kiss me, aren't you?" she whispered, her breaths sounding labored.

"Every morning and every night. Should you allow it, of course."

*Allow it?* Why, she'd probably be *ordering* him to do so!

"What about when you leave for your club?"

Adam blinked when he realized he was about to ask, *What club?* "If I am welcome to do so, my lady, then I shall kiss you whenever you wish me to." And because she was gazing at him with such expectation in her eyes, he leaned closer, placed his hands on either side of her thighs so they gripped the edge of the bench, and he kissed her. He meant only to give her a quick kiss—a peck, really—but once his lips were on hers, he found he didn't wish to let go. He wanted nothing more than to continue kissing her. Continue until one of them had to come up for air.

Since he was able to breathe through a kiss, he had every intention of continuing to kiss her, but the coach came to a sudden halt, the force of which had Diana nearly tossed into his lap. Her arms were suddenly pressed against his shoulders in an effort to stop her forward momentum.

"Oh!" Her blue-gray eyes were round with surprise, and it took every ounce of self-control Adam possessed to keep from gathering her into his arms and kissing her senseless. "My lord, please forgive me," she managed to whisper. "I should have been—"

His lips were on hers again, a quick kiss to stifle whatever she was about to say. "You need never apologize for ending up in my arms," he whispered. About to kiss her again—or rather, pick up where he had left off—he realized the driver had already stepped down from the box and was about to open the door.

There wasn't enough time to put the young lady to rights on the opposite bench, so he merely pulled her so she ended up sitting next to him, her skirts becoming twisted as he did so. He moved to get up from the bench, well aware of the bulge that had formed against his doeskin breeches. Keeping himself bent over, he gathered up the boxes and bags and moved to open the door at the same time it swung open from the outside.

The driver had stepped back to allow his passengers to depart. Adam quickly descended the two steps and turned to offer his hand. The woman didn't make a move to stand up, though. "Sweeting?" he ventured. "Is something amiss?" He cursed himself for having helped himself to the second —or was that the third?—kiss. He had probably scandalized her with the first. Now she was probably regretting ever having met him!

Although she didn't look regretful. She was staring at him with an expression of awe he rather hoped he would pay witness to many times over the course of their lives.

Diana blinked.

*Sweeting?*

No one had ever used the endearment with her. Not even her father, who had called her mother 'sweetheart' the entire time she'd lived in the household he provided them. She had even once asked her mother if the man knew her given name. *Why, he might not*, the woman teased and then sobered, as if she just then realized it was possible her lover didn't know her given name.

The following day, Diana heard her father refer to her mother as 'Lil' at least three times.

The memory of her parents brought a grin to her lips, but it also reminded Diana that she and the viscount hadn't yet been properly introduced—the viscount still didn't know her name!

Or who her father was.

# CHAPTER 12
# A COUNTESS PROVIDES A
# BIT OF GUIDANCE

*t Worthington House*
When Lady Lancaster's coach pulled up in the half-circle drive in front of Worthington House, the front doors opened even before Sims had a chance to step down from the box. He had the town coach door opened for his mistress, giving her a nod and offering a hand on which she placed her gloved hand as she stepped down. Although he took note of her tear stained face, he said nothing.

"I've no idea how long I'll be," she warned.

"I'll make my way to the stables, then, my lady," he replied with a nod. "I hear the earl acquired a matched pair of greys last week, and I'd like to take a quick look, if I might."

Elise allowed a smile. "Of course," she agreed before making her way to the front door. Although the rain had stopped, she realized she had left her umbrella at Godfrey's townhouse. She had half a mind to send Sims after it, but wondered if Nigel—or his master—would see to its return. "Bernard, you're looking young today. How is that, do you suppose?"

The butler of Worthington House blinked, his usual staid manner proving he'd been caught off-guard by the remark.

"Much obliged, Lady Lancaster," he replied with a deep bow. "I'm to tell any callers that Lady Torrington is in the nursery, and should you wish to see her, I'm to escort you there."

Amused by the thought of the new mother directing her butler to say such a thing nearly had her giggling. "I know where it 'tis, of course. No need for you to announce me," she added as she gave up her pelisse to the man. Her hat, firmly pinned in place, would have to remain on her head.

The unmistakable sounds of babies had her grinning before she had reached the top of the stairs. On her way to the nursery, she overheard the countess telling her daughter she was the most beautiful creature on the planet and then telling her son he was the most handsome. She could just imagine their faces alighting in delight at her personal attention. How many aristocrats spent this much time with their children?

The infectious sounds of baby giggles had Elise pausing before she made her presence known to the countess. She hiccupped a sob as she poked her head around the corner of the open door. "I am told you're only receiving visitors if they come here," she said with a watery grin.

Adele glanced up from the two babies she held, her surprise at finding she had a visitor apparent in her facial expression. The babies gurgled again, the one looking in her direction giving her a huge grin.

"Oh, they're simply adorable," Elise added as she curtsied and entered the room. She hurried to stand before the countess. "And you're looking especially fine," she added.

Giving a roll of her eyes, Adele sighed. "As are you. I haven't seen you in an age," she complained. "And you have to forgive me. I'm not about to attempt to stand up while holding both of them," she added as she indicated her children.

"You're forgiven, of course," Elise replied. "Now, which one am I allowed to hold?" she asked as she set aside her reticule.

"Take Angelica, if you would," Adele offered, lifting the arm that held the twin girl. "She spends far too much time in the company of her father. Why, I fear she'll be smoking cheroots and drinking scotch before she's a year old," she complained lightly.

Elise giggled as she took the wide-eyed girl from Adele. "Surely you don't allow him to hold her while he's smoking," she countered.

Adele gave a shake of her head, the movement followed with rapt attention by her son. "Of course not, but I've found him in his study holding her in one arm as he's reading aloud from a book on modern farming techniques," she claimed with a lifted brow. She shuddered, as if the very thought of the topic was reprehensible. "I can just imagine the two of them conversing on the subject when she's old enough to speak."

This last sentence seemed to amuse the twin boy, George, for he suddenly erupted into a series of gibberish punctuated with kicks and giggles.

Not able to help herself, Elise giggled, tears streaming down her face as her giggles turned to sobs.

Alarmed, Adele stared at the duke's daughter. "Whatever is the matter?" she asked. The sudden change in his mother had George's nearly invisible brow furrowing, and he looked as if he were about to cry. Before he could do so, Adele lifted him to her shoulder.

"Thorncastle finally proposed," Elise managed between sobs, her distress having a profound effect on the girl she held. Angelica, rather confused by the change from giggles to sobs, stared at the woman who held her, apparently trying to decide if she, too, was expected to cry or if she should merely watch from where she rested in Elise's arms.

The news wasn't completely unexpected. Adele had heard during tea that morning that someone had sent a letter to Elise asking for her hand in marriage. Adeline, Marchioness of Morganfield, had shared that bit of *on-dit*, although she hadn't divulged just who the guilty party was. Knowing now that it was Lord Thorncastle, Adele supposed the most common response to hearing such a claim would be, *What took so long?*

"I thought you'd be thrilled," Adele countered, her face betraying her surprise.

"I was," Elise replied, lifting Angelica to her shoulder so she could pat the baby on the back. She was afraid if she didn't, the poor girl would break out into tears of her own at any moment. "Until he told me he'd thought I'd had an *affaire* with Lord Reading," she countered with a hiccup.

Adele's eyes arched up in surprise. "Whatever gave him *that* idea?" she asked in surprise.

"The very same idea that had him believing I'd had an *affaire* with your husband," Elise replied. She blinked, realizing she hadn't intended on bringing up *that* particular point.

Frowning, Adele angled her head to one side. "You mean, you didn't?"

It was Elise's turn to blink. "Of course not!" She stared at the countess a moment, confusion evident on her face. "*You* thought I'd had an *affaire* with Torrington?"

Adele shrugged the shoulder that didn't have a baby resting on it. "Truth be told, yes. You're a widow, and he only ever bedded widows until he married me," she reasoned.

Elise blinked again. "I haven't been a widow that long! I solemnly swear, I was *never* in the company of your husband in such a manner," she stated firmly. "And I cannot believe you thought I ever was. Especially since you were being courted by him when Lancaster died!"

Ignoring Elise's bit of a tirade, Adele shrugged again. "You don't find him appealing?"

Elise allowed an audible gasp, shocked at Adele's response. Despite finding the woman's husband a rather personable gentleman and handsome in the typical Grandby fashion— most all the Grandby men were handsome—she had never given Milton, Earl of Torrington, any consideration in that regard. The family ties were too close. "He's *family*, Adele.

Although we're not directly related..." She paused as she considered the family genealogy. "At least, I don't think we are directly, we certainly are by marriage in a number of ways. Why, it would be like being with a *cousin*," she added, giving an involuntary shudder.

Apparently appeased by the explanation, Adele lowered George back into her arms and gave a grin when she realized he was sound asleep. "Is that all Thorncastle did wrong? Think you'd had an *affaire?* Or two?" she whispered.

Elise sighed, lowering Angelica to discover the girl's eyes quite wide and studying her as if she were memorizing her. The thought that she, too, could have a baby like Angelica nearly brought tears to her eyes again. "You sweet creature," she whispered, which had the baby grinning before her head fell against Elise's shoulder. Within a moment, the girl was sound asleep. Elise turned her attention back to the countess and sighed. "I suppose," she replied in a whisper.

"You two were meant to be together," Adele said quietly. "You told me yourself years ago."

Elise's eyes widened, remembering that she had told Adele —and several other acquaintances back in the day—that she and Godfrey Thorncastle had declared their love for one another before she was even fourteen years of age. How odd to be reminded of it now, after so many years and a bad marriage.

"He adores you. He doesn't have eyes for anyone else," Adele went on. "Why, I don't even think he employs a mistress. In fact..." She paused as she seemed to realize something. "I have never seen Thorncastle in the company of a woman. At least, not while he's been in London." Her eyes widened in alarm, but before she could put voice to a query, Elise waved a staying hand in her direction.

"He is not, I assure you," she said, thinking perhaps Adele was about to wonder if Godfrey Thorncastle was a molly.

"Well then, you have your answer. Marry the man, Elise. You know you love him. He loves you. What more is there?"

Elise regarded her friend for a long moment and finally sighed. "You make it sound so easy—"

"Do not make it harder than it is," Adele warned. "You can go on living the life of an independent woman, but should you choose that path, you will never have one of these," she said quietly, indicating the babe she held. "At least not legitimately."

Elise gave a sideways glance to the sleeping babe she held and nearly broke out bawling. Instead, she allowed a heavy sigh and gave Adele a wan smile. "Perhaps I'll speak with him on the morrow," she allowed.

Adele grinned. "Should I put these two in their cribs and ring for tea?" she asked in a whisper.

Shaking her head, Elise said, "Thank you for the invitation, but I think I shall go home and read a book," she murmured.

With that, she rocked herself out of the chair and carried Angelica to her crib. Once the babe was covered with a light blanket and tucked up against a pillow, Elise took her leave of the countess and of Worthington House.

# CHAPTER 13
# A CONVERSATION
# OVER ICES

*M*eanwhile, at Gunter's

"Coming, darling," Diana said to Adam as she regarded him from the town coach, remembering how she had referred to him on the steps at White's. The word had come so easily, she hadn't even given her reply a second thought. Probably because her mother used to use the endearment when replying to Father.

Adam's gloved hand closed around hers as she stepped down from the town coach. "Thank you, sir," she managed as she gave a nod to the driver. She was about to retrieve a coin from her reticule to give to the driver, but Adam passed one to him before she could. Glancing up, she realized the man had dropped them off directly in front of Gunter's. Why, he had even driven the town coach all the way around the square so that they were deposited on the pavement in front of the shop rather than in the street on the opposite side under the maple trees.

"Much obliged," Adam said before leading his intended to the front doors. They opened as if by magic, two waiters stepping aside to hold each one of them open.

Determined to keep her eyes in her head—she had only

ever been to Gunter's with her mother, and that had only been two times in her youth—Diana found she also had to keep her mouth closed.

The thrum of the mid-afternoon crowd seemed to die down as they made their entrance. Aware of eyes turning their way, of heads bent in quiet query, Diana struggled to hold up her head and scan the room without making eye contact with any of the patrons. She wondered if anyone would take note of how dated her gown might be, and then remembered the spencer was one of this Season's designs— her one splurge when she received her last pay from the school.

One of the men who had opened the front door stepped in front of her and led them to a small table at the back of the shop. He held a chair for her before Adam could even reach the table, and Diana seated herself.

Having removed his short top hat, Adam placed it on the extra chair at their table. His dark hair appeared nearly black, although the touch of gray at his temples was more pronounced. "I don't think I've ever seen this place so busy," he remarked as he turned to regard the menu board. "What's your pleasure, my lady?"

Well aware several patrons had made note of their appearance in the popular confectioner, Diana had half a mind to take her leave of the place—as fast as she could run. What if she was recognized? What if one of her students happened to be enjoying an ice at this time of the afternoon?

Given the hour, though, none of them had better be at Gunter's. They had better be in either Miss Betterman's painting class or learning French from Miss Anders. Besides, the viscount's easy manner and affable presence was a welcome respite from spending her days in the company of other teachers and students. Assured there could be no one who would recognize her, Diana took a breath and relaxed a bit. Thought of how easy the kiss had happened in the coach. She couldn't remember a time when she had felt so at ease in the company of a man.

Not that she had ever been in the company of a man in such a manner.

She blinked. Why, besides her father, she hadn't spent this much time with a member of the opposite sex!

Ever.

"Or perhaps you're only interested in... a lemonade or—"

"Oh, I'd adore an ice, of course. Strawberry," Diana interrupted with a nod. "I apologize for taking so long to decide. There are just so many flavors from which to choose," she added with a sigh.

Adam regarded her with an arched eyebrow. "My second-favorite flavor," he murmured, his teasing voice suggesting the other flavor might not even be on the menu.

When the waiter appeared to take their order, Adam saw to it as Diana dared a quick glance around. She shouldn't feel guilty for having come, she decided. These people were no better than she. Even the aristocrats—and she wasn't even sure there were any besides the gentleman who sat almost across from her—were simply other people who had the good fortune to be born to it. As for being seen in the company of one—other than her father—well, stranger things could happen, she decided.

"A penny for your thoughts, my lovely," Adam whispered, his head angled in her direction.

Diana blinked, about to claim he would be short-changed when she watched as his eyebrows arched up on his forehead. She nearly blinked again at hearing his endearment.

*My lovely.*

Goodness, the man had said it as if he believed it! Well, she did maintain a passing resemblance to her youngest aunt, and that woman was still rather lovely despite being in her thirties.

"Do not try to deny it," he admonished her. "I could practically see the wheels turning. Solving a particularly vexing math problem, perhaps? Or inventing a new dance? We could use one of those," he remarked in a lowered voice. "Something along the lines of a waltz, but a bit slower. More... intimate."

Allowing a grin at his salacious comment, Diana shook her head. "I was deciding I shouldn't feel at all... uncomfortable... about being here at Gunter's," she replied.

It was Adam's turn to blink. "Are you supposed to be teaching a class right now?" he asked in alarm, not even considering he might be the reason she seemed ill-at-ease.

Diana allowed an impish grin. "It's my day off, actually. Much to the relief of my arithmetic students."

"Ah, but not to your dance students, I should think," he countered.

Her grin widening to a smile, Diana angled her head. "It all depends on those who have two left feet, I suppose," she replied her thoughts on the poor student who had been paired with Lord Graham's son at last night's ball. "Four of my students were in attendance at Lord Weatherstone's ball last night, but they did nothing to embarrass me," she added.

Adam's eyes rounded. "You were there? How is it I didn't find you then?" he asked, straightening in his chair.

Diana shook her head, realizing she probably shouldn't have said anything. "I was merely watching from the balcony. I wasn't... I wasn't an invited guest," she explained.

"I was not there long. I didn't even dance," Adam countered, his voice betraying regret. "Had I seen you, though, I would have asked you for at least three."

"Bounder," she accused lightly, knowing he couldn't have asked for more than two dances. It just wasn't done.

She watched as Adam gave a slight shrug, his amusement apparent in the crinkles at the edges of his eyes and in the slight lift on the left side of his lips. Considering what she had just said—again—she wondered if he was always this easy to converse with. She could almost imagine being married to him. Meeting for the morning meal in a bright and comfortable breakfast parlor. Conversing over a spot of tea in the afternoon. Enjoying a bit of banter over dinner. Waiting for him to join her in the parlor...

Well, maybe not the parlor but perhaps somewhere more comfortable.

... After he finished his port and a cheroot.

Well, maybe not the cheroot.

"Do you smoke cheroots?" she asked.

Adam blinked before giving his answer a good deal of consideration. "On occasion," he answered rather carefully. "Never in the house, of course. Usually at White's."

"You don't have one after dinner?" Diana countered, leaning away from him when the waiter reappeared with their ices on a tray. "With your port?"

The viscount allowed a chuckle, giving a nod and a coin to the waiter after the decorative cups were set down on the round marble tabletop. "Only when I've dined at my club, my lady," he allowed. He took a breath and sighed. "I take my cues from my father, you see. And he takes his from my mother." This last was said with a wink as he leaned forward and dipped a spoon into his ice. "*Bon appetit*, my lady," he added as he watched her admire her mound of strawberry ice in the round crystal-stemmed cup.

"*Bon appetit*," she murmured in reply, lifting her spoon to stab the ball of smooth red ice. She wondered at the viscount's words. She couldn't imagine an earl following the dictates of his countess. Was it possible for a man to have so much regard for his wife that he would give up smoking in the house? Smoking in his study?

After Adam swallowed his first bite and displayed an expression of appreciation, he leaned toward her again. "Do you know who my mother is?" he asked in a whisper, as if her identity might be a secret to anyone but those in the *ton*.

Nodding, Diana angled her head and furrowed her brows as if in thought. "Patience Waterford, sister of Harold Waterford of Horsham and daughter of a well-regarded businessman from the Horsham District. Her niece, Olivia Waterford, is married to Michael Cunningham, son of Viscount Cunningham. Miss Waterford married Mark, Earl of Aimsley, the year —or two, rather—after her come-out, having gained his notice at a ball where it has been said they danced every dance despite the rule that they dance only two together." This last was said with an arched brow, as if she found the news scandalous. She was about to continue with a remark about the Comber children when Adam held up a staying hand.

"My father insists it was only two dances, but he made sure they were the longest sets of the evening," he explained quickly, as if he felt the need to correct her mistaken impression. "Which is what I would have done last night with you, had I known you were in attendance."

Diana was sure she saw his eyes twinkle. Goodness! Did the man have any idea how endearing he was? Why, his entire face lit up when he spoke of his parents.

"They're hopelessly in love, I tell you," he went on. "My mother has my father wrapped about her pinky, and her forefinger, and all the others he hasn't yet decorated with rings from Rundell and Bridge," he claimed with a sigh. "In fact, I think he's just bought her some kind of newspaper," he murmured, his brows furrowing. "He claims he couldn't give me the particulars—some secret that must be kept for the protection of us Combers—except to say that my mother was a natural and would probably earn him enough blunt to stay solvent should we ever have another year without a summer." He sobered. "Forgive me. I didn't mean to bring up... money," he whispered quickly.

Not the least bit offended at the mention of blunt, Diana regarded him for a moment, rather surprised at his sudden silence. "I rather enjoy hearing you speak of your parents," she murmured in reply, leaning towards him so their heads nearly touched. "It seems to make you... happy," she said. And human.

Faith, but if this went on much longer, she would be asking *him* for his hand in marriage!

Adam nodded. "It does," he agreed. He allowed another chuckle before leaning back in his chair. Only a spoonful of his bergamot pear ice remained in the bottom of his crystal dish, and he toyed with it using the point of his spoon. "I do hope our marriage can be as pleasant as theirs," he whispered.

Diana inhaled softly at hearing his words, said with such longing that she thought he might shed a tear. "As do I," she replied, resisting the urge to snort when she considered the unlikely scenario.

*He doesn't even know my name!*

*What will he think when he discovers—?*

"Enough about me and my disgustingly-in-love parents. What of you?" He paused a moment, his eyes taking on a look of mischief. "No. Don't tell me. Allow me to guess," he said. "You're from... Kent."

"Marylebone," Diana corrected, realizing he would learn the truth of her at any moment and see to their quick departure from the shop.

Or perhaps just his.

"Marylebone," he repeated. "Your father was a... vicar—"

"Manages an estate." She wasn't about to admit just how. Or how large.

Adam angled his head, obviously impressed. "And your mother was the daughter of a... baron," he guessed with an arched eyebrow.

Diana's eyes widened. "A baronet," she whispered, rather surprised at how close he had come on that point. She supposed her mother's illegitimacy wasn't really an issue any longer.

"They met at a garden party—"

"The theatre."

"And fell in love at first sight."

Blinking, Diana shook her head. "I rather doubt that," she

argued. "In fact, I do believe my mother had reason to slap my father across the face before the second act had finished."

"Because she was already in love with him," Adam stated with a firm nod. Noticing how Diana stared at him in disbelief, he added, "Women always do that when they're in love with a man." When he saw that she was about to put voice to a protest, he added, "I have that on good authority. My mother said as much when she told me of the first night she danced with my father. She slapped him across the face. Hard right hand to his left cheek." He pantomimed the hit using his own left hand so it nearly impacted his left cheek, his head suddenly jerking to his right. "Left a mark for days," he claimed, as if he'd been present for the assault. "That's according to my father. Mother said she already knew she would be his countess, but she wanted him to know she wasn't going to simply agree with everything he said."

Diana wasn't sure if she should laugh or cry at his comment. "Indeed?" she managed for lack of a better reply.

And yet they had danced two of the longest sets of the evening.

Adam slowly settled back into his chair, his gaze suggesting he regretted having told her the story. "Although I don't relish the thought of you slapping me across the face, I would abide it should you decide it... *necessary*," he ventured. "Do keep me informed as to your intentions."

This last was said with entirely too much hope, Diana thought, which had a burble of a chuckle erupting before she had a chance to cover her lips with one hand. "You make it sound as if you would *welcome* it!" Aware she had captured the attention of nearby patrons, she had a thought to simply slide down and out of her chair and through the floor in an effort to disappear from the room.

But Adam's broad smile and matching laughter had her keeping her seat just then. His laughter was infectious, the deep rumble sending frissons of pleasure through her entire body. That she could have said something he would find so humorous as to conjure such laugher was both a surprise and a delight. "I cannot imagine what you might do to deserve such treatment, my lord," she managed after a time.

"Oh, I can," he countered with a mischievous grin. "Why, if we weren't in such a public place, I might try it right now."

Diana sobered as she stared at the viscount. Part of her wanted to know exactly what he might try while alarm bells were keeping the rest of her mute. At his arched eyebrow, though, she blinked. "If we weren't in such a public place, what might you try?" She was almost afraid of his answer.

Adam swallowed. He hadn't expected her to put voice to such a question. Why, he merely made the comment so he could watch in wonder as her face turned pink. She was so lovely with color on her cheeks, with her blue-gray eyes wide, as if in shock. "I am not a rake, my lady. Not a libertine, either. I was merely thinking of the..." Here, his voice lowered to a whisper. "The kiss we shared in the coach. I should hope that we indulge in one at least once a day, every day, for the rest of our lives," he stated, his eyes never leaving hers.

The remaining few spoonfuls of her strawberry ice long forgotten, Diana stared at Adam for nearly fifteen seconds before she allowed a nod. "I would like that, as well," she admitted on a barely audible sigh.

What could it hurt to admit such a thing? It wasn't as if she would ever see the man again after this day ended. Once he had paid the bill for their ices, he would put her into a hackney and send her back to Warwick's. He would then return to White's to retrieve his mount and ride off to—

"Where do you live?" she asked, not realizing just how forward the question sounded until the words were out.

Adam feigned shock, an impish grin the tell that he found her question more amusing than scandalous. "I have a little bachelor house in Green Street. Although it would probably suit the two of us..." *with a great deal of renovation and decoration,*

"... I would prefer we take up residence in a larger townhouse. Perhaps in South Audley or Curzon Street." He didn't add that they would move into Aimsley House in Park Lane once he had inherited the earldom.

Diana's eyes widened again. "Rather expensive addresses," she murmured before realizing she still had a few spoonfuls of the strawberry confection in her dish, the edges of the ice having melted so it looked like a pink sunny-side-up egg. She lifted the middle onto her spoon and brought it to her lips. "Are you quite sure we can afford such a home?" she asked before finishing off the ice. "Since you admit to not keeping your own ledgers."

Rather surprised—and impressed—that she was so comfortable speaking of finances, Adam angled his head to one side. "Although I have already taken a seat in Parliament—by way of a writ in acceleration—"

"What is that?" Diana asked, unfamiliar with the term.

"Ah. When the majority of Parliament gets a bit long in the tooth, they like to lower the average age by having a few of us younger nobles take a seat before we inherit. I have my father's viscountcy, you see, so they let me in early," he explained. "Now, I'll admit I have no other source of income besides the allowance my father affords me every month," he added carefully. "But it's more than enough. That is, if I'm not spending my afternoons at Tattersall's."

The mention of the auction house specializing in horses had Diana giving a start. "How many horses do you own?" she asked, her eyes widening.

Leaning back in his chair, Adam regarded the teacher with an arched brow. "Three in my own stables, although I'm thinking we may have to find you a suitable mount," he replied, excited about finding her the perfect horse. "A bay, perhaps? Or would you prefer something smaller? A Welsh pony?" At her sudden look of disappointment, Adam realized she would only be satisfied with the very best horseflesh. "An Arabian?" he offered. Dressed in a hunter green riding habit, she would look stunning atop an Arabian, he considered. *She would look stunning atop me*, he amended, ever so thankful he was sitting and not standing as he imagined her straddling him, her riding habit draped artfully off to one side as she rode him to a fast and frantic finish. He failed to stifle the odd groan that erupted from his throat just then.

"I wouldn't require anything quite that fast," Diana countered, wondering what he was thinking just then. He had the most interesting expression on his face. Adoration and lust and...

She straightened in her chair. "What, pray tell, are you thinking this very moment?" she demanded to know.

Aware his face had taken on a decidedly reddish cast, Adam sighed. "You, in a hunter green riding habit," he admitted. He didn't verbally complete the scenario, deciding she would most probably slap him across the face.

At least then he would know she felt affection for him. Probably loved him, if his mother's words were true.

Angling her head to one side, Diana considered his words. "I haven't actually owned a riding habit since I was twelve," she murmured, remembering her mother's insistence that she and her older sister have them fashioned by her favorite modiste. She could count on one hand how many times she had worn the ensemble before her mother died of typhus.

Sobering, Adam leaned forward so their heads nearly touched over the table. "We'll have a modiste pay a call the day after we're wed and have one or two made for you."

Diana's eyes widened again. He loved seeing her blue-gray eyes like that, filled with wonder and delight and...

"You bounder!" she accused.

It was Adam's turn to widen his eyes. "Why ever would you say that?"

Her serious expression turned to one of amusement, and she was nearly giggling when she finally replied, "The very last person you're going to want paying a call on us after our wedding is a *modiste*," she replied. "Why, I expect you won't want to see the light of day for at least..." She suddenly stopped, her hand moving to cover her mouth as her eyes once again rounded.

*Damnation!* What was she saying?

What must this man think of her cheeky manner? Her conversation laced with mentions of money and inappropriate comments that suggested there could be days of post-wedding debauchery?

"At least three days," Adam agreed with a nod. "You make a good point," he stated before he realized what he had spoken out loud. *Faith!* The poor woman probably wouldn't marry him given his inappropriate topics of conversation. Money and the acts that took place in a marriage bed and behind locked doors —not to mention the number of comments that were double entendrés (even if most of them weren't intentional).

"But after that, I shall allow the visit," she agreed with an impish grin.

"I do believe we'll make the perfect couple," Adam stated in a whisper.

"As do I," Diana agreed on a sigh. She sobered. "About my mother—"

"The daughter of a baronet?"

"Yes," Diana replied, rather surprised he would remember the detail. "She..." Diana stopped, realizing how close she was to telling him the truth about her parents. Once he learned it, she was quite sure he would take his leave of her and never see her again. "She died when I was but fourteen years of age," she said in a hoarse whisper, deciding not to mention what she had done for a living in her younger years. Before James Burroughs decided to make her his mistress.

Adam blinked, resisting the urge to take her into his arms just then. "Your father must have been heartbroken," he stated with a nod.

Diana angled her head to one side, rather stunned by his words. Only a man who had come from parents who felt affection for one another could say such a thing. "He was," she agreed, remembering how her father had spent days locked away in his apartments, his eyes red and bleary the nights when he came out to check on her and her sister, Daisy. "He didn't take a wife until nearly three years later."

"Devoted, then?" Adam suggested.

"Very," Diana countered before he had finished his reply. She couldn't help but notice how his eyebrows arched up in surprise at her simple word. "I was rather surprised he held my mother in such high regard, and that he was so devoted to her for so many years. Not many men would be so, but my father was," she added before burying her top teeth into her lower lip. "I suppose I should expect the same devotion from my husband." The words were out before she had a chance to censor them, nearly hissing at how they must sound. Faith, but the viscount probably thought her far too outspoken to be an aristocrat's wife. "Knowing all that, I suppose you wish to call off our betrothal," she suggested on a sigh that carried as much disappointment as it did hope.

Adam blinked, dismayed she would think such a thing. Instead of answering it, he thought to discover something else first. "Have you and your father's new wife forged a friendship?" he asked quietly, as if he truly cared for her. Her stepmother might be the reason Diana no longer lived under her father's roof. Why she was teaching arithmetic and dancing at a finishing school instead of living under his protection.

Noting he didn't put voice to a reply suggesting he might wish to call off their betrothal, Diana wondered how to respond. She didn't know if her father's new wife even knew of her existence. "We've not even been introduced," she whispered, wondering if everyone seated in Gunter's had heard her earlier words. She couldn't help the wash of red that she knew suffused her face just then.

Of course, Adam didn't put voice to an immediate reply. And he probably wouldn't, she thought, crestfallen. He would be looking for a way out. A way to extract his offer of marriage and take his leave of the confectioner's shop so their brief liaison would go mostly unnoticed.

Diana couldn't blame him.

She was relieved they had the unpleasantness of truth out of the way before he had paid the one-and-twenty pounds for the special license.

"I am truly sorry," she managed, her eyes bright with unshed tears.

The man before her frowned. "But, why?" he countered with a shrug. "Your father's marriage changes nothing as it applies to us," he reasoned in a whisper matching hers. "Does it?" he added uncertainly.

Diana blinked. And blinked again. Had he completely missed her comment of requiring devotion—fidelity—from a husband? She had always thought her chances of an advantageous marriage were dashed, so she had given up hope of any marriage at all. As for her father's marriage, it only brought the man up to snuff as far as Society was concerned. That her step-mother had born her father an heir was probably most important. "I suppose it does not," she countered in a quieter whisper.

Adam considered her words. Rather saddened she had thought it necessary to bring up the matter of fidelity, he decided he didn't want her preconceived notions of his future fidelity—or lack thereof—to put a damper on what he had decided was one of the best afternoons of his life. "No, it does not," he finally replied. "As for my intentions, my lady, I promise I shall take my wedding vows very seriously," he said with solemnity.

Diana did something she never thought she would do in public in her entire life. She leaned forward and kissed the viscount. A peck on the corner of his lips, really, but a kiss, nonetheless.

Adam stared at her for several seconds, his expression unreadable as he considered her words. And her attempt at a kiss. "You're determined to make me fall in love with you before I take my leave of you, aren't you?" he murmured with a hint of sadness. "It isn't enough that I'm going to make you my wife? And be a devoted husband?"

Frowning, Diana thought perhaps she had underestimated the man. "Perhaps," she agreed with a slight smile. "Perhaps I will," she admitted, not realizing just how hopeful her words sounded.

# CHAPTER 14
# A BUTLER KNOWS BEST

*ack at Thorncastle's townhouse* Nigel waited until his master disappeared into his bedchamber before he entered the study to remove the tea tray. As he suspected, the viscount hadn't availed himself of any of the remaining Dutch biscuits, nor had he poured himself another cup of tea. He had, however, been writing at his desk.

The butler knew the telltale signs of Lord Thorncastle whilst he wrote missives. The constant murmuring. The occasional long pauses of silence as he considered what to write next. The sound of parchment being crumpled into a small ball and tossed into the tall basket positioned at the side of the oak desk.

Lifting the tea tray from the table, Nigel took a quick look around before making his way to the basket. He dared a glance down, noting the only thing in the bin was the recently crumpled parchment the viscount had been writing before he put voice to his frustration. *Dreck!* he had heard the man call out. Dipping a bit, the butler reached the ball of parchment and plucked it from the bin.

The tea tray in both hands and the crumpled missive

stuffed into a pocket, the butler made his way out of the study and down to the kitchens.

A missive needed to be ironed and mailed on the morrow. Or, since he could probably spare a footman, perhaps it could be delivered to a certain townhouse in Curzon Street before the clock struck eight. Along with a certain royal blue umbrella he had noted was still in the urn in the vestibule.

Nigel certainly couldn't trust his master to know what was best when it came to his future. Godfrey Thorncastle had proven he was quite inept when it came to members of the fairer sex. The man needed all the help he could get.

## CHAPTER 15
## TWO LOVEBIRDS PART WAYS

*Meanwhile, back at Gunter's*

Having never felt quite as calm as he did at that moment, Adam Comber regarded the woman who sat across from him and allowed a smile. "I look forward to our life together," he murmured. "The sooner, the better, of course," he added, as if he intended to have them married once they left the confectioner's shop.

Diana considered the man's claim. "When do you expect that will be? I do have to teach tomorrow," she said, a hint of humor in her words. The viscount might believe what he was saying, but despite the bit of hope she had felt the moment she kissed him, she still wasn't convinced he was anything more than a bounder. At any moment, it would become apparent this was all just a lark. All just a ruse to spend an afternoon in a young woman's company.

Wouldn't it?

"Oh," Adam replied, his brows furrowing. "Well, given I cannot procure a special license today, what about the day after tomorrow?"

Diana blinked. "Saturday?" She gave a quick thought as to

what she might have had planned and finally allowed a grin. "Saturday would be... perfect."

Adam allowed a huge grin. "I shall pay a visit to the archbishop's office on the morrow." He suddenly frowned. "It will have to be after Parliament." He considered some of the other tasks he would need to accomplish before they married and realized he really needed to be on his way. "Let me escort you to the coach. I'm sure you have much to do, too."

Although his manner was still friendly, Diana thought he seemed ready to dismiss her. This was it, then. He would put her into a hackney and make some excuse about needing to be somewhere else.

Fighting the tears that threatened, she stood up and made her way through the confectioner's shop, giving a nod to the waiter who opened the door. The Floris town coach was still parked at the curb, the driver immediately hopping down to open the door. She gave him a nod before climbing inside.

"Back to Floris, my lord?" the driver queried.

Adam regarded the man a moment before pulling a coin from his waistcoat pocket. "Could you take us to Warwick's Grammar and Finishing School? And then take me to White's?" he asked as he offered the driver the coin.

At the sight of the blunt, the older man arched an eyebrow. "For this, I would take you to Chiswick."

Adam allowed a chuckle. "You're a good man."

The seat on which Adam had been sitting was covered in packages and bags, so it didn't surprise Diana when he moved to sit beside her. It did surprise her that he was even in the coach.

"I do hope you don't mind," he said as the driver shut the door. "I just... I wish to spend as much time as possible as close to you as I can," he whispered as he took one of her hands in his. "I won't see you again until..." He paused and frowned. "Well, I'll have to see you tomorrow. To let you know about the arrangements for Saturday," he reasoned.

Diana's soft inhalation of breath was barely audible. "I look forward to it," she whispered, realizing she meant it.

The ride to Glasshouse Street went faster than either of them expected, so it was a bit of a surprise when the coach suddenly came to a halt in front of one of the boarding houses for the school. When Adam made the move to get out before her, Diana pulled his arm back. "You cannot be seen escorting me," she whispered, her head shaking. "At least, not yet," she added when she paid witness to his look of confusion.

Adam finally gave her a nod of understanding. "Then I shall kiss you here." And before Diana could reply, his lips were on hers in a searing kiss that would leave no doubt as to what they had been doing during their last moments together. Not to anyone who would see Diana's bee-stung lips and the high color on her cheeks.

When Adam finally pulled away, he sighed. "Let me help you with these parcels at least," he said as he gathered the boxes and bags. Once Diana was out of the coach, he draped the handles over her wrists and the boxes into her arms. "Sleep well, my sweeting."

"You, as well, darling," she replied with a teasing grin. She continued to stand at the curb and watched as the town coach merged into traffic. Adam had opened the window and was watching her, his hat held in one hand.

*This has been the best afternoon of my entire life*, Diana thought as she watched the coach depart. The viscount continued his farewell by waving his beaver through the open window. *If he's not careful, he's going to lose that expensive hat,* she thought as another coach passed between them.

And then he was gone.

Rather shocked at the sense of disappointment she felt at seeing the last of Adam Comber, Diana chided herself. She was sure she would never see the man again, and she had reminded herself of that very thought on several occasions during their time together. But the afternoon had been enjoyable. His company had been unexpected. Once she finally accepted he wasn't going to take his leave of her in Jermyn Street, she had begun to relax and take pleasure in his easy manner and friendliness—when she wasn't concerned about propriety.

He had been so attentive as he squired her about—interested in everything she had to say—and he behaved as if they had known each other their entire lives.

Even to the very last moment as he gave her the packages from the shops in Jermyn Street, he had reiterated how much he was looking forward to their life together as man and wife. And then he had given her another kiss on her cheek—"Since your hand is unavailable at the moment"—and bowed from inside the Floris coach.

After another moment on the curb, her packages held against the front of her body and dangling from her wrists, Diana wondered at the profound sense of loss that had her nearly in tears. Why would she feel such disappointment when she had told herself all day nothing would ever come from the viscount's attentions? He was a bounder. He had probably already forgotten her.

Not that he ever knew her name.

They hadn't been properly introduced!

Diana sighed and finally made her way to the front door of Alpha House. Relieved when the housemaid opened it so she wouldn't have to, she still had to juggle the packages and bags through the opening.

"Oh, my lady, it looks as if you've spent a bit o' coin today," Mae commented with an arched brow as she moved aside.

Giving the maid a nod of agreement, Diana stepped into the small vestibule and paused, wondering why she held so many packages. She had only bought a pair of slippers, a comb, and a toothbrush! "Indeed," she agreed, hurrying off to her rooms with the thought that the viscount had accidentally given her all of his purchases!

Once she had divested herself of the colorful boxes and

bags—the pile on the bed made for an impressive display of Jermyn Street's finest shop names—she stripped the gloves from her fingers. She pulled out the two packages she knew were hers, unwrapping the comb and toothbrush from their tissue wrap and sliding the box of shoes beneath the edge of the bed.

Three boxes were left. Peeking into one, she quickly closed it, quite sure it was filled with fine lawn and lace. The night rail. The rather ornate night rail that had been on display in the modiste's shop, with several layers of lace around the neckline and bottom flounce.

But why would she have the box? Unless...

She shook her head. Certainly the viscount wouldn't have purchased the garment for her. How improper! Which meant he had probably purchased it for someone else.

Which was just as improper!

Frowning, she opened the next box and found a hairbrush nestled in a cloud of tissue paper. She pulled her hand away as if she'd been burned, and then glanced at the comb she had set on her dressing table. The two items were made from the same wood, their grains and coloring matched perfectly.

The viscount had bought the matching hairbrush!

She gingerly opened the last paper bag with the ribbon handle, knowing before she even pulled out the bottle what it was.

Perfume.

"Limes," she whispered as she read the label. "Oh, dear." *Viscount Breckinridge, what have you done?*

# CHAPTER 16
# A MISSIVE IS DELIVERED

*ater, at Elise's townhouse*

When Merry appeared in her mistress' bedchamber at half-past eight o'clock, her ladyship was pretending to read a book. Merry frowned as she attempted to make out the title from where she stood with a cup of tea.

"It's *The Story of a Baron*," Elise announced from where she sat next to the fireplace. "I figured it was past time I read the book that everyone else in the *ton* seemed to find so interesting," she commented. Elise didn't add that she had owned the book for some time but never had the wherewithal to actually read it, concerned she might find herself depicted as one of the characters. So far, she had only determined that three of the leading characters were really Lord and Lady Sommers (although Lady Sommers was really nothing like the character of Geraldine Porterhouse portrayed in the book) and Lord Everly (whose fictional portrayal as Lord Afterly was really quite spot on). If she hadn't heard the gossip in Lady Torrington's parlor, she might not have made the connection, though. Having been away from London for so much of the past eighteen years meant she was unfamiliar with the current crop of debutantes and young bucks.

Merry took note of the woman's tear-stained cheeks and gave an exaggerated sigh. "Was he really a brute?" she asked as she set the teacup on the nightstand. After all the years with Viscount Lancaster, Merry hoped her ladyship's next association would be with someone who was a bit more loving. A bit more loyal. And far more monogamous. Otherwise, why would she bother? Far better she be an independent woman.

Elise blinked. "A brute?" she repeated, thinking there was no such character in the book. Perhaps the beast hadn't yet been introduced.

"The man who proposed to you," Merry clarified. When Elise frowned and shook her head, the maid allowed a sigh. "Did he say something stupid?" she queried.

Elise blinked. How was it that maids knew men were generally stupid? The butler who was in charge of the household and staff seemed to be a rather intelligent man. The single footman even seemed to possess a modicum of brains.

So from where had Merry developed her poor opinion of men?

"I am married," Merry reminded her, as if she could read Elise's mind.

Her ladyship blinked again, rather startled to be reminded that, yes, Merry had indeed married. At least a year ago. "A groom in Lord Mayfield's stables, no?" she remembered. "At Harrington House?"

It was Merry's turn to blink, rather surprised her mistress remembered such a detail. "Indeed. He might know everything there is to know about horseflesh, but he knows little else," she commented with an arched eyebrow.

"Is he a good lover?" Elise asked aloud, almost regretting having put voice to the query.

Merry seemed to give the question some consideration before allowing a nod. "Once I set him straight on proper positioning, I suppose," she answered, her voice hinting at humor. "Seems he thought the only way to take a woman was from behind, so I had to clear up his misunderstanding on that matter."

Slumping back into her chair, Elise rather wished she'd had the temerity to set her late husband straight on the matter. She couldn't help but wonder how Godfrey preferred making love. She couldn't imagine him treating a woman like a horse, mounting her from behind and rutting as if she were some kind of animal. But she really had no idea of his skills or lack thereof. Truth be told, she couldn't recall hearing much *on-dit* about the man. Any, really.

A knock at door had both of them giving a start. Merry hurried to the door, opening it just a bit. A white envelope was slid through the opening, along with a royal blue umbrella, and she took the items. Despite not knowing how to read, she gave the writing on the envelope a glance before hurrying to give it to Elise. "A missive for you, milady," she said. "And your umbrella," she said *sotto voce*, an arched eyebrow suggesting she thought her ladyship had left it behind intentionally.

Elise frowned at the insinuation and took the bright white note from her maid. Studying the inked lettering by the light of the candle lamp on the dressing table, she didn't recognize the script, nor did she notice the faint evidence of wrinkling in the parchment. "Did the post just now get delivered?" she asked, her brows furrowing.

Merry shook her head. "This late at night? A courier would have delivered these, milady," she countered as she moved to put the umbrella in the dressing room. "Or a footman, perhaps. The posts were delivered earlier this afternoon."

With a bit of trepidation, Elise popped the unembossed wax seal from where the corners had been joined. Slowly unfolding the missive, she frowned as she began to read, struggling to ignore the crossed out words (rather difficult considering they were quite evident) and concentrate instead on the words she could make out.

*My dearest Elise,*

Elise inhaled sharply. There was only one man on the entire planet who would address her in such a manner.
Godfrey Thorncastle.

*I wish to apologize for my mistaken assumptions as to how you have been living your life these past eighteen years. I admit to having assumed a woman of your poise and beauty would be a draw for any man, as you certainly have always been for me. I admit to having believed everything I have read in print, thinking it was the truth, for otherwise, why would it be printed?*

*Thanks to your tutelage, I know better now. I have not been employing the traits of a critical thinker. I apologize and ask, nay, beg your forgiveness. It's too bad I didn't employ critical thinking eighteen years ago. Had I done so, I could have avoided so much heartache and disappointment on both of our behalves.*

*You see, I have always believed we would one day be married.*

*I love you.*

*I love you.*

*I want you to be my wife. I want to live the rest of my life with you. I want you to be the mother of my heir (should we be so blessed) and daughter (who will be beautiful despite my share of her).*

*Please forgive my mistaken assumptions. I thought the worst only because my fellow aristocrats can be such rakes when it comes to beautiful women like you. Even if you had engaged in an affaire, please know this. It would not have made a difference to me. I love you, Elise. I shall always love you. Please marry me. I love you and only you, Elise.*

*Yours forever, Godfrey.*

Elise dropped the parchment onto her lap. Aware that Merry had been watching her the entire time she had been reading and rereading the letter, she gave the maid a quelling glance. She turned her attention to the dying flames in the fireplace, wishing they would provide her with a sign of what she should do.

The man's plea was obviously heartfelt. But how could he have thought her to be a... a *wanton?* Quick to bed any man who showed interest when she was married to Lancaster? As if any usurper to his property would be tolerated? Why, if she had been discovered having bedded any other man during their marriage, she was quite sure Lancaster would have challenged said man to a duel in Wimbledon Common. And he would have won. The man was a crack shot and made sure everyone knew it.

"Is it from your true love?" Merry asked with too much enthusiasm.

Allowing a sigh, Elise shook her head. "It's from Lord Thorncastle," she stated. "A declaration of love and stupidity, I suppose," she added when she noticed her maid's look of confusion. "He was the one who proposed in the missive I received yesterday morning."

Her eyes widening, the maid regarded her mistress for several moments before finally allowing a nod. "Two letters of love in two days? Why, he must truly feel affection for you, my lady," she sighed happily.

The maid obviously believed in true love despite having married a man who lacked horse sense. Or perhaps had too much of it.

Elise allowed a sigh of frustration. "I suppose," she agreed with not a lot of enthusiasm. The idea of returning to the viscount's townhouse on the morrow didn't appeal to her in the least, but neither did the thought of penning a reply.

What would she write? *I was about to accept your offer of marriage before you made a cake of it. Before you put voice to words that only emphasized how thoroughly and completely stupid men of your ilk can be.*

What made him think the worst of her in the first place? Possessing poise and beauty didn't mean she was an idiot! She was a widow, though, and she supposed the actions of a few had the man thinking she would welcome a lover into her bed.

There was a time—a very brief time, shortly after Lancaster's death—when she would have been amenable to the idea of taking a lover.

Loneliness did that to a woman.

Made a person consider situations in a different light. Made for some poor choices in bedmates. Made the nights feel longer and darker than they should have, even if they had been just as long and dark before a husband's death.

At least Godfrey had apologized. Rather profusely. His note was quite clear in that regard.

Elise sighed. She supposed she owed him another opportunity to state his case. Another opportunity to properly propose. It didn't mean she had to accept his suit, though. Didn't mean she had to give him an answer anytime soon, either.

There were conditions that had to be met.

Glancing at the clock on the mantel, she set aside the book and quickly stood. "Have Draper arrange for the town coach. I'm going for a ride," she stated.

Merry blinked before her eyes rounded. About to put voice to a protest—it was nearly nine o'clock—she took note of Elise's fierce expression and thought better of it. "Yes, milady." She hurried to the door and disappeared down the hall.

Elise regarded her reflection in the cheval mirror, rather relieved to find her face didn't appear as strained as it had when she first returned from Lord Thorncastle's townhouse. She leaned closer, examining the tiny lines at the edges of her eyes, and the corners of her mouth. The blue irises darkened at the thought of what she was about to do—pay a nocturnal visit to Godfrey Thorncastle.

*You naughty girl, you*, she thought.

As for the dinner gown she wore, she thought it rather appropriate for the occasion. Either the viscount would be caught tongue-tied and unable to put voice to more ridiculous assumptions, or he would not.

She rather hoped he had learned his lesson.

## CHAPTER 17
## A SON CONFERS WITH A MOTHER

*Meanwhile, at Aimsley House*

Adam Comber regarded the front entrance of Aimsley House with a wary eye. He would one day inherit the mansion in Park Lane, although given his father's good health, he didn't expect to for many years. The cream stucco appeared in good condition, the white around the windows a pleasant contrast. The black wrought iron fencing just at the edge of the pavement could use a good cleaning, but he expected his mother might have already put it on her list of things to which the butler needed to do.

Patience Aimsley always seemed to have lists, but then, he supposed organized women did. He rather imagined his betrothed would do the same. He rather hoped she would.

The front door opened before he could use the brass knocker. Hummel stepped aside as he said his welcome, and Adam gave the butler his hat. "Is the countess in residence?" he asked.

Hummel nodded. "She is in her salon."

Adam gave a nod and hurried to the end of the central hall, ducking his head around the last door's jamb. "Have you a few minutes for an errant son?" he queried.

Patience looked up from her escritoire and gave him a broad grin before standing up. "That all depends. What have you gone and done *now?*" she asked in feigned dismay as Adam leaned down and bussed her on the cheek.

"Found my future wife," he replied as he led her to one of the floral upholstered chairs.

The countess didn't sit down, though. Instead, she whirled to face him, a look of shock on her face. "You're serious," she whispered.

Adam nodded. "I am." Despite trying to keep an impassive expression, he was soon smiling.

Blinking, Patience finally took a seat—practically falling into it—and watched as Adam took the adjacent chair. "Well. It's past time I suppose," she said with a feeble smile. She suddenly frowned, though. "Did you get a child on her? Is that why—?"

"No, Mother. That's not it at all," Adam replied with a shake of his head. And a rather shocked look. He supposed he shouldn't be surprised she would think the worst of him, though. He hadn't exactly been a model son through the years, but at least his best friend, Felix Turnbridge, had seen to getting him out of trouble when necessary. "I met her outside of White's, and I just spent the most pleasant day of my life in her company." He described how they had shopped and enjoyed ices at Gunter's, noting how at ease he was in her company.

Patience watched as her son described the young lady, rather fascinated by how his face seemed to light up as he did so. "Do I know her?" she asked after a time. In his entire recitation of his afternoon with the woman, he never mentioned her name.

"Perhaps. She's a teacher at Warwick's. Dancing and arithmetic," he added proudly. He knew the topic of Warwick's wasn't her favorite—his sister, Emelia, had experienced a rather unfortunate incident with the former dancing instructor

—but he felt relief in seeing his mother didn't allow a grimace or any other outward sign of disapproval during his description. Either she was fine with his news, or she would make an excellent card player. Adam wasn't quite sure as he soldiered on. "She's agreed to keep our household books," he stated, as if that may have been one of the primary reasons for considering her as a wife. "Anyway, after Parliament ends tomorrow, I plan to pay a visit to Doctors' Commons. Apply for a special license so we can skip the banns and all."

Patience regarded her son with a wan smile, tears nearly coming to her eyes. "I was beginning to wonder if this day would ever come," she said with a sigh.

Adam's eyes widened. "Why ever not? Just because I've waited until I'm almost thirty isn't very different from others of my ilk," he added defensively.

Shaking her head, Patience sighed and allowed a grin. "It's not that. It's that you seem to be in love. First, your sister. And now you."

A rush of color suffused his face just then. Leave it to his mother to notice what he hadn't quite admitted to himself. "Oh, I rather I doubt that," he allowed, not about to admit he wouldn't know if he was or wasn't. How did one know such a thing? He frowned, though, wondering about his sister. He'd only seen her once since her return from Switzerland. "Emelia's in love? When did that happen?"

Patience gave her son a quelling glance. "Probably during Lord Weatherstone's garden party a couple of months ago," she replied.

Adam continued frowning. "Hmm," was all he said. He was about to ask if he knew the man but remembered the real reason for his visit. "I wondered if I might fetch Grandmother's ring? The one she said I was to give my bride when I found her," he added.

Arching an elegant eyebrow, Patience regarded her son with a look of surprise. "I'll get it for you. It's a bit out of fashion, though. Are you sure you don't want to find something a bit more modern?"

"Quite sure. I think it will suit my sweeting perfectly," he replied.

Patience thought it interesting Adam didn't mention the woman's name, but she figured she could sort it after a day or two. She was in the business to know such things, after all. "You do realize I'll have to include an article about you in the next issue of my newspaper," she warned with a grin.

Adam blinked. "About that. Just what kind of rag has father purchased on your behalf?"

The countess angled her head to one side. "It's still a secret, dear. But let's just say I'll be far more fair and lighthearted in my reporting than the last editor." She wasn't about to tell him that the last editor had been his best friend, Felix Turnbridge, and that the newspaper she now owned was *The Tattler*. Lord Fennington would soon be her son-in-law. Adam's brother-in-law. Any printable gossip would now be hers to share—or not.

Adam stood up when his mother moved to her escritoire. She opened one of the small drawers on top and pulled out the gold ring on which was mounted a single diamond. Although it was terribly out of fashion—there was little in the way of embellishment—the diamond glimmered in the light from the candle lamp mounted on the small desk.

Patience handed the ring to Adam. "Are you quite sure you don't want to get her something more modern?" she asked again.

Her son shook his head. "This will suit my sweeting, I assure you. Thank you for keeping it on my behalf."

The countess continued to regard her son for another moment before leaning in. "Whatever you do, promise me you won't be greedy on your wedding night, or you may find your bride won't welcome you back into her bed for a week or more," she warned with an arched brow.

Adam blinked, understanding almost immediately to what

she referred. He and his betrothed had talked as if they would spend three days in bed, though. Three days before a modiste would come to make her some bride clothes. "I will take care, of course. I promise," he replied, rather glad his red face wasn't so apparent in the low light of the salon. He leaned over and kissed one of her cheeks.

"You'll bring her for dinner," Patience ordered.

"I will," Adam agreed, deciding now wasn't the time to ask if an apartment in Aimsley House might be available.

For now that he was giving marriage a good deal of thought, he rather doubted his betrothed would have much in the way of a dowry, and he wondered if his allowance would cover a wife.

Questioning his decision, Adam gave his mother another kiss on the cheek and bade her good night before heading down the hall. He didn't take his leave of Aimsley House, though.

His curiosity had him seeking his father.

# CHAPTER 18
# A LATE NIGHT VISITOR

*T*en o'clock *in the evening at Lord Thorncastle's townhouse* Nigel was about to extinguish the gas lamp in the vestibule when the sound of a town coach had him pausing. A quick glance out the front widow that looked out onto Bruton Street confirmed his suspicions. Someone was paying a visit to one of the houses along the street, and given how the town coach was suddenly parked out front of Thorncastle House, he realized his master probably had a visitor.

As to whether or not Godfrey Thorncastle would receive said visitor was unknown. The man had spent most of the evening in his bedchamber and then in his study, examining the bottom of a crystal tumbler that had held several fingers worth of scotch—several times. The fact that the man could do so and still remain upright in his favorite wingback chair was a testament to how often the man imbibed. What else did he have to do on evenings such as this, though? He was unmarried. He didn't employ a mistress. He only ever left at night if he was invited to play cards at White's or share someone's box at the theatre. As for brothels, well, Nigel was quite sure the man avoided the pleasure palaces only because he never spent the night somewhere other than in his own bedchamber.

He often wondered if perhaps his master preferred the company of other men, but Lord Thorncastle had never entertained any at the townhouse, even for dinner.

Even before the brass knocker made a sound, Nigel opened the front door. Garbed in a dark mantle with a hood hiding her face, the butler wasn't even sure it was a woman until Lady Lancaster passed over the threshold, lifted her head, and gave him a nod. A calling card appeared in one of her gloved hands and she offered it. "Is Lord Thorncastle receiving callers this evening?" she asked, removing her mantle in a flourish even before he could respond.

The usually unflappable butler was suddenly flapped as he struggled to take the mantle from her, his gaze sweeping down her rather scandalous dinner gown and back up to her elaborate coiffure. He was about to put voice to a response when she said, "I'll take that as invitation to find out for myself." Then she simply glided past him, making her way to the very room where she had met with his master less than eight hours ago.

*She read the letter*, Nigel realized, his eyes lifted heavenward for a moment as he prayed Lord Thorncastle wouldn't make a cake of whatever was about to happen.

Hanging the mantle on one of the hooks on the vestibule wall, Nigel was half-tempted to eavesdrop on the couple's conversation, but he instead decided to simply take a seat in the hall and wait.

*E*lise paused on the threshold of the study, sure Godfrey was in the room. Although she probably should have allowed the butler to announce her arrival, she had no patience for the niceties.

The pale light from a dying fire was the study's only illumination, and given the dark leather, wood furnishings, and deep green Turkish carpeting, very little light made its way to the doorway. Once her eyes adjusted from the brighter light in the hallway, she realized her prey was sitting in the very chair he had been sitting in when they had shared tea earlier. She briefly wondered if he had even moved since then. *But of course he has. He had to get up to write the letter*, she reasoned.

Although she had half a mind to take a step back and have Nigel announce her, she decided instead to simply close the door and make her way to where she had been sitting earlier. *Return to the scene of the crime*, she thought with not a lot of humor. Dressed in the deep red satin dinner gown and bedecked with a diamond and ruby necklace, a diamond bracelet, and diamond and ruby earbobs, she very nearly glittered in the firelight.

She angled her head as she regarded the viscount. When he didn't look up right away—she thought perhaps he was napping—Elise curtsied. She was about to lower herself onto the divan but thought perhaps she should remain standing. Godfrey Thorncastle might be a viscount, but at the moment, she needed to make him think she outranked him.

"I received your letter," she said without preamble.

Godfrey gave a start, the amber liquid in his tumbler nearly sloshing over the edge of the glass. The man seemed to blink several times, as if he couldn't believe what he was seeing. It was as if the devil himself had dressed his naughtiest and most beautiful enchantress and delivered her from thin air to stand before him. He was nearly blinded by the flashes of light that sparkled from the jewels she wore. "I didn't send a letter to the devil," he managed to get out, his voice sounding rather foreign to his ears. Worse, his tongue seemed to get in the way of his words, and his vision seemed blurry around the edges.

"You're *foxed!*" the enchantress accused as her gloved hands went to her hips. The motion only enhanced her décolletage, which had his nether region responding in a manner unsuitable for mixed company.

Godfrey's eyes widened in... well, not horror, certainly, for the red-clad vision before him was quite beautiful.

And quite incensed.

His body responded at least, although two parts did instead of the usual one. His member jumped to attention—something that only happened when he thought of Elise Burroughs—as did his legs, which had him standing up rather awkwardly. He bowed, the response so automatic, he didn't have to give it a second thought. Rather fortuitous, since the issue of his erect member had him wondering how to hide said evidence when he returned to a standing position. The crystal tumbler would have to do the trick, he decided, the hand holding said tumbler moving so it held the nearly-empty glass directly in front of the placket of his breeches. "Elise," he murmured in awe. At least, he hoped it sounded as if he were in awe.

He was. Truly.

For he had spent several hours that day thinking he might never see her again. "You look... ravishing," he murmured, hoping his voice sounded clearer than the slurred words that made their way to his ears.

Elise allowed a sigh as she removed her hands from her hips and slowly sank into the divan. Two things had made themselves most evident just then. Besides Godfrey's member, the man had spent the evening imbibing in what smelled like rather good scotch. "Is there any more scotch?" she asked, thinking she could do with a finger's worth.

Godfrey blinked, partly because he understood her query perfectly and partly because he sympathized with why she would ask such a question. "Indeed," he answered, moving as steadily to the credenza behind his oak desk as he could manage given his overactive nether region and his inebriated state. He poured a rather generous dollop into one of the tumblers he found on the silver salver. Lifting the glass, he took it to her, giving her a nod as he placed it into her gloved hands. The position afforded him a glance down the deep, thin canyon that made up her décolletage, although he was careful to keep his glance brief.

He was still trying to hide his nether region with his own glass of scotch. Or what little was left of it. A passing thought had him realizing that Elise could probably see through the nearly empty tumbler. When he realized her gaze was directed at his glass—well, he supposed there was a slight chance she was admiring his onyx ring—he gave up trying to hide anything and finally sighed. "I cannot help it, my love," he said in an apologetic voice. "I was… thinking of you, and then you were suddenly here. Like magic."

Elise took a sip of scotch before she directed her gaze back up to his face. He looked ever so sad, she thought. Pitiable, almost. "Perhaps you've simply conjured me into existence," she replied in a quiet voice, deciding it was as good a reason as any to explain her decision to pay a call on the viscount well past calling hours.

"If that were the case, then you would be here all the time," he replied, sounding ever so sober. "Every day. Especially at night."

Her eyes widening at hearing his words, Elise angled her head and regarded Godfrey for a moment. "Truly?"

The viscount nodded. "Oh, Elise. I've been such a fool," he said, settling into the chair directly across from her. "I thought the worst of you because I thought the worst of those with whom I thought you were spending your evenings."

Wincing, Elise thought she might have made a mistake in coming. Despite their earlier words, he still seemed to believe she had carried on *affaires*. "Until two years ago, I was married. From the time I was sixteen years old," she countered, her voice rather firm. "I was completely faithful to Lancaster." *Because I had no choice.*

"I know that," Godfrey responded with a nod. "I've known that all along. It's just…" He paused as he took in a deep breath. "I allowed my imagination to get the worst of me. As easily as I conjure you in my mind's eye, I conjure others whom I believe are just as besotted with you as I am."

"Yet I am not in their homes well past calling hours," she whispered. "Nor have I ever been." She thought to add that last bit just in case he might think she made it a habit of visiting the homes of unattached men. At night. Or whenever.

Godfrey straightened as he regarded her with an expression of contrition. "I do apologize for my overactive imagination."

Elise considered *how* he said the words more than the words themselves. *Overactive imagination* suggested a creative sort. Or a dreamer. "You're forgiven," Elise murmured. She gave a nod and then sighed. "Now, about the letters you've sent—"

"Letters?" he repeated, rather relieved his words were no longer slurred. "As in, more than one?"

Elise blinked. "Letters, yes. Two of them."

The viscount's brows furrowed into a single line, his expression suggesting he was either experiencing a massive headache or he was extremely confused. He scratched his head and was about to put voice to another query when Elise angled her head to one side.

"I received one yesterday, before the Weatherstone ball. The one in which you first proposed marriage," she clarified. "The other one arrived just tonight. I read it about an hour ago." She frowned then, wondering if he had forgotten he had written the declarations of love, or if he had written them whilst deep in his cups and had no memory of doing so.

Godfrey blinked before he suddenly returned to his feet and made his way to his desk. In the near-dark, he gave a quick glance over the surface and then reached down to lift up the basket where he was quite sure he had tossed the last letter he had written to Elise.

The basket was empty.

"What is it?" Elise asked from where she was still seated in the divan.

"Seems there's been some other kind of magic happening here," he murmured, quite sure he had crumpled up his last letter to Elise in a fit of frustration. He set the basket back down onto the floor and returned to his chair. "Was the last letter you received a bit... wrinkled, perhaps?" he asked, his expression still displaying his confusion.

Elise blinked at hearing his question. "Are you suggesting the letter was never intended to be read by me?" *Oh, damnation.* The only reason she had decided to make the trip to see Godfrey at the ungodly hour of ten o' clock at night was because the second letter had been so... heartfelt. So full of contrition and longing and, dare she think it? *Love?*

The viscount allowed a shrug. "Eventually. I just thought to rewrite it. I wanted to be... clear about my apology. About..." He allowed the sentence to trail off before allowing a long sigh.

"I thought your words were crystal clear," Elise whispered. She took a sip of the scotch and had to suppress the urge to choke as the white-hot liquor made its way down her throat. "Which is why I decided to pay a call." Her last words were pitched a bit higher than normal.

Godfrey's eyes widened. "Go on," he urged as he leaned forward.

Elise leaned forward as well, rather glad when their knees nearly touched. The low table on which the tea set had been earlier that afternoon was pushed off to one side, apparently to give Godfrey more leg room in front of his favorite chair. "I wish to give you my answer and state my conditions." Despite Godfrey's suddenly pale appearance, Elise soldiered on. "I will accept your offer of marriage. In fact, I thought perhaps we could simply skip the formalities and marry by special license."

It was Godfrey's turn to blink. "Tomorrow?"

Elise sat back and angled her head to one side. "Well, perhaps in a week or so, actually," she hedged, not having thought that far ahead. "Besides, I rather doubt you can obtain a license and get married on the same day. Can you?"

The viscount shook his head. "I've absolutely no idea. I've never been married before, nor have I been tempted enough to even look into the matter," he admitted, not realizing how his words would sound. "At least, not since I was sixteen," he clarified.

Elise frowned before straightening on the divan. "Then why have you proposed to me?" she countered, ire evident in her question. *Did James put him up to it?* she wondered, her thoughts of her brother rather uncharitable.

Godfrey blinked twice, realizing just then how his words must have sounded. "I've never been tempted by anyone *but you*," he clarified. "And until two years ago, you were married," he added with a curt nod.

"But I've been out of mourning for a year!" Elise replied, her anger even more evident.

Closing his eyes—he couldn't bear the thought of her being angry with him yet again—Godfrey stilled himself. How should he reply?

Admit to being a coward?

Not yet. Perhaps never.

"If I had proposed a year ago, would you have given my suit any consideration?" he whispered. "Honestly, Elise. I thought you were enjoying the life of an *independent woman*," he whispered, trying hard not to make the words sound like an accusation.

Her expression softening a bit—there had been a hint of gossip about her return to London back then—Elise studied the crystal tumbler she held. She remembered how her brother, James, had reacted to her claim that she would be living the rest of her life as an unmarried woman. As a duke, he couldn't exactly allow her to live without some sort of protection. Lancaster hadn't exactly left her with much of an inheritance, but with careful budgeting, she could have lived a rather comfortable life in the capital. Instead, James had set her up in a townhouse, ordered the town coach, and given her an allowance as a means to keep her close, keep her from appearing as if she was living completely on her own.

It was all about appearances, after all.

"I *wanted* to be an independent woman," Elise finally acknowledged with a nod. "I was tired of being married to a philandering husband and wondering if there was enough money to pay the servants. Tired of his drunkenness and his cruel words. Praying I wouldn't find myself with child, because I didn't want to have to protect it from the beast—"

"Jesus, Elise," Godfrey whispered hoarsely, the curse a testament to his ignorance of the life she had lived as the Countess of Lancaster. "I had no idea. Had I known..." He swallowed, wondering what he might be capable of doing. "I would have—"

She held up a staying hand. "You're right. I would not have considered your suit back then," she admitted with a nod, saving him from making any kind of chivalrous claim. "But another year has passed, and circumstances have changed, and now you have proposed marriage."

"I shall pay a visit to Doctors' Commons on the morrow and see to a special license," Godfrey stated.

"Tomorrow is Friday," Elise reminded him. "Won't you be at Parliament?"

"Not all day," Godfrey countered. "Would you consider a ceremony on Saturday, perhaps?" he asked, his voice sounding rather hopeful.

Elise resisted the urge to inhale sharply. She hadn't realized he would take her suggestion so seriously. *What would the gossips think?* "I suppose," she hedged. "Although a sudden wedding will have the tongues wagging. Why, they'll think we *had* to marry," she added as her eyes widened. She took a swallow of scotch and found it went down far easier than the first sip.

Godfrey gave a shrug, realizing he rather liked the idea that some in the *ton* might think such a thing. "Let them think we had an *affaire* that's left you *enceinte*," he replied with a nod, his face brightening. "It will be our secret that we didn't."

Giving him a quelling glance and about to say something

along the lines of, *it doesn't quite work like that,* Elise rather enjoyed seeing Godfrey's expression just then. It was the first sign of joy she had seen on his face since the first day he had kissed her. He was rather handsome when he looked like that.

Happy.

The expression faded when he suddenly frowned, and the moment was lost.

"You said you had conditions."

Elise inhaled softly, rather surprised he remembered. "Where will we live?" she asked. "You see, I refuse to spend the entire year living in the country." She dared a glance around the room in which they sat, knowing the study would always be his domain. This might be the only time she was welcome here.

"Would you be amenable to moving in here? With me?" His enthusiasm had him looking as if he were ten years younger than he was. "We could live here year-round if you wish. We'd never have to go to the country."

Elise blinked. "Do you ...? Is there enough room for me?" *Enough room for a family?*

Godfrey's eyes widened. "I should hope so. There are four-teen rooms here," he claimed. His eyes went skyward before he allowed a sigh when he remembered Elise had never toured the townhouse his family had owned since its original construction. "You'll have your own bedchamber, of course, and then there's mine. A bathing chamber. And a couple of guest bedchambers, a nursery and a salon. Those are all on the first floor. And then, down here, there's a small ballroom. A breakfast parlor, and a dining room, and the parlor. Kitchen, butler's pantry, and study," he counted off, giving a nod when he had finished the inventory of rooms. He held his breath a moment. "You're welcome to redecorate should you decide you don't like the colors or... or the fabrics... or anything, for that matter. Throw out anything you don't think is suitable. As long as..." He paused, his expression sobering.

"As long as...?" Elise prompted, wondering at the sudden change in him. Why, he looked as forlorn as he had when she had first arrived.

"As long as you don't throw *me* out, I suppose," he finally said.

Elise sighed before leaning forward. She placed a hand on his knee, giving it a shake. "I won't," she whispered. "That is, unless..." She stopped, her lips set in a thin line.

"Unless?" he prompted.

"I will not abide another philandering husband," she stated, her chin thrust out in defiance. "It's one of my conditions. Despite his vows and his assurances to my brother, Lancaster was never faithful to me. You have to promise..." She stopped when she paid witness to his expression of surprise. "What? Is that too much to ask? Because, if it is..."

Godfrey had to suppress the urge to laugh at her, but not for the reason she would assume. "Elise, please. I will be faithful to you to until my dying day," he vowed, slowly getting to his feet. "And beyond. I promise."

The empty tumbler dropped from his hand and rolled onto the carpet as he covered the space that barely separated them. His hands were suddenly beneath her arms, pulling her up to her feet. Despite her gasp of surprise, he embraced her, his arms pulling her hard against the front of his body before Elise quite knew what was happening.

Not having been held so close in a very long time, Elise closed her eyes and reveled in the sensation of his heat permeating the satin of her gown. Her own arms lifted to wrap around his shoulders, one hand moving to his head as her fingers speared the waves of his hair. "Then I make the same promise to you," she murmured. She pulled away so she could look into his eyes when she said her next words. "I have only ever been with one other man, and that was my husband," she added in a whisper. "He was a very poor lover. I never knew..." She paused as a flush covered her face. She might have attributed it to the scotch, but she knew it was embarrassment at the topic of her comment. "You shall have to teach me what I need to know to please you in bed."

Left momentarily speechless, Godfrey tried to form the words he thought he should say just then, but instead he pulled her against his body again. "Jesus, Elise. I've a mind to..." He clamped his mouth shut, knowing he would never do what his overactive imagination had him imagining just then. At least, not until after they were wed. Even then, he wasn't sure he would manage that particular feat.

"Oh, we really can't tonight," she said with a shake of her head. "I've no other clothes with me, and my coachman is out front..." She paused before allowing a nervous giggle. "But that's probably not what you meant just then, is it?" she added uncertainly.

Godfrey kissed her then, his mouth taking possession of hers in a soft, slow kiss that seemed to send heat to every part of her body. The heat was necessary, though, as her entire body seemed to shiver beneath his hold. Desire bloomed while the front of her body molded to his. When his lips moved to her jaw and then to her neck, Elise allowed a quiet sigh. "I think I shall make kisses another condition of our marriage," she managed to get out in a hoarse whisper.

"You needn't, I assure you," he countered, dipping his tongue into the hollow of her throat, just above where her pendant lay against her heated skin. "For I would make them one of mine."

Elise allowed another gasp as his tongue trailed down to the neckline of her gown. She felt her nipples harden behind the fabric cups of her corset, and she gasped again. "Have you others?" she asked as she used one of her hands to guide one of his to her breast. She inhaled sharply when he gently cupped it, molded it slowly.

"Others?" he repeated, finally pulling his lips away from her chest.

"Conditions?"

"Have you?" he countered, his brows furrowing as he brushed the edge of his thumb over her pebbled nipple. Despite the low light from the fireplace, he could see the silhouette of it through the dark red satin. He had half a mind to cover it with his mouth, but reason had him straightening instead. He would ruin the gown if he did. And he wanted to see her wearing it again. And again.

"I want a baby. Two, actually," Elise whispered. "Maybe more."

He blinked. "Of course," he nodded. "I need an heir," he agreed with a nod. "Do you suppose...?" He swallowed, his head falling forward so his forehead rested on hers. "Would you be agreeable to sharing a bed? At least, whilst we sleep? For I think I shall want to hold you all night long. Keep you warm. Keep you safe."

Nodding, Elise lifted her head and kissed him as she had done earlier that afternoon. "I think I'll make a condition of it," she murmured. "Unless you snore, and then we shall have to renegotiate."

Godfrey grinned before sucking in a breath between his teeth. "Oh, how I wish I was married to you already. If I don't send you home this very instant, my lady, we shall be saying our wedding vows without benefit of a bishop up in my bedchamber," he warned.

Elise had half a mind to allow him to do so, but reason prevailed when she remembered how she was dressed. She would have to return to her townhouse at some point, preferably about the same time as she would if she were attending the theatre. Tomorrow was Friday. There would be morning callers.

"I'll let my brother know I'll be vacating my townhouse," Elise said, a twinge making her wonder if she was doing the right thing. She allowed Godfrey to lead her to the vestibule.

"I've already asked and received his permission," he replied as he lifted her mantle from the peg and held it for her. "Third time's the charm?"

"What did you say?" Elise asked in alarm.

Godfrey blinked and allowed a one-shouldered shrug. "Your brother has finally given me permission to marry you. Which is another reason why my proposal occurred when it did."

Elise nodded, a mix of anger at her brother and surprise at Godfrey thinking he needed the duke's permission leaving her discombobulated. "Good night," she murmured.

Godfrey settled his lips onto hers and kissed her. "I can hardly wait to do this every single day for the rest of my life."

Giving him a wan smile, Elise nodded her agreement and took her leave of Thorncastle's townhouse.

Her future home.

Once she was settled in the squabs of her town coach, Elise thought about Godfrey's words.

*Third time's the charm.*

Had the man really asked for James' permission to marry her that many times?

Perhaps she should keep the ducal townhouse, just in case something happened. Just in case she was making a huge mistake in finally marrying Godfrey Thorncastle.

But in the meantime, she needed to have a word with James.

## CHAPTER 19
## A SON CONFERS WITH HIS FATHER

*Meanwhile, back at Aimsley House*

Adam strode through the hall, his boot heels sinking into the Axminster carpet runner decorating the center of it. On either side of him, the faces of past Aimsley earls and their countesses stared down at him. A few Breckinridge viscounts were scattered among the portraits, only one of which had a matching viscountess. *Grandmother*, he thought as he paused to gaze at the woman he could barely remember from his youth.

Had her raven hair been allowed to show instead of the ornate wig featured in the painting, Adam realized she and Diana could have been related. Given the common ancestors of so many aristocrats, perhaps they were. Both had heart-shaped faces that looked as if they could be made of porcelain, with wide-set eyes and rosebud lips meant for kissing. Grandmother's were set in a teasing grin he recalled seeing several times.

He regarded the painting for a moment longer, frowning before he stepped closer. The ring tucked into his waistcoat pocket was featured in the painting, although the artist failed to capture the brilliance of its single diamond. The pendant at the hollow of her throat included a single gem, although it was impossible to tell just what kind of stone the gold setting surrounded.

Sighing, Adam stepped back, about to move on when he did a double-take. Why, he was quite sure his grandmother was winking at him. He moved closer, studying the brush strokes around her eyes, noting the tiny lashes and crinkles at the corners. She had been a handsome woman. Probably even pretty in her younger years. *What had his grandfather deciding she would be his countess?* Had their marriage been one of convenience? Or one of mutual affection? Given her expression, he rather hoped it had been a happy union. He thought of what his intended might look like in forty years. She would still be beautiful. He was sure of it.

When he was convinced his grandmother's portrait wasn't winking, he finally gave the matron a bow and continued his trek down the wide hall.

He ignored several marble busts he was sure were watching him—as a child he half-expected one or more of them to come to life—and finally stopped at the half-opened door to his father's study. Ducking his head past the opening, he was relieved to find Mark, Earl of Aimsley, at his desk. The man gripped a pen in his right hand and was furiously writing.

"One more line and then you can interrupt," the earl commented without taking his attention from the parchment in front of him.

Adam stood just inside the door, deciding to wait there rather than take a seat in front of the desk. He hadn't yet determined how he was going to broach the subject he now thought to discuss with his father. At first, he had merely thought to inform the earl that he had decided on whom he was going to marry. Now, though, he had another concern.

When Aimsley glanced up, he did a double-take. "Well, if this isn't a surprise. What the hell brings you to Aimsley House on this fine night? Nothing good happening at White's?" he asked as he waved his son to the chair in front of his desk. He was about to ask if Adam needed an advance on his allowance, but decided against it when he saw the serious expression on Adam's face.

The oldest son shook his head. "How did you know Mother was the one?" Adam blurted as he took the proffered chair.

Aimsley blinked and stared at his son for a moment before turning to retrieve a decanter and two tumblers from the credenza behind his desk. Without saying a word, he poured a generous amount into each crystal glass and offered one to Adam. He lifted his own glass and said, "To ladies and their pinkies."

Adam frowned but lifted his own in salute. "To pinkies," he repeated, a hint of uncertainty in his voice. The scotch burned the back of his throat, but the smoky scent filled his nostrils at the same time the liquid heat seemed to fortify him. When he inherited the earldom, he would be sure to stock this scotch, he decided. He had a passing thought he could buy a bottle from Berry Bros. to have at his townhouse, but he rather doubted his allowance would cover the cost.

Watching his son for a moment, the earl finally sighed. "I think it was a bit of love at first sight coupled with a good deal of lust."

Adam blinked, rather startled by his father's candor. "Lust?" he repeated, not so sure he wanted to hear what his father had to say about meeting his mother.

"Oh, God, yes," Aimsley replied before taking a sip from his scotch. "That woman could have led me around by my—"

"Father!" Adam interrupted, stunned at what the earl was suggesting. "You make Mother sound as if she was a... a *courtesan*," he scolded, the last word said *sotto voce*. He had almost said something else, but decided he didn't want his father knowing he knew such a word.

The earl seemed to think on the comment for a moment and was about to agree but gave a chuckle instead. "Pretty much," he agreed with a grin. "Wanton is probably a better term, though. She still is." He sobered, though, and gave a shrug. "I loved her. She loved me. Proved it to me several times before we were even wed," he added with a naughty grin. "So I ruined her to ensure we would."

Adam's eyes rounded. Stunned at hearing that his mother, a paragon of propriety, would have bedded his father before their wedding had his head shaking in disbelief. "You're joking," he accused. Why, he had half a mind to challenge his father to a duel for impugning his mother's honor like this!

Aimsley gave him a quelling glance. "Haven't you done the math?"

Adam blinked, wondering if his father had somehow overheard his conversation with his betrothed at Gunter's. "What math?"

The earl rolled his eyes. "Jesus, Adam. You were born seven months after the wedding," Aimsley said with far too much amusement. "Surely you must have sorted that out by now."

Truth be told, Adam hadn't sorted the timing of his birth because he had never thought to do so. He was about to put voice to the thought but his father spoke up before he could.

"Tell me about yours now. And don't try to claim you haven't got one. You wouldn't have put voice to such a question if you weren't *finally* considering matrimony," the earl stated firmly. "About damned time, too. If I'm two-and-fifty, you have to be about thirty." He suddenly frowned. "You haven't ruined her, I hope?"

Adam rolled his eyes. "Of course not!" Then he realized what else his father had said. "Two-and-fifty? That means you got married when you were..." Here Adam had to stop and attempt to do the math in his head while his father watched with baited breath.

"Two-and-twenty," Aimsley finally said with a hint of impatience. "I take it you skipped school the day they taught simple arithmetic," he accused. He was well aware of Adam's truancy at Eton, but now he was growing concerned that perhaps the boy had missed more instruction than he thought.

Adam was about to explain that he had never been good at mathematics, but he wanted to get back to the matter at hand.

His betrothed.

"It's true that I have proposed marriage. Mother knows—I just came from speaking with her—but given my future wife is an instructor at Warwick's, I rather doubt there will be much of a dowry—"

"Instructor?" Aimsley repeated, a scowl forming on his still-handsome features. "Where in the world did you meet her?"

Adam sighed. "Outside of White's. I spotted her as she was walking past the bow window, on her way to Jermyn Street."

"A ten?"

Blinking at his father's quick query, Adam frowned before he remembered what the number meant. "A seven, actually. At least, that's what I thought at first. I amended it to a nine after I spent the afternoon in her company," he added with a sigh. The woman was really a 'ten', but he didn't want his father thinking she was leading him around by his cock. Or that she already had him wrapped around her pinkie. Which she probably could if she wanted him there.

He was going to make it his mission to be sure he was wrapped around that pinkie. Or the other one. Both, if that were possible.

Aimsley nodded, apparently satisfied with the explanation. "Do I know her?"

Screwing his face up in concentration, Adam tried to determine if there would have been a reason for their paths to cross. "I doubt it. She replaced the dance instructor who was fired over what he did to Emelia," he commented, deciding it was safe to tell his father that much. "Oh, and she also teaches arithmetic."

This last bit had Aimsley straightening in his chair, a look of appreciation making his features appear far younger than his fifty-plus years. "Well, that's good enough for me," he said with a nod. "God knows, you certainly cannot do math." He paused for a moment and then frowned, realizing just why Adam was in his study.

Perhaps the boy *could* do math.

"You're here for an increase in your allowance, aren't you?" he asked, suspicion evident in his voice.

Adam managed a look of contrition. "It's possible we can live in my townhouse—"

"No, it's not."

"In which case, I won't require more funds than I'm currently receiving—"

"You'll need more rooms within a year. A nursery, certainly."

"A bit of budgeting and careful spending, and we'll be fine."

"If you think for one minute I'm going to allow your nine-of-a-bride to live in that hovel you call a townhouse, you are sorely mistaken," Aimsley announced as he pulled a ledger from the edge of his desk and opened it.

"It's hardly a hovel," Adam countered, rather relieved his ploy at gaining a larger allowance seemed to have worked. "There are seven rooms!" He scowled as he sat back in the chair. "You really think it's a hovel?" he asked in a quiet voice, rather offended by his father's assessment.

Aimsley lifted his gaze from the ledger and regarded his oldest son for a moment. "You're a viscount. You're already serving in Parliament. It's hardly suitable for you to be living in Green Street if you're married. You need an address closer to Hyde Park or Grosvenor Square," he argued. He took up his pen and began to scribble, his writing as furious as when Adam had first come into the study.

"Do you know of a townhouse available for let? Close to Park Lane or to the Square?" Adam asked carefully. "North Audley, perhaps?"

"No, but there are agents for that sort of thing. See to it you let them know you're in the market." He completed his writing and then lifted a cheque from the desk's blotter. "This should be enough to cover the first year's lease," he said as he handed over the cheque.

Adam leaned forward and captured the document, one brow rising in surprise at the amount. "Only one year?" he questioned. Good God! He could live in Green Street for five years with what he was holding in his hand!

"You are obviously unaware of what's happened to the rents in the fashionable districts," Aimsley responded, one eyebrow arched in warning.

Giving his father a nod, Adam said, "Thank you. I shall be sure to find the very best property." He paused a moment and then took another breath. "Would you by chance have an Arabian in your stables you'd be willing to loan me on occasion?"

Aimsley blinked. "*Loan* you?" he repeated. "What happened to your three nags?"

Angling his head to one side, Adam gave a shrug. "None of them are a suitable mount for my bride-to-be, and she doesn't have any horses of her own," he explained.

Leaning forward with his hands clasped on his desk blotter, the earl took a calming breath and let it out slowly. "I shall have your brother see to something appropriate. He's at Tattersall's just about every afternoon. We'll make it a wedding gift."

Adam's eyes widened again. "You'll do that?" he asked in surprise. "Thank you. And thank you for the cheque. I'll see to an appropriate house on the morrow."

About to resume what he had been doing when Adam interrupted him, Aimsley regarded his son for a moment. "Whatever you do, honor your vows, son. Don't be seeking comfort in the arms of another, and you will find your bride far more willing to provide comfort, if you take my meaning." His arched brow emphasizing his warning, Aimsley pulled the parchment back to the blotter and resumed writing.

Adam leaned back in his chair and considered his father's words, offended by his implication. "I am not a rake," he stated firmly. "Nor have I been in the habit of bedding anyone other than the few women to whom I have made contracts for their services. Those few contracts have all ended,"—the last one nearly six months ago, he didn't add—"And I find myself quite in love with my betrothed," he went on, determined to make his father understand how serious he was about marrying.

Aimsley lifted his head from what he had been writing and regarded his son for a moment. "You have a reputation from your days at university and before," he replied, his voice quiet.

"That was nearly thirteen years ago!"

"Reputations are hard to overcome," Aimsley countered with an arched brow.

Adam sucked in a breath. None of his exploits at Eton or at university had involved women. None had been about debauchery or scandalous acts. They had all been simply pranks pulled to make fun of those in power at those institutions. Pranks in the name of fun and frolic. Nothing serious. Nothing that should have followed him to the ripe old age of thirty. "Obviously," Adam replied sadly.

"Did you really put a dinner gown on the statue of Aristotle?" Aimsley asked then.

Blinking several times, Adam shook his head. "It was Plato, as I recall, and only after we learned he preferred young boys to the company of women," he added with an arched brow that nearly matched his father's. He wasn't about to tell his father he had stolen the gown from a window display in a modiste's shop, especially knowing the gown had been safely returned and purchased almost immediately after the well-publicized incident.

Aimsley laughed out loud, tears collecting at the corners of his eyes and threatening to spill out after a moment. "Fennington has your mother believing it was you who dressed

Aristotle, but I have a sneaking suspicion Fenn was the one who did it."

Appreciating his father's assessment, Adam nodded. "You have that right, Father. He also dressed the statues of Hippocrates and Euclides, but he'll never admit it," he said *sotto voce*.

Adam took his leave of his father's study, rather glad he left the man chuckling in his wake.

He soon sobered after he left Aimsley House, though. He had a townhouse to find and let, although he had half a mind to wait until after the wedding.

Wouldn't it be better to have his wife with him when he shopped for a new home?

## CHAPTER 20
## A SISTER CONFRONTS A BROTHER

*The following morning*
"Has the Duke of Ariley left for Westminster?"

The question had Jarvis angling his head to one side. The butler of Ariley Place stepped aside as the rather impatient sister of his master stepped into the vestibule.

"His Grace has not, my lady." Realizing he couldn't claim the Duke of Ariley wasn't in residence, he added, "He's in the breakfast parlor." He would have led her there, but Lady Lancaster was already halfway down the hall of the Park Lane mansion that housed James and Helen Ariley, their two-year-old son, William, and their baby daughter, Rose.

A copy of *The Times* hid her brother from view as Elise entered the brightly colored breakfast parlor. A footman stood at attention near the sideboard, but he bowed to Elise and seemed unsure of what to do next.

"Might I have a word with you?" Elise asked, saving the footman from having to make a decision.

The newspaper moved aside to reveal her brother's grinning face. "Are best wishes in order, perhaps?" he asked as he stood up. He moved around the table with his arms held out as if he intended to give his youngest sister a hug.

Elise allowed him the hug but did not return it. "Finally, if I'm to understand my betrothed's comment," she countered with an arched brow. "Third time?"

James inhaled as if to reply but let the breath out in a *whoosh*. He turned to the footman, and with a quick nod of his head, the servant disappeared into the butler's pantry.

"Join me for breakfast?" James asked, his manner unlike any he had shown her before. Ever. He moved to the sideboard. "As I recall, you like your eggs coddled, your toast dry, and your bacon rather overdone," he said as he started to dish up a plate.

Blinking at her brother's act of servitude, Elise angled her head in defiance. "Scrambled, buttered, and just a hint of crispness," she countered before allowing a sigh of frustration. "You're not going to allow me to be angry with you, are you?" she half-asked as she moved to take the chair next to his.

James set a filled plate in front of her and bussed her on the side of her head. "No," he replied. He returned to the sideboard and poured a cup of coffee, adding milk and sugar before he brought it to her. "But, dear sister, do allow me to explain myself," he begged.

Elise lifted a fork, almost tempted to stab him with it. "Explain yourself, then, brother, for I have spent a rather sleepless night wondering how I might make your son the current Duke of Ariley."

About to continue the teasing, James suddenly sobered. Light-complected and with hair color that matched hers—although showing more gray at his temples—the seventh Duke of Ariley could have easily passed for a man ten years younger than his seven-and-forty years. He stood nearly six feet tall, his back still straight and his belly still as flat as it had been when he inherited the dukedom in 1785. "I thought I was doing right by you," he said quietly.

Rather surprised at his soft words, Elise lowered the threatening fork. "How?"

James allowed a shrug. "I knew Thorncastle and you were

fond of one another, but he was about to leave for Cambridge when he first asked father and me for your hand, and..." He stopped when he saw how Elise's eyes widened.

"He asked for permission when I was... *fifteen?*" she asked in a whisper.

"Aye. But then, so did Lancaster. He was already an earl, and I thought I was doing right by you. Making you a countess," he added. "If I'd had any idea Lancaster was a dishonorable man, I never would have agreed to the match," he added before Elise could argue.

"And the second time? When was that?" she asked, thinking it had to have been in the last few months. Godfrey wouldn't have asked whilst Lancaster was still alive.

"The week after Lancaster died," James replied simply.

"*What?*" Elise couldn't help the surprise in her response.

"He thought there would be a line of suitors asking for your hand when you completed your mourning," the duke explained with a sigh. "He thought every unmarried man in the *ton* wanted you for a wife. Still does, I think," he added as his brows furrowed into a single line. He shook his head as if to clear it, unaware of the effect his words were having on his sister. "You had just returned to London the day before and told me that very night of how awful your marriage was. I couldn't imagine you would welcome talk of another marriage so soon, so I told him to wait a couple of years. Exactly two years later to the day, he showed up and asked again."

Suddenly lightheaded, Elise stared at her brother in disbelief as gray took away the edges of her vision. Her head bobbed before she heard his next words.

"Oh, no you don't," he said as he straightened in his chair and reached over to steady her. "Don't you go fainting on me, sister," he said just as his wife entered the breakfast parlor. He moved to stand up, attempting to hold onto his sister at the same time.

"Good morning... Oh! Elise!" Helen, Duchess of Ariley, said

with a bright smile as she moved to greet her sister-in-law. Her smile soon disappeared when she realized Elise seemed about to faint. She quickly moved to stand behind her, unbuttoning the back of Elise's gown before loosening the ties of her corset. "Someone's maid was a bit too enthusiastic this morning," she said to her husband, an arched brow punctuating her comment. She reached up to buss him on the cheek. "Breathe, Elise," she added, rubbing the younger woman's shoulders.

Elise's vision finally cleared, and she dropped her head back to give the duchess a wan smile. "Good morning, Helen," she whispered. "I can't say as I blame my maid, though," she added as she angled her head to regard her brother with a look of reproach. She allowed a sigh and was about to admonish him, but James shook his head as if in warning before she had a chance to do so.

"Had I known then what I know now, I would have given him permission the first time he asked," James stated as he held out a chair for his wife. "Although, I think I wouldn't have actually allowed the wedding until after you'd had a chance at a come-out and a Season or two," he added, his manner suggesting he wasn't teasing.

"It wasn't just because you wanted to be rid of me? I am the youngest. I suppose Lancaster's offer was—"

"It wasn't that at all," James said. "But he was an *earl*. I truly thought you would prefer the title of countess over viscountess."

"Now I'll have both," she whispered.

James dared a glance at Helen, who still stood behind Elise. "I'll be gaining a new brother soon," he said by way of explanation.

"Viscount Thorncastle has proposed again, I take it?" Helen guessed as she moved to the sideboard to help herself to some breakfast. "Well, it's about time, is all I can say. The man's been in love with Elise since..." She stopped and glanced about. "Is it the footman's day off?"

James was at her side in an instant, taking the plate from her and filling it on her behalf. He jerked his head in his sister's direction by way of explanation.

Nodding her understanding, Helen moved to take her seat at the table. "When will you wed?" she asked as she moved to take Elise's hand in hers. "And where?"

Elise allowed a wan smile. "Eighteen years later than we should have, so... possibly tomorrow. Depends on whether or not he can obtain a special license. As to where..." She allowed a shrug. "I've no idea."

The stunned looks of both her brother and sister-in-law had her allowing a wan smile.

"Because you have to?" her brother asked in alarm.

"Ariley!" Helen admonished him.

Elise gave her brother a quelling glance. "I could only wish," she replied with an arched brow before tucking into her breakfast.

The response only had her brother glowering despite his wife's attempt to calm him. "Really, Elise. Talk like that will have the tongues wagging."

Not about to claim she didn't care about gossip, Elise gave a sigh. "I'll marry him. If we're so blessed, I'll bear him an heir and a spare," she said quietly.

Helen regarded her sister-in-law for a moment. "He loves you, Elise. You can do no better."

*No better?*

What if *not* remarrying at all would be better?

But Elise considered how much she wanted a child of her own. How much better life might be with a man who felt affection for her.

Finishing her breakfast, Elise took her leave of Ariley Place and headed for her home. If she was going to marry Godfrey Thorncastle, she wouldn't be living there much longer.

There was packing to do.

## CHAPTER 21
## TWO VISCOUNTS IN SEARCH
## OF THE SAME

*L*ater that day
Godfrey Thorncastle removed his robes and peri-
wig, ignoring the light conversation carried on by his
fellow lords in the dressing chamber in Parliament. Despite
having spent that day's session in a boisterous discussion about
parliamentary reform, no one seemed particularly upset by the
proceedings.

Without so much as a farewell to any of his colleagues, he
took his leave of the building and hailed a hackney—at the
very same time Adam Comber, Viscount Breckinridge, did so.
In fact, the two attempted to climb into the conveyance at the
same time, each giving the other a stare of annoyance.

"I am in a terrible hurry," Thorncastle warned the younger
viscount, one foot on the step.

"As am I," Adam countered. "I've absolutely no idea how
late the Archbishop of Canterbury's office is open," he argued.

Godfrey blinked and removed his foot from the step. "It
seems we have the same destination in mind," he replied as he
called out, "Doctors' Commons," to the driver and stepped up
and into the coach. He waved the younger viscount in and
watched as Adam removed his top hat and gave him a nod.

"Much obliged, Thorncastle," Adam murmured. "I had hoped today's session would end a bit earlier."

"As had I," Godfrey agreed as he removed his top hat and set it on the bench, at first wondering why Lord Breckinridge would even be at Parliament. He hadn't yet inherited the Aimsley earldom.

When Adam noted Godfrey's expression, he said, "Writ of acceleration. Seems the age of those in the House of Lords was getting a bit high, so I agreed to step in," he explained.

Godfrey nodded, rather impressed a younger aristocrat would agree to give up his freedoms early and take on the responsibility of Parliament. "Can't say as how I would expect you to be in need of a special license, though," he said.

Adam considered the comment. Given his reputation, he thought Thorncastle's words were said in jest. "The same might be said for you," he countered with an arched brow. "May I inquire as to the identity of the lucky woman?" Why, he hadn't heard—or read—a bit of gossip mentioning Godfrey Thorncastle. But the viscount was a bit long in the tooth, and it was probably well past time the man saw to populating a nursery.

"The widow, Lady Lancaster," Godfrey offered carefully. "And the name of yours?" He half-expected Breckinridge to make some off-color remark, so he was rather surprised when the man gave him a look of appreciation.

Although the younger viscount seemed ready to reply, he suddenly frowned. His brows furrowed deeper before he gave his head a shake. "Damnation!"

That wasn't quite what Godfrey was expecting to hear. He rather doubted any women were bestowed with such a name, although he supposed there were some unlucky men who used the term to describe their wives on a daily basis. "What is it?" the older viscount asked in alarm.

Adam's eyes darted to one side, as if he were trying to remember something. "She's a... teacher. At Warwick's," he replied finally.

Rather stunned by the reply—pleasantly so—Godfrey straightened in the squabs. "However did you meet her? Or is she a family friend, perhaps?"

The younger viscount's attention still seemed on his mind's eye as he replied, "At White's." He shook his head. "Oh, this is not good. Not good at all. I cannot..." He looked up suddenly and stared at Godfrey. "I don't—"

"Good God, man, what has you looking as if the devil just walked over your grave?" the older man asked in concern.

Adam stared at Godfrey for a long moment before finally admitting, "I don't remember her name," he whispered. "In fact, I don't believe she ever offered it." His eyes widened. "Do you suppose I can still obtain a license without knowing her name?" he asked, his voice filled with hope.

Godfrey shook his head, wondering if Breckinridge might have been deep in his cups when he proposed marriage to the finishing school teacher. "I rather doubt it," he replied. "Pray tell, may I inquire as to how you... came to propose marriage to a woman to whom you hadn't been properly introduced?" Why, certainly a teacher at Warwick's Grammar and Finishing School would know the rules of polite Society!

But did Lord Breckinridge?

Now looking as if he might be sick, the younger viscount regarded Godfrey for a moment. "I don't know that I exactly *proposed* marriage so much as that we came to an agreement to marry," he explained sheepishly. "She knocked on the door at White's..." He paused when Godfrey raised a gloved hand.

"Forgive me, but now I know you were either foxed or have dreamt up this woman," Godfrey stated. Why, it was just like how he had conjured Elise into existence the night before. Although Elise had actually been a real woman—not a figment of his overactive imagination. But Lord Breckinridge's woman? Knocking on the door of White's? Why, there wasn't a woman on the entire planet who would deign to do such a thing! "Women are not allowed—"

"She didn't try to get *in*," Adam countered with some annoyance. "She merely wished to know..." He paused and allowed a short bark of laughter.

"Wot?"

Adam allowed a grin. "She wanted to know what number had been assigned to her. She paid witness to me standing in the bow window, you see, and thought to learn how I found her face and figure."

Godfrey rolled his eyes, never an advocate for the practice that ranked women in such a crass manner. There was only one woman on the entire planet for whom he would ever hold up all the fingers of both hands. "And how did you find her?" he asked, curious.

"Oh, a 'ten', once I was out of White's and escorting her to Jermyn Street," Adam replied with a nod. One of his eyebrows dipped low. "Although, I am ashamed to admit I first thought her a mere 'seven'. I cannot believe that I did not believe her to be a 'ten' from the start."

The words were said with such apology, Godfrey couldn't help but feel a bit sorry for his fellow viscount. "My Elise has always been a 'ten'. I've thought of her as such since she was but... thirteen years old, I believe," he said with a sigh.

Adam regarded the older viscount for a moment, rather stunned to hear the man had held his affianced in such high regard for so many years. The man had to be in his mid-to-late thirties!

*Why hadn't he married her when he was younger?*

Adam was about to put voice to the query when an idea struck him. "Would you be amendable to a quick stop in Jermyn Street? I'm quite sure I can discover my betrothed's name from a clerk in one of the stores we visited," he explained.

Frowning, Godfrey pulled his chronometer from his waist-coat pocket. "I don't suppose we could just stop at Warwick's?" he suggested carefully. "Perhaps one of the students there—"

"Capital idea!" Adam cried out, his face brightening. "I cannot believe I didn't think of that first," he said. "She lives there, in fact," he added with a nod, although he hadn't been able to watch from the departing coach long enough to know in which building she lived.

Not about to inform the younger viscount that Warwick's was made up of at least a half-dozen separate buildings, Godfrey lifted his cane and tapped the trap door above their heads. When the driver's head appeared, silhouetted against a cloudy sky, he said, "Glasshouse Street. Warwick's."

The man frowned but gave a nod. "And then to Knightrider Street?" he queried.

"Yes. We'll pay for your time whilst you wait, of course," Adam called up to the man. "I'll pay," he amended when the trap door shut and he noticed the expression on Godfrey's face.

"How is it a woman could agree to marry you when you didn't even propose *and* you did not learn her name?" Godfrey asked then.

Adam gave a shrug, deciding not to explain that he planned to more formally propose once he had the special license. His grandmother's ring was in his pocket. "I admit I was a bit... *predisposed* to the idea of needing to find a wife post-haste," he admitted with a shrug. "And she appeared, as if I had conjured her!"

"Lost a bet, did you?" Godfrey asked, one of his bushy eyebrows lifting with the query.

Shaking his head, Adam sighed. "I was reminded by my very best friend that I had agreed to the terms of a bet many years ago, although I myself don't stand to gain anything but a wife from it. If I don't marry, he stands to lose a great deal of blunt, and he cannot afford to do so," he explained. "But I assure you, I really do wish to marry the woman I met yester-day. She's... *brilliant*. Teaches arithmetic and dance to the daughters of the *ton*," he said proudly.

Frowning, Godfrey wondered who might have the unlucky aspect to be Lord Breckinridge's best friend.

And then he realized he knew just who held that honor.

Or dishonor.

"*Fenn?*" Godfrey said suddenly. "Why ever would you allow the Earl of Fennington to set such terms in a bet?" he asked in dismay. He knew the earl wasn't as bad off financially as some were led to believe. The man had income from some kind of concern, for his fortunes were nothing like they had been when he had first inherited the Fennington earldom. Godfrey knew this because the earldom had owed his viscountcy a rather large sum—a sum that had been paid in full just the year before.

"He is my best friend!" Adam replied in surprise. "He has seen to rescuing me from any number of scrapes ever since we were at Eton," he added then, remembering the times when Felix Turnbridge managed to get him out of trouble with school officials by taking the blame for Adam's wrongdoing. Or the times his friend had seen to his safe return to their rooms despite how drunk he had been, or the time he had taken a punch for him when Adam's debauchery with a high-flyer angered a particularly high-ranking city official—who was apparently married to the woman. "In fact, I do believe my mother holds him in higher regard than she does me," Adam added as he considered his history with Felix. This last was said as if he were pleased, but his countenance soon sobered. "I've not been the best behaved heir," he admitted.

Jesus! Was it any wonder he'd overheard his mother praying—nay, begging—that his father, Mark Comber, Earl of Aimsley, be allowed to live to the ripe old age of sixty or beyond? She probably couldn't countenance the idea of her oldest son inheriting the Aimsley earldom.

The fact that Adam had agreed to a writ of acceleration probably had her confused, but she didn't realize how truly interested he was in the politics of government. In the negotiations and the wrangling and the give and go.

*I really have to prove I can do better*, he thought then. Marriage to a respectable woman would go a long way toward proving he was past his days of debauchery and disappointment. The young lady he sought wasn't a member of the *ton*, it was true, but having taught the daughters of the *ton* at least meant she could pass for one. She certainly spoke like one. She acted like one. Why, she even *looked* like one, although Adam found her visage far more pleasing than he did those of the current crop of debutantes. Pleasing and perfect, her heart-shaped face the epitome of an English miss.

He couldn't help that he imagined that same face in a fit of ecstasy beneath his body. Couldn't help that he had imagined her waking up next to him just that morning, her tousled hair resting over his bare chest and her large, beautiful eyes regarding him with the mischief she had displayed whilst they were shopping just the afternoon before. Damn, but she looked like an angel first thing in the morning!

"I really have not been the best behaved son of an earl," Adam remarked, attempting to tamp down the sudden arousal he felt at the thought of his true love. Of course, she hadn't been with him that morning, but his imagination could certainly place her in his bed. Place her beneath him as he worshipped her body and brought her to ecstasy time and time again as proof she was the only woman for him. The only woman from now until the day he died.

There was a moment when he thought he might wince at that last thought, but when he didn't, his eyes widened and he allowed a brilliant smile.

Godfrey scowled at the man who was suddenly smiling like some sort of idiot. Were any of the heirs to aristocratic titles 'well-behaved'? "Which begs the question," Godfrey said with some annoyance. "What does Aimsley think of you taking a wife?" he asked.

Adam blinked and then glanced about the interior of the hackney. "I spoke with him last night. To let him know about my intentions to marry."

"And did you?"

The younger viscount nodded his head. "I did. Like you, he was a bit surprised, but he was moved to help in the matter of my finding a larger townhouse for my betrothed."

"Why the hurry?" Godfrey asked, realizing it was really none of his business, but he was curious as to why the younger viscount seemed so determined to marry quickly. Marriages made in haste weren't the most welcome of events.

"I promised my betrothed I would see to a special license today," Adam explained. "I have no intention of disappointing her on our second day of acquaintance."

*Second day?*

Well, they couldn't be marrying because a babe was on the way, Godfrey realized. Perhaps Breckinridge had ruined the chit upon their first meeting, although it didn't seem likely.

The hackney turned a sharp corner, which had Godfrey daring a glance out the dirty window to his right. "Well, Lord Breckinridge, it seems you now have the chance to learn the name of your betrothed," he said with an arched brow. "Ten minutes. No more," he warned as he once again removed his chronometer and took note of the time. The more he thought of Elise, the more he wanted to be married—and without further delay.

There was something to be said for quick weddings.

He could understand the other viscount's pursuit of his apparent true love. But what possessed a man to decide a certain woman was the one? The one to whom he could pledge undying love and affection? Pledge his life and protection?

Pledge fidelity?

If Elise could forgo a formal wedding in St. George's or St. Peter's, then Godfrey would see to marrying her on the morrow. But he couldn't do so if he didn't have the damned license!

Adam nodded at the older viscount's ultimatum. Ten minutes. "Understood." He grabbed his hat and quickly took his leave of the hackney, the conveyance still moving as he did so.

Godfrey watched the ne'r do well as he raced to one of the buildings that made up the Warwick's campus, wincing when he realized the man was headed not for a classroom building, but rather for one that housed those that boarded at the school. He half-expected to hear peals of giggles or blood-curdling screams when the door was answered, but all was quiet as he watched Adam Comber interact with the woman who answered the door. She was probably a house maid, he thought as he watched from where he sat.

Well, of course, the house maid wouldn't scream, Godfrey thought with a roll of his eyes. She was probably setting the time and date of an assignation with the viscount!

Godfrey was about to return his attention to the interior of the hackney when he noticed Breckinridge giving the servant a deep bow. And then the man disappeared inside the building!

*What? Does Breckinridge intend to tumble the maid in exchange for the information?* Godfrey thought with some annoyance. Before he could form another uncharitable thought about Breckinridge, though, a young woman appeared from one of the other buildings followed by several younger women who walked behind her, their white gowns a testament to their youth. He was reminded of a mother swan and her string of goslings, although this mother swan didn't seem to give those in her charge a backward glance to be sure all of them followed. Indeed, the one in the lead didn't wear white, but rather a bright pink gown and an expression that suggested she was either a rather happy woman or very relieved.

Definitely not a mother.

On impulse, Godfrey opened the hackney door and called out to her. "Miss? Might I have a word? I'll be quick," he said, daring a glance up and down the street to be sure there weren't any coaches that would run him over should he step out of the hackney. He used his cane to tap on the ceiling above. When the driver's head appeared, he said, "I'll be no more than ten minutes," he said, tossing a sovereign up to the man.

The startled driver caught the coin and gave him a nod. "Vera good, guv'nor," the man replied.

The woman in pink paused in mid-step and frowned. She urged those behind her to continue on their way. Although she didn't step off the curb, she stayed where she was and waited for Godfrey to join her, apparently noticing the quality cut of his clothing and his aristocratic bearing despite his having stepped down from a hackney.

Godfrey bowed, his top hat tucked under one arm, before he reached for her hand and bestowed a kiss on the back of it. "Forgive me, my lady, but I wondered if you might know the name of the woman who teaches arithmetic and dancing at this establishment?"

The young woman's eyes widened, and she suddenly took a step back. "Perhaps," she hedged. "Might I be told who wishes to know?" she asked, her suspicion obvious.

"Lord Thorncastle, at your service," he said, giving his head a bob. "I ask on behalf of the man who wishes to marry her," he added, mostly because he wanted to see how she reacted to such a claim.

He wasn't disappointed, for the young woman blinked several times.

"Miss Diana Albright teaches those particular subjects," she answered before daring a glance up and down the street. "May I ask how you came by such information, my lord?"

Something about her manner had Godfrey thinking she might just *be* Miss Diana Albright. Her manner of speech was impeccable. Her bearing was perfect. Why, the woman could pass for any daughter of the *ton* in her third or fourth Season. "Are you aware of a betrothal between Miss Albright and a viscount, perhaps?" he asked as he angled his head to one side.

When the young woman took a step back and dipped her head, Godfrey knew he had her. "I was on my way to secure a special license so that I might marry the woman I have always wanted as my wife, you see," he started to explain. He took delight in seeing how her large eyes widened and regarded him with a bit more respect than he deserved. "When a young viscount insisted he be allowed to share the hackney so that he, too, might secure such a license."

"Lord Breckinridge," she breathed.

Her head also angled to one side, and the expression of surprise coupled with embarrassment had Godfrey understanding why it was Adam Comber thought her a 'ten'. Why, she was positively gorgeous in an elegant, youthful sort of way. She could have been Elise if Elise wasn't twenty years older and wiser. Why, this young woman had the same glow about her that Elise seemed to exhibit at that age, a sort of *joie de vivre* that suggested she took joy in the simple things.

"He escorted me on a shopping trip in Jermyn Street yesterday, and then took me for an ice at Gunter's," she admitted, her cheeks pinking up as she made the admission.

Godfrey prided himself on having guessed correctly. Now he only had to confirm a few details to ensure Adam Comber wasn't the bounder he suspected he might be. "Did the viscount speak of... marriage?" Godfrey asked gently.

Diana nodded, her eyes darting off to one side. "The entire time he was in my company, my lord. I didn't do anything to encourage him, I assure you," she said with a shake of her head, as if she thought he had been sent to break off any arrangement that might have been made. "At least, I don't think I did," she added in a worried whisper.

"He thinks you're a 'ten'," Godfrey stated, deciding he would tell Elise the very same thing when he was next in her company. Why, his betrothed deserved to know what he thought of her. That he thought her the most beautiful woman on the planet. The only woman who he would ever deign to consider as his viscountess. The only woman he would ever marry.

"A 'ten'?" she repeated, her eyes wide. Diana visibly swallowed, as if she couldn't decide what she should think of such a statement. "Pray tell, is that... a good number? Or—"

"The very best, I assure you," Godfrey murmured with a nod. "My betrothed is a 'ten', in fact. She has been her entire life." He dared a glance toward the house in which Breckinridge had disappeared. "Might I inquire as to what you thought of Mr. Comber?" He turned to watch her reaction, puzzled by how she gave a start at the mention of Elise. Her wide eyes mesmerized him, as did a face that sported one of the prettiest blushes he could ever remember seeing on a young lady. One that reminded him of how Elise had looked back when they first spoke of marriage all those years ago.

Nearly twenty years ago.

"Truth be told, I thought him a bounder, my lord," Diana admitted sadly. "I certainly didn't expect he would return with a special license. Why, he doesn't even know my *name*," she said. "What was I supposed to do when he merely thought to spend his afternoon in the company of a young woman with nothing more in mind than a passing fancy?"

"That I was a fool in love for not having learned your name *before* taking my leave of you," Adam stated from behind her. His top hat held in both of his hands, the younger viscount dared a glance at Godfrey before turning his attention to the young woman who had whirled about and was now gazing up at him in surprise.

Godfrey cleared his throat. "Miss Diana Albright, might I introduce you to Adam Comber, Viscount Breckinridge?" he said in his most somber voice. He hadn't yet decided if he was doing the young woman any favors by introducing her to the viscount.

To the bounder.

"I'm honored to make your acquaintance," Adam said as he

bowed deeply. He reached for her hand and brought it to his lips.

"I didn't think you'd come," Diana whispered. "I thought—"

"Please don't say you thought I was insincere in my pursuit of you," Adam countered, his brows furrowing. He didn't let go of her hand, but rather held onto it as he gazed at her.

The young woman shook her head. "Oh, I *believed* you. Especially after what you said at the tea shop. But when you still hadn't asked as to my name, I figured you were merely a—"

"A bounder," he finished for her.

She nodded, realizing he had overheard the remark. "I apologize—"

"Don't," he interrupted with a shake of his head. "I was a fool to let you out of my sight yesterday," he said in a whisper. He suddenly frowned. "And yet, if I'm to secure a license for us to marry on the morrow, I really must take my leave of you again." He looked up, expecting to find Thorncastle standing behind her and pointing at his chronometer in a fit of impatience. Instead, he noticed the man was back at the hackney, cane in hand and regarding the sky with a look of awe.

Adam followed his gaze and grinned as the clouds parted and the afternoon sun lit the walkway on which they stood. The bright rays also lit Diana's face. She appeared almost angelic as light painted its way over her visage. "Seeing as how we have His blessing, I shall be on my way," Adam said with a good deal of sadness. "Do tell me, though, how might I find you tomorrow?"

Diana rolled her eyes and pointed to the building from which Adam had emerged only moments ago. "There," she said with a nod. "But don't think I'll marry you wearing any of the gowns I own," she warned him.

Blinking, Adam angled his head first left and then right. "Shopping in New Bond Street tomorrow then?" he suggested with an arched brow. "After a walk in the park? Wedding on Sunday?"

Diana dared a glance at the hackney, wondering when Lord Thorncastle thought to marry his betrothed. They would require witnesses no matter when they married. She was about to ask if they might serve in that regard, but decided she needed to discuss it with someone else first. She rather hoped her aunt was watching this bit of spectacle from where she sat in the parlor of Alpha House.

As for marrying on a Sunday, was that even possible?

Adam watched as Diana seemed to ponder his suggestion. He knew it was probably scandalous to suggest he accompany her as she shopped for a gown, but he felt relief that she didn't seem the least bit bothered by the suggestion. They had just spent the afternoon prior in several shops in Jermyn Street.

A giggle erupted from the dance teacher, and she finally allowed a nod. "Come fetch me at ten o'clock, my lord," Diana replied as her face colored up in a blush that matched her pink gown.

"Truth be told, you're rather lovely in the gown you're wearing right now," Adam said with a grin. "Are you quite sure we can't be married later this afternoon? Or this evening, perhaps?"

"Tomorrow at ten," she countered with an arched brow. An arched brow he was quite sure she had learned from his mother.

"Ten o'clock," he agreed. He paused a moment before leaning down to buss her on the cheek. "I shall count the hours," he promised.

"Can you count? That high, I mean?" she countered, a brilliant smile appearing to give away her tease.

"Why, of course..." His face took on the look of a man who realized he'd been the butt of a joke. "I shall show you just how high I can count," he warned, his lips coming down onto hers.

Although Diana's first thought was to pull away—anyone from the school could have paid witness to the kiss—she allowed the brief intimacy. At that moment, she found she really didn't care who saw them. She would in a moment or two, but the few seconds of his kiss were as if time had stopped and only they existed. Only they mattered.

"He might be able to count, but he surely cannot tell time," Godfrey called out from where he stood next to the hackney. This time, he really was pointing to his chronometer, Adam noted when he reluctantly ended the kiss and spun around.

Adam lifted Diana's hand to kiss the back of it. "I'm off to the archbishop's office. Please don't change your mind, Miss Albright," he warned as he hurried off to join Godfrey in the hackney. "I wish to spend the rest of my days with you. Counting them!" he called out before disappearing into the coach.

Diana stood and watched Adam as he leaped into the hackney, shaking her head. *Bounder,* she thought with a roll of her eyes. Two fingers went to her lips, though, as the effects of his kiss seemed to linger there.

Once the hackney had turned the corner and was gone, she made her way to the Alpha House parlor, wondering if Viscount Breckinridge would ever feel for her the kind of love Viscount Thorncastle felt for his true love.

*Let me count the days.*

## CHAPTER 22

## A TEACHER CONSIDERS HER FUTURE

*A few minutes later*

"What in the world was that all about?" Elise asked as she dared another glance out the front window of Alpha House, the building in which the teachers of Warwick's Grammar and Finishing School lived if they didn't have homes in London. "Was that Lord Breckinridge?" She knew there had been another, older man with the viscount, but from her vantage and the mere glimpse she had of the man, she didn't know who he might be.

Her goddaughter and second-oldest niece dipped her head before giving it a nod. "It was," Diana Albright acknowledged. "He insists he is on his way to the Archbishop of Canterbury's office with the intent to procure a special license. He intends to marry me, my lady," she said in awe.

Elise's eyes widened before she dared a grin. Having been told the same thing the night before by Godfrey, she knew exactly how Diana felt. "He is the one, then?" she asked as she dared another glance out the front window.

"He thinks so," Diana allowed with a mischievous grin. "I insisted I could not marry him in any of the gowns I own. Told him to be here at ten in the morning to take me shopping."

Elise's eyes widened in appreciation. "If he appears at ten, then you'll know he's sincere in his intentions," she replied, not sure if she should put voice to the most obvious question. "What then?" she asked instead.

Diana inhaled sharply and then suddenly sobered. "I suppose I shall marry him," she whispered, uncertainty coloring her voice. She couldn't help the rush of excitement she felt at the thought that a viscount—and a handsome one at that—wanted her as his wife. That he would seek her out to learn her name when she had done nothing to encourage him.

Well, other than to knock on the door of White's to learn who he might be. To learn how she ranked in his estimation.

Her brows furrowed as she remembered Lord Thorncastle's comment.

*He thinks you're a ten.*

*The very best.*

Elise reached out with an arm to pull her niece into a light hug. "He knows, then?" she half-questioned.

Diana stiffened in her arms, immediately understanding her aunt's query. "No. I... I've not told him. He knows very little about my family," she whispered. "I mentioned Mother had died and that my father had remarried..." She allowed the sentence to trail off, her lower lips trembling when she remembered how she had spoken of her father and his new wife. As if they were no longer part of her life.

Perhaps she had left the viscount with the impression she was estranged from her father.

To some extent, it was true. She hadn't paid a call on him since his marriage to Helen, nor did she dare. What if the duchess was in residence? How would she explain her reason for wanting an audience with James, Duke of Ariley? Would her father have told his duchess he had not just one, but two illegitimate daughters?

Probably not, if what her mother had said to her was true. The female members of the peerage didn't want to know their male counterparts had engaged in sex with anyone but them, even if they secretly knew they weren't the first in their bed. Or the only after they were married.

If only her mother was still alive! Lily Albright would know what she should do. Provide counsel and a shoulder to cry on if her words proved what Diana suspected.

That she shouldn't give Viscount Breckinridge's proposal another minute of thought. That his words were merely those of a man in lust with her. That he would come to his senses—or someone would remind him he should be seeking a proper daughter of the *ton*.

The death of her mother had been hard, the courtesan having protected Diana and her older sister from the vagaries of illegitimacy, raising them as the daughters of a duke.

The daughters of the Duke of Ariley.

There was a reason James had waited so long to marry and sire a legitimate heir. He had been secretly in love with his mistress, Lily Albright, and carried on a private life with her until her death in 1809. He bestowed gifts on his daughters for their every birthday and Christmas, and saw to funding dowries they could either use for the purpose of marriage or for living independent lives.

Diana would gain the use of hers when she turned five-and-twenty—if she didn't marry before then. As for her older sister, Daisy, Diana expected she had already opted to take the money for herself. She couldn't imagine Daisy ever marrying, if only because she had at one time assumed her older sister would follow in their mother's footsteps. But Daisy Albright had instead used the skills their mother had taught her and secured a position in Whitehall.

Diana knew her sister was a spy for the Foreign Office, but she was sworn to secrecy on the matter. Probably no one besides Matthew Fitzsimmons, Viscount Chamberlain, or some of Daisy's associates could say exactly what Daisy did in exchange for her pay.

As for her own situation, Diana thought teaching at a finishing school would prevent anyone from discovering her relationship to the Duke of Ariley. From deciding they wished to court her for her dowry. For the money she would gain the following year when she reached her majority.

Diana thought to merely bide her time teaching, and then, when her account at the Bank of England was suddenly flush with funds from her father, she would decide if she should buy a house and live in luxury near Hyde Park, or buy a small estate in Kent and live in the country.

She had never given thought to being married. Her older sister had certainly never thought of matrimony, but then, Diana didn't think Daisy could given what the woman had to do in her various guises as a spy. Her work required her to act as an enchantress. A mystery woman. A mistress.

Daisy's only hope for an advantageous marriage would be if one of her fellow operatives decided he could overlook her status as a ruined woman and make her his wife. No, far better that Daisy continue her life as an independent woman. She had bided her time until her monies were deposited in her account the year before.

Even if Daisy couldn't take full advantage of the funds at the time.

She had been on an assignment in York for nearly two years. Once she had helped see to the arrest of a man involved in smuggling illegal liquor into York, Daisy had returned to London to see Diana and had then taken her leave of the city with a promise she would return once she had either taken another assignment or resigned her position.

Diana was still waiting for her sister's return to London. Perhaps the announcement of her wedding to a viscount and heir to an earldom would force her sister to reappear in the capital.

Perhaps not.

*This wedding isn't really going to happen*, she reminded herself. A viscount wouldn't marry an illegitimate woman.

Would he?

Pulling away from Diana so that she could regard her niece, Elise managed a wan smile. "You'll have to tell him, Di. I've no idea how Aimsley will react—I don't know the earl well at all—but I believe his mother will be quite pleased to learn her new daughter is a Burroughs," she whispered. She rather imagined Patience, Countess of Aimsley, would be relieved when told her oldest son had settled on anyone to be his wife. Her son was nearing thirty, after all.

But Diana wasn't a typical daughter of the *ton*. She wasn't a debutante, nor was she one who'd had her come-out years ago and was almost a spinster.

Nor was she a widow.

But she was an illegitimate daughter of the *ton*.

When Diana didn't respond, Elise angled her head and allowed a wan smile. "A penny for your thoughts," she said quietly, watching her goddaughter for signs she might be changing her mind about marrying Adam Comber.

"I rather wish my sister were here." When she realized how her words might sound to Elise, she quickly shook her head. "I meant no offense, of course!"

"None taken, I assure you," Elise said with a shake of her head. "I rather imagine Daisy will return when she's of a mind to do so. I do believe she felt..." Elise swallowed, knowing her secret niece had felt soiled after her last assignment.

It hadn't been the first time Daisy Albright had been sent into the field with an assignment to bed a man in exchange for information, but it was the first time she had been sent to spy on the wrong man.

To bed the wrong man.

To act the part of a mistress. To take his money, and live in elegant quarters he paid for, and then betray him—despite feeling affection for him. Too late, the poor woman realized how the man despised her for apparently leaving him to pursue a richer master. Because he thought she was greedy—trading his affections for a nicer townhouse, larger jewels, more pin money—when, in fact, she was only doing her job.

Daisy couldn't tell the man, a marquess, why, of course. She could never divulge her duty for King and country without giving up her true identity.

Better the man never know. Especially now that he was married.

Elise gave a start when she realized Diana was passing a hand before her eyes. "A penny for *your* thoughts, I should think," she countered. "Where *were* you just then?"

Coloring up a bit, Elise allowed a sigh. "Thinking of your sister. I do believe she felt as if she had betrayed someone for whom she had developed a tendré," she murmured before allowing another sigh. "But the man is married now, to a proper young lady." She grimaced at this last, giving her head a shake. "I didn't mean that quite how it sounded. It's just..." Elise sighed. "I don't think the Marquess of Plymouth would be a very pleasant man for Daisy. He's far too serious," she remarked. Elise gave her younger niece another smile. "How soon do you suppose Breckinridge will wish to marry?" she asked, changing the subject in an effort to take her mind off Daisy.

Giving a slight shrug, Diana said, "Sunday, he says. Is that even possible?"

Elise's eyes widened. "*This* Sunday?"

"He suggested tomorrow."

Elise considered this bit of information. Why, she might be married on the morrow if Godfrey could somehow secure a license and convince her they shouldn't wait. She hadn't expected such enthusiasm from a man who at first seemed so... *sad* about having to marry. "You might be in good company," she answered. "I have decided to wed again."

Diana gave a start. "I thought you were going to be an independent woman!" she chided in feigned shock.

Rolling her eyes as she recalled her words to that effect, Elise finally allowed a shrug. "Thorncastle has proposed."

The younger woman's mouth dropped open in a most unbecoming manner as one of her hands came up to point toward the front window. "Godfrey Thorncastle?" she clarified. "The viscount?"

Elise's gaze followed the young woman's finger. She was about to admonish the girl for pointing as well as for the look of shock on her face when she considered the reaction. "How is it you know Lord Thorncastle?"

"I just met the man! He was the other gentleman with Lord Breckinridge," Diana claimed. "He's the one who properly introduced us, I might add," she said happily. She suddenly sobered. "He was also the one who forced Breckinridge to hurry back to the hackney lest they be too late to Doctors' Commons."

At first dismayed to learn the news that she had missed seeing her betrothed by mere moments, Elise was soon giggling. "It won't matter the time they get there," she said, her gaze going to the clock on the fireplace mantel. "Unless they've made an appointment, the archbishop's office will be closed in just a few minutes."

The sense of disappointment that Diana felt just then had her convinced of something that, until then, she wasn't quite sure about.

She wouldn't mind marrying Adam Comber.

Otherwise, why would she experience such a sense of disappointment at hearing there would be no special license? The office would no doubt be open Monday, at which point the viscounts could secure their licenses and they could all be wed Tuesday.

At least, they could if Adam still wished to do so once he learned Diana was illegitimate.

And that her father was a duke.

"It's just a few more days," Elise said in a whisper.

Diana nodded. "I know." Although she tried to feign ambivalence, she certainly didn't feel ambivalent. *Perhaps I really do wish to marry.*

# CHAPTER 23
# AN AFTERNOON IN THE PARK

*The following morning*
When the housemaid knocked on Diana's door, the young woman looked away from the mirror above her dressing table and glanced at the small clock on her nightstand. Stunned to see it was exactly ten o'clock, Diana had to suppress the urge to run to the front door. "Come!" she called out, stabbing another hairpin into her topknot. At least the spirals at her temples were holding despite the humid weather.

The door opened a few inches and the maid leaned in. "There's a gentleman at the door for you, Miss Albright. Says he's a *lord*," the older woman said in awe.

Diana allowed a grin. "That would be Lord Breckenridge," she replied, rather surprised Mae Thatcher would display such awe when most of the girls who attended Warwick's Grammar and Finishing School were daughters of the aristocracy. Certainly lords and ladies visited the girls on occasion. Of course, those girls who boarded whilst attending the school lived in the other buildings positioned along Glasshouse Street, six or eight in each house, while the house in which Diana lived was shared with several other instructors at the school.

"Well, you're not going to keep him waiting, I hope?" Mae

half-asked when Diana didn't move to get up from the dressing table. "Why, if one of the others happens on him in the vestibule—"

"I suppose I shall have to hurry," Diana said with an arched brow, realizing Mae was convinced another one of the teachers might appear to sweep the man off his feet. She couldn't imagine who, though, as two of the teachers were old enough to be his mother and the other made her distrust of members of the opposite sex known at every opportunity.

She gave her hair one last look in the mirror before topping it with a smart, blue hat. Decorated with small silk peacock feathers, the hat had been a gift from her father on the occasion of her twentieth birthday along with a note to pay a visit to Madame Suzanne's shop for the matching carriage gown and pelisse. *Perhaps I'll see you wear it in Hyde Park or at Hatchard's,* her father had written in the accompanying note. *It's been far too long.*

It had been too long since she'd last seen her father. She never dared pay a call on him at his house, though, for she was afraid his duchess might be there. Or that the woman would discover she had paid a visit. The very last thing Diana wanted was to have Helen, Duchess of Ariley, learn her husband had an illegitimate daughter or two.

She hadn't even considered the duchess might already be aware of her and her sister. The thought hadn't crossed her mind.

Diana stood up. "Will I need an umbrella, do you suppose?"

Mae blinked. "Not today, miss. Why, I don't think there's a cloud in the sky!"

"A parasol, then," Diana countered as she helped herself to the bright blue pelisse and the matching lace parasol. Giving the maid a wink, Diana hurried out of her room and to the vestibule.

She found Adam pretending to study the landscape

painting over the fireplace in the parlor, one of his hands resting on a hip as the other took purchase on the mantel.

"You're rather punctual this morning, my lord," she said from the threshold. "Good morning."

The viscount whirled about, his happy expression suddenly changed to one of awe. "I wanted to arrive much earlier, my lady," he murmured, hurrying to join her. He reached for her hand, and that's when Diana realized she hadn't remembered the ensemble's matching gloves. The kiss he bestowed on the back of her bare hand sent shivers of delight racing up her arm, though, so she didn't mind her oversight so much.

She managed a curtsy, stunned when he moved to place a kiss on the corner of her mouth. "Why would you wish to be here before ten o'clock in the morning?" she asked, aware of how a blush crept over her face at his show of intimacy. "You probably wish you were still abed."

Adam feigned offense. "In the event I might be allowed to help you dress, of course," he said with a naughty wink. He sobered suddenly. "I am teasing, of course. I've never actually assisted a woman in dressing." Although he was far better at the undressing, he hadn't done such a thing in a very long time. When he caught what he thought was a look of disappointment on Diana's face, he added, "But I certainly intend to learn once we're married."

The blush on her face deepened. "You are a bounder," she accused, her grin widening.

"Aye. But yours and only yours," he stated with a nod. His hands went behind his back, as if he didn't trust them to remain at his sides. "Your gown is gorgeous, my sweeting. In fact, if I spotted you in New Bond Street, why, I would assume you were a duchess."

Diana gave a start, almost tempted to ask, *What of a duke's daughter?* but decided it was too early to broach that particular subject. She was really looking forward to spending the day with the viscount. Her news, which might send him straight to his club, never to be seen by her again, could wait until later.

"I'll be sure to let Madame Suzanne know your good opinion," she said with a nod. "I need to return to my room for a moment. It seems I've left my gloves behind," she said as she curtsied.

"Might I join you? I must admit to a certain curiosity about how the teachers here at Warwick's live, especially now that I see you have such fine art in your parlor." He indicated the landscape with a wave of his hand. "A Fitzsimmons, is it not?"

Diana blinked as she gave a quick glance at the painting. Lady Samantha had indeed done the work, an idyllic scene of a field outside a village in the Cotswolds, although there were no sheep included in the painting. "Indeed. The Marchioness of Plymouth completed it whilst she attended school here," she said, referring to the former Samantha Fitzsimmons.

Adam offered his arm, which had Diana noticing how closely in color his waistcoat matched her pelisse and carriage gown. He noticed as well. "I promise, I did not have a spy tell me what you planned to wear today," he said as he let her lead the way to her room.

Startled she was actually allowing a man into any part of the house other than the parlor, Diana almost asked if he could return there to wait for her. His presence was most improper! But once she was in her room—Mae had obviously finished up and left to see to another teacher—the man stopped short at the threshold and held his hands behind his back as Diana retrieved the gloves from a highboy.

"I didn't expect such fine furnishings in a teacher's rooms," he commented as he first studied the four-poster bed, imagining what Diana must look like as she slept in it. He dared a thought of how he would look holding her in it, but when his loins suddenly tightened, he forced himself to think of cold water and what it might feel like to be doused by a bucket of it. He turned his attention to the high boy. "Are these all... yours?"

he asked as his gaze swept the modest-sized room. Besides the wardrobe, bed, dressing table and highboy, there was also a velvet wingback chair and a bookshelf stuffed with leather-bound books. A rose-colored carpet covered nearly the entire floor.

Following his gaze, Diana gave a shrug. "They are. A gift from my father when I accepted the position here," she replied, remembering the note that accompanied the surprising delivery.

How had the Duke of Ariley learned she had secured the position? Did the man have informants beyond the gossips who frequented his men's club?

*Men are the best gossips*, her mother had always said.

Since the quarters had already come furnished with a cot and a few other shabby pieces, the movers were forced to divest the room of its existing furniture to make way for the grander pieces. The old stuff had found new homes in other rooms throughout the house.

"He must have been very proud of you," Adam remarked, one of his eyebrows furrowing. *Faith!* From the conversation they'd had at Gunter's two days before, he knew her father managed an estate.

But where? Did the man even live in town?

And if he did live in London, Adam wondered if he should do right by the man and seek his permission to marry Diana.

Adam chided himself that he hadn't even considered requesting her father's permission to marry her. During their time at Gunter's, the conversation about her family had been limited to her late mother and the fact that her father had remarried, apparently recently.

Rejoining him at the door, Diana nodded. "He was rather proud," she agreed, deciding it was better he be left thinking her father and her were estranged. She had no intention of telling him who her father was, at least, not yet.

Adam seemed to show a hint of relief. "I had hoped I

wouldn't have bad news this morning, but there's been a bit of a... a hiccup," he hedged as he escorted her down the hall to the vestibule.

"Oh?" she replied, deciding not to admit she knew he'd been unable to secure the special license.

*Or had the man changed his mind about a quick wedding? About a wedding at all?*

"Despite our best efforts to make it to the archbishop's office yesterday, Lord Thorncastle and I were too late," he said sadly.

The disappointment she felt at hearing the confirmation was more for her Aunt Elise than for herself. Although Elise didn't seem particularly excited about her impending nuptials to the older viscount, there had been the moment when Diana realized the woman did feel affection for Thorncastle. Probably had for many years. Now was their chance to finally marry. To make the life together they had been denied all those years ago.

"Which simply means we'll marry another day," Diana said with a bright smile. She still didn't believe the man would actually marry her—especially if he learned the truth of her parentage—but her curiosity had her wondering if he might offer a completely different proposal.

One that involved *carte blanche*.

Should he do so, she would then know his true character. Once offended, she would make her ire known in how hard she slapped the man across his too-handsome face.

And then she remembered his comment about women who slapped men across their face.

"You don't seem too terribly disappointed," Adam hedged as they took their leave of the building and made their way to a glossy black town coach parked at the curb. The Aimsley crest was emblazoned in bright gold paint on the door.

Diana gave a slight shrug as she allowed him to assist her into the coach. "I have learned never to take anything for granted, my lord," she replied. "And not to expect too much from anything."

The viscount paused before joining her in the coach. The comment implied she knew far more about life than she should for a woman so young. "But, why?" Adam countered as he climbed in behind her, rather happy to find she had left space for him on the seat next to her. He settled into the squabs even as he regarded her.

"I am never disappointed. Or rather, *too* disappointed," she said with a sigh.

Adam considered the response. "Then it seems you must not look forward to anything either. In the event it's cancelled or otherwise altered," he reasoned, his brows furrowing.

Diana gave a start. "Oh, but I do," she countered, hoping he wasn't referring to their wedding. If she wasn't careful, he might end their betrothal before it had ever begun just because he sensed she was ambivalent. "I just... I just try not to hang my every hope of happiness on things over which I have no control."

Allowing a sigh, Adam took one of her gloved hands in his. "I should never want you to be disappointed," he commented. "Especially in me."

Her eyes widening at his words, Diana felt a strange tug in her chest. Reason told her she shouldn't give it a moment's notice—mathematically, this was not a union that had any hope of happening—but she couldn't help the bit of unreasonable hope that flared just then. "If I expect you to be a bounder, and you are, what then?" she replied with a teasing grin.

Adam brought her gloved hand to his lips and kissed the palm. "I do not believe I shall live up to that expectation," he replied, a strange twinge twisting somewhere in his chest. Without even thinking, he brought his lips down to hers and kissed her. Perhaps he thought to seal his words with the kiss, to further prove himself, although a kiss was entirely inappropriate given the circumstances. He realized it almost immediately, but when he was about to hit himself upside the head and apologize, he found Diana staring up at him in wonder. And before he could hit himself upside the head, her lips were suddenly back on his, her free hand moving to his shoulder as if she needed something on which to hold.

Lost in the sensation of her lips on his, on how her soft breaths washed over his cheeks, how the light citrus scent of her filled his nostrils, and how his arm had moved to wrap around her back, Adam had no idea how much time passed, nor was he aware the coach had yet to move. And he might have stayed lost in her kiss far longer if the coachman hadn't opened the trap door above.

"Where to, milord?" the man asked, his weathered face replacing the bit of blue sky made evident from the open door.

Adam blinked as he jerked away from Diana. She seemed nearly as startled as he felt, and he felt as if he'd been caught with his hand in the biscuit jar. "Hyde Park," he called up.

When he turned his attention back to Diana, she was regarding him with an expression that suggested she had been the one caught with her hand in the biscuit jar. "You honor me," he murmured, hoping she would simply continue what they had been doing when they were interrupted.

Her pulse pounding in her ears, Diana wondered what had her behaving so. She had kissed the man! She had displayed the sort of wanton behavior her mother had warned her could lead to the worst possible outcome!

But Adam's response was completely unexpected. From what her mother had said, when given such an invitation, a man would think it his right to ravish her, to have his way with her, to take her virtue and claim it was all her fault. Instead, Adam simply stared at her with a besotted look.

*You honor me.*

"I cannot believe I just did that," Diana managed in a hoarse whisper.

"Me, neither," Adam replied in wonder. "But may I be

allowed to suggest you do it whenever the fancy strikes you? Because, I'm quite sure I won't mind." He tried but failed to think of places where he might mind being caught unawares by being kissed out of the blue, but damn if his brain couldn't come up with a single example just then.

A blush suffused Diana's face. She couldn't be sure if he was teasing her or if he was serious. This was maddening!

Straightening in the squabs, she turned her attention to the window, dismayed at finding the curtains spread open. Anyone on the street might have seen her kissing the viscount. "Is this why we're riding in a town coach instead of a phaeton? Or a curricle? So that you might have your way with me?" Suspicion colored her voice.

Adam allowed a sigh of frustration. "I thought only to escort you on a walk in the park. And since I've yet to procure a phaeton, a town coach was the only conveyance available to get us to the park."

Diana's brows furrowed. Didn't every young buck own a phaeton? Red or yellow, with a pair of matched greys to pull it? Before she could put voice to a query, though, Adam allowed another sigh.

"My father owns a phaeton, of course, but he's rather proud of it. Won't allow me or my brother the use of it."

Not quite sure why, Diana felt like giggling just then. Had she a brother, she was quite sure her father wouldn't allow him the use of his phaeton, either. But the reminder that Adam had a brother had her curious. "Have you seen him since the war? Your brother, I mean?"

Adam allowed a shrug, secretly pleased she was no longer suspicious of his motives on this fine day. He grimaced, though, at the thought that she might know Alistair. "He and his wife were my mother's guests for dinner last week. I think because she wanted time with her grandson. Have you met Alistair?"

Diana dipped her head. "Only in passing. His bride was a student at Warwick's my first year there. She brought him to the school shortly after they were wed. To introduce him to some of her former classmates at the soirée they hosted."

"Ah. Showing him off, no doubt," Adam commented. The hint of jealousy in his voice couldn't be missed.

"I think she wanted to show that a man had deigned to marry her," Diana countered, her words carefully chosen. At Adam's look of confusion, she added, "There were some who thought Lady Julia rather proud, but I never found her to be so. At least, not any more so than the other girls at the school."

Adam seemed to give her words a good deal of consideration. "Given Alistair's position, I hardly think she could be too proud," he agreed.

Although Alistair had been an officer in the British Army, he had returned from Belgium having made a promise to fund the widow and children of a fellow soldier who had died in his company. When their father, Mark Comber, Earl of Aimsley, refused to help with the monthly stipend, Alistair sold his commission and invested the funds in a five-percenter. Furious at learning Alistair had sold the commission, the earl disowned him, and so Alistair was forced to take a position as a groom in the Harrington House stables.

When Julia Harrington, daughter of the Earl of Mayfield, spotted him, she thought him too handsome to be a groom and decided to make him into a gentleman. She didn't know his true identity—didn't realize he was already a gentleman, given his status as the second son of an earl—so when Alistair agreed to be tutored in dance lessons and be fitted for clothing appropriate for Lady Mayfield's ball, Julia had a project to keep her occupied. She never expected to fall in love with her student, and Adam was quiet sure Alistair never intended to take a wife when he was six-and-twenty. But he had—even claimed to be in love with Julia. And now he was the father of a baby boy, too!

"I hear he is quite well regarded by those looking to buy a horse," Diana said as a way to keep up her end of the conversation.

"Aye. When I finally buy my own phaeton, I'll have him pick out the horses for me," Adam agreed. "Besides his work at the Harrington House stables, he's a consultant at Tattersall's," he added. "Available for hire." Although he would have made the comment with a hint of derision in the past, he decided he couldn't begrudge his brother his success at finding his niche in life. It wasn't as if Alistair would ever inherit the Aimsley earldom—Adam would gladly fill his father's shoes when the time came, for he had been raised with an appreciation for politics and what it took to run an earldom.

"Do you always travel by town coach?"

The question had Adam blinking as he realized he'd been caught woolgathering just then. "I don't, actually. I have my own horse. A bay. And you?"

Diana shook her head. She rather doubted she could afford to keep a horse on her meager earnings. "There's no mews at the school, so I usually just walk where I need to go."

This seemed to bother Adam. "Without benefit of a companion?" he replied, remembering she had been alone the day before yesterday when he had joined her outside of White's.

"I am old enough to walk by myself," she replied curtly. Should she require protection, she knew who to go to for it. Whose name she could drop if required.

"I shall escort you at night, of course," Adam stated.

Diana's eyes widened. "I never go walking after dark. Not even with a link boy," she claimed. She was quite sure the young boys who carried lanterns at night had arrangements with footpads so they could share in whatever gains could be made from a quick robbery.

"I am relieved to hear it," Adam replied just as the town coach came to a halt. He reached over and opened the door, stepping out and turning to offer her assistance. "When must I return you to Warwick's?"

His grip on her hand had Diana giving a start. Would it

always be like this? His simple touch sending shivers of delight up her arm. And then she chided herself for thinking there would be much more to his attentions. Certainly he would grow bored of her. Realize he would require a daughter of the *ton* to be his viscountess. His one-day countess. And if he didn't, what would he think when he learned the truth of her?

Well, she rather doubted it would ever come to that.

"Before dark, I should think," she replied with an arched brow.

Adam allowed a broad grin. "Touché."

Diana frowned. "I thought we were going shopping."

Taking the hand she had placed on his arm into one of his, Adam nodded. "We will, my love. But I think a walk in the park on such a fine day is called for."

They set off on the crushed granite path, one of Diana's hands on his arm whilst she held her parasol aloft with the other. They spoke of everything and nothing and sometimes walked in silence. So when they were suddenly hidden from the rest of the world by hedgerows, they both stopped and regarded one another for a moment.

"I've something to ask you," Adam whispered, nervousness apparent in his manner.

A sense of disappointment settled over Diana, although she chided herself for the reaction. She had expected he would decide against marriage and instead offer *carte blanche*. She had even thought that earlier this morning. So why did her chest suddenly hurt? Why did her breath catch in her throat, and her heart suddenly feel as if it was being crushed? Why did she feel as if...

"Will you marry me?"

Diana blinked and stared at Adam, unable to form a coherent response just then. This wasn't the question she was expecting!

"I know we've already agreed to marry, although I cannot help but think I forced you into it when we were in Jermyn

Street," he went on. "It was terribly unfair of me. To put you on the spot like that. Of course you would think me the worst bounder. But I wish to be your bounder. And only yours." He reached into a waistcoat pocket and pulled out the gold ring he had retrieved from his mother, the ring his grandmother had insisted he give his bride.

Diana's gaze darted from the ring to his face and back to the ring. "Where... where did you get that?" she queried, her voice breathy. For a moment, she thought she might faint.

"My grandmother. She told me I was to bestow it on the woman I was to marry," he replied, reaching for one of her gloved hands. He used his free hand to pull first one and then another finger free of the glove. Then he tugged again until the garment came free of her hand. He slid the ring onto her fourth finger and then raised it to his lips to kiss it. "Will you be my wife, Diana? I promise I'll let you do all the math. In fact, I may require it of you." This last was said in an almost apologetic tone, as if he regretted having to make the request.

His final words finally had Diana taking a breath, his attempt at humor bringing a grin to her face and clearing the gray from the edges of her vision. "Yes, yes, of course," she replied with a nod.

Their kiss might have lasted the rest of the afternoon, or perhaps just a moment. Diana had no sense of time passing, no sense of anything else in the world but just the two of them.

When he wrapped his arms around her body and pulled her against the front of him, she rested a cheek against his shoulder and marveled at how her curves seemed to fill his voids. At how his hard body accepted her softer body.

A kiss on her forehead had her raising her face to his. She regarded him with a wan smile. "Who will you tell first, do you suppose?"

Adam took a deep breath, rather surprised by the query. "I told my mother Thursday night," he replied in a hoarse whisper, his words quiet. "She seemed happy for me. Demanded that I bring you for dinner." He paused a moment. "She and my father recently acquired a newspaper, although she claims she cannot tell me which one. It's all very secret," he said with some amusement. "She did let me know she would be including an article about us, though. And my sister recently returned from Switzerland, and while I thought she would be thinking of the Season and potential husbands, it turns out she's already betrothed."

Diana heard the bit of surprise in his voice, as if he thought it odd that his sister might have beaten him to the altar. "Since she is your sister, you must be pleased for her," she ventured even as she wondered which newspaper his mother might have acquired. And why.

"I am, of course. I do think Cupid must be on a shooting spree, though, because my best friend told me he has decided to take a wife."

"Your best friend?" Diana repeated, wondering who that might be. He hadn't made mention of the man while they were at Gunter's.

"Felix Turnbridge never ceases to amaze me," Adam replied, his voice still quiet. "We were best mates growing up." He paused a moment, thinking the two hadn't been so close of late. Not since Felix had inherited the Fennington earldom and all the debts that went with it.

Well, at least this marriage would help alleviate some of that debt. All the proceeds from the bet that required Adam to marry by thirty would be in Felix's hands whenever their vows were said.

"You don't suppose your mother's preoccupation is due to your sister's acquisition of Lord Fennington as a husband?" Diana suggested with a lifted brow, the corners of her mouth turned up in a teasing grin. When she saw how his brows furrowed and his face darkened, the grin disappeared. "I apologize. I thought you would approve..."

Adam stared at her, his confusion apparent. "How is it you

can suggest such an arrangement?" His mother had mentioned his sister was in love—was even betrothed—but she hadn't said anything about Fennington being the groom! Christ! His sister had barely had her come-out. Felix hadn't said a thing, although Adam hadn't seen the man since...

Just a few days ago.

At White's.

But Felix hadn't said a thing about marrying his sister!

Diana wondered at Adam's look of confusion, at how he seemed bothered by the suggestion that his sister might be betrothed to the Earl of Fennington. If the two were best friends, certainly he would find the match agreeable.

*Wouldn't he?*

"I heard it mentioned at school yesterday," she explained. "Apparently Lord Fennington was allowed to propose marriage after eight weeks of courting Lady Emelia."

Adam shook his head. *Eight weeks?* Emelia had only been back in England for a bit more than that, given her return from attending finishing school in Switzerland. "Damn him," he murmured, not intending for Diana to overhear his curse. Given the dowry Felix would collect from marrying Emelia, the earl would no doubt be left debt-free. Debt-free and flush with funds to live a rather comfortable life. And yet Felix had implied that he was in need of the funds from the bet he would collect when Adam married.

The cur!

"I apologize. I didn't mean to upset you..." Diana whispered.

Adam hugged her harder. If what she said was true, he didn't *have* to marry. Felix would do just fine without the money from the bet.

Adam didn't feel a bit of relief, though. In fact, he was more determined than ever to marry.

He was quite sure he wanted to marry.

He knew he wanted to.

A new determination replacing the one he had felt earlier

that morning, Adam kissed Diana with a fervor that took her by surprise, robbing her of breath and leaving her light-headed. When he finally pulled away but left his forehead touching hers, he whispered, "I am quite sure I love you."

Diana swallowed, rather stunned by his words. She nodded, not sure what had just happened. "I am quite sure I may be in love with you as well," she murmured, realizing she meant every word.

His renewed kiss lasted far longer than any they had shared before. And it might have gone on longer except a drop of rain landed on Diana's cheek.

The splash had the two stepping back from one another, their startled expressions turning to laughter as Diana held up her parasol, and the two hurried off to the town coach.

It was pouring by the time they were safely inside, their labored breaths soon turning to murmured promises and kisses to seal them.

# CHAPTER 24
# A SUNDAY BY THE SERPENTINE

*Sunday afternoon in Hyde Park*

Elise inhaled slowly, her face lifting to regard the puffy clouds directly overhead. Although she held an open parasol, she didn't hold it over her head as she regarded the late spring sky. She rather hoped she would find a sign from above, an indication of whether what she was planning was right or wrong. Good or bad.

"May I be allowed to say you're a vision on this fine morning?"

Whirling around to find Godfrey regarding her from a few feet away, Elise allowed a wan smile. "I certainly don't feel like one."

Godfrey's top hat was suddenly in one hand as he afforded her a deep bow. He hurried up to join her as she dipped a quick curtsy. She placed a hand on his proffered arm, and he bussed her on the cheek.

"Pray tell, what has you bothered? I do hope you're not having second thoughts," he countered, one brow furrowing in concern. He certainly hoped she hadn't changed her mind about marrying him. Having pulled some strings, he had been able to secure an appointment on the morrow with a bishop about a special license and had arranged a time to be married on Tuesday morning in St. George's.

It was amazing what was possible on a Saturday if one was persistent.

And had some blunt.

Elise gave a slight shrug as they walked the crushed granite path through Hyde Park. She had entered the park from the northern gate closest to South Audley Street, walking alone for nearly a half-hour knowing that Godfrey would join her at some point near the Serpentine. Given how quickly he had found her, she wondered if he had been following her from the time she left her townhouse. "Are you quite sure about this? About us?" she finally responded.

Attempting to swallow the sudden lump that had developed at the back of his throat, Godfrey found it difficult to speak. "You *are* having second thoughts."

"And third and fourth and... oh, Godfrey. I am honored you still hold me in such high regard. That you still claim to want my hand in marriage. But it's been years—"

"Only about twenty," he countered quickly, pausing to face her. From the manner in which he said the words, twenty years might have only been twenty days.

Elise boggled. "You're a bounder," she accused, although she managed a grin.

"I am not. I merely know my own mind," he replied, hurt by her rejoinder. "And my heart."

Staring at him a moment, Elise realized he believed every word he said. He believed they would simply pick up where they left off before she was forced to marry Lancaster. As if the intervening years had never happened. Never left their scars or their life lessons on either of them.

If she married him, what would happen after a few days or weeks? When his vision of her changed to see the reality of how she was now? Would Godfrey still find her appealing? Still find her desirable? Still think of her as a vision?

She rather thought not. She wasn't a chit fresh out of the schoolroom. An innocent who believed in true love. Too much had happened during those years with Lancaster. Her heart hardened and her distrust of men having made her a bit of a cynic, she no longer believed in it.

Or in destiny.

"I envy you," she murmured as she turned to resume their walk.

Godfrey frowned. "Because I know my own mind? I rather think you are well in possession of your own." He fell silent for a moment before adding, "What does it tell you to do?"

Elise sighed. "Run away. Stay. Travel. Marry and have babies..." She inhaled sharply as tears collected in the corners of her eyes.

"What does *your* heart tell you to do?"

Aware that his other hand had come to rest atop the gloved hand she had placed on his arm, Elise dropped her gaze to it. Such a large hand, it completely covered hers. She thought of the protection he would provide, a different sort than what her brother claimed to offer. She thought of the kiss they had shared and the sensations it had stirred in her. Of his misconceptions of how she had lived her life and her misconceptions of his.

She had to admit to a hint of jealousy at thinking of Godfrey with another woman. Any woman.

No woman would be good enough for Godfrey Thorncastle. He was a fine man. A gentleman of impeccable manners and grace. Of infinite patience and kindness. He honored her with his lifelong affection, and yet, she couldn't bring herself to accept him without reservation.

The thought brought her up short.

"I don't believe I am worthy of you," she murmured, the tears finally dripping from her eyes. She wasn't even aware of them at first, at least not until Godfrey suddenly stopped and pulled a handkerchief from his waistcoat pocket. He pressed it to her cheek.

"And here I was afraid I wasn't worthy of you," he murmured as he wrapped an arm around her shoulders and pulled her close. The need to comfort Elise overruled any thought of propriety—although there were no signs of anyone else in this part of the park, someone could come upon them at any moment. And if they did? What was the worst that could happen?

He would be forced to marry the woman he loved. *I should have done this years ago*, he considered as he moved his other arm around her waist.

Elise didn't resist his hold, but instead allowed a sigh as he embraced her. Rather glad she had opted to wear the smaller straw hat with an upturned brim and short feather instead of the larger bonnet festooned with flowers, she now wondered if the single feather was tickling his face. She angled her face to look up at him, but before she could put voice to any query, his lips were suddenly on hers.

His kiss, barely there and rather tentative at first, might have ended when she moved to face him more squarely. But he tightened his hold on her and deepened the kiss. A moment passed—or perhaps it was several—before a slight moan emanated from the back of her throat and he suddenly pulled away.

"I apologize," he whispered, giving his head a quick shake. He glanced around them as if he had just then realized they were out in the open, barely hidden by the trunk of a tree and a hedgerow. Although there were distant sounds of children and their nurses close to the water's edge, no one paid witness to their clinch.

"Don't you dare," Elise countered in a hoarse whisper, shocked at how her body responded to his hold on her. Her breasts felt swollen behind her stays, the space between her thighs throbbing with need. The sensations were foreign to her, as if parts of her body were awakening for the first time in her life. "Don't," she repeated in a softer whisper.

Godfrey allowed a slight grin, heartened to hear her words and to see tears no longer brightened her eyes. Emboldened, he resumed the kiss, pulling her tighter when one of her hands reached up to rest against his cravat. Her fingertips delved into the hair just beneath his top hat, separating the slight waves and sending delightful skitters through his scalp.

When he pulled away the second time, it was to take a breath and regard her with an expression of awe. "Do you suppose we might kiss like this often?" he asked in a whisper.

Dazed, Elise angled her head and finally allowed a nod. "I do believe I shall make it a requirement of you." She would have added a comment about deciding she would marry him, but realized it was unnecessary.

His grin broadening into a smile, an expression that youthened him by at least ten years, Godfrey lowered his head until their hat brims touched. "I look forward to learning of your other requirements, especially after Tuesday."

Elise gave a start. "Tuesday?" she repeated.

Godfrey nodded. "That's the day you're going to marry me. The day after tomorrow."

Elise couldn't help the blush that colored her face, nor the sense of relief that seemed to settle over her just then. Marriage was in her future, is seemed.

At least she no longer dreaded the thought.

# CHAPTER 25
# A DAUGHTER REGRETS

*The following Tuesday*

Diana entered the narthex of St. George's church and paused a moment. Awed by the quiet, cavernous sanctuary bathed in a golden light, she felt as if she were merely an inch high. She gripped her bundle of late spring flowers in her white kid gloves and allowed her gaze to take in everything.

She had never stepped foot in this hallowed hall before. When she was a child, her mother had told her illegitimate people weren't allowed. Because her mother was also baseborn, she and her mother and sister had never attempted to enter a church. Had they wished to do so, she was quite sure her father would have seen to some sort of arrangement. Her father could see to anything, she supposed, but Lily Albright had long ago accepted her place in Society. And so they had simply spent their Sundays in quiet solitude, reading books and taking long walks in the park.

Why had she allowed Adam to talk her into marrying in this particular church? In any church, for that matter?

Because Thorncastle wanted to marry Aunt Elise in this church, she remembered then. This was the church in which most aristocrats married. And since she and Adam would be acting as witnesses to the Thorncastle wedding, it only made sense they would say their vows here, as well.

When Diana finally dared take another step forward, she concentrated on the huge altar at the front of the church, wondering if that's where she would be saying her vows on this bright, sunny day.

"You're a vision," Adam's voice came from somewhere to her right. "In fact, I thought perhaps you were an angel."

Diana blinked as she turned to regard him, stunned she hadn't noticed him leaning against the wall. He looked far too handsome—dark and dangerous—a devilish gleam in his eyes. Her insides did the flip she remembered from the first day he had met her.

Had that been just five days ago?

*What am I doing here?* she thought, a hint of panic gripping her. *I am going to marry this devil.*

Rather than feeling as if she should be casting up her accounts, she instead felt a flare of desire for the man who was regarding her with an appreciative expression. An expression that had a blush suffusing her entire body. *Do not fear it,* her mother had said on one occasion. *That desire for a man, for the power you have over him is all the power you will ever possess.*

Until this moment, Diana had never understood her mother's comment. Now, seeing the way her betrothed beheld her in the dimness, she understood her mother's words completely. Perhaps later, she would put them to good use. She only wished she had allowed her mother to teach her more about pleasing a man.

Daisy had learned, of course. She was older. More worldly. And she'd been eager to do so, as if she intended to use her power to seduce men for a living. Although Diana knew Daisy hadn't taken up the occupation as mistress to some aristocrat, Diana also didn't quite know what her sister did in her guises as a spy to make her way in life.

Daisy had come into her majority already, though, and had accepted their father's settlement with the promise she would not gamble it away or spend it all in one place. Diana expected she might one day receive an invitation to a house party in Kent or Bath or Brighton and finally see first-hand how Daisy had spent the money. Or perhaps she would be sent a ticket to travel to some exotic location and discover her sister was the owner of a plantation or extensive estate or a palace. None of those seemed likely, however. Daisy had never struck her as a woman who pined for the elegance in which she'd been raised. The opulence that surrounded them in their youth because of who their father was.

Diana gave her head a shake as if to clear her mind and stared at Adam. She took in his topcoat and elaborately embroidered waistcoat, its silver and gold threads twinkling in the dim light of the narthex. "As are you," she countered as she hurried over to him. "Why, you'll blind an angel with that waistcoat," she teased with an impish grin. "And if not the waistcoat, then with that pin," she remarked, openly admiring the diamond cravat pin that winked from the folds of a snowy white neck cloth. She reached up with a gloved finger to touch the gem, quickly pulling away her hand when she realized it was entirely inappropriate to be standing so close to the man.

"Do you think it's too much?" he asked with concern, stepping back to look down at his ensemble. Even his black Hobys reflected what little light there was in the entryway, a testament to how much time his valet had spent shining them that morning. "I wanted to wear my very best since I knew you would be wearing the gown you bought Saturday," he murmured, his voice kept low in deference to their surroundings. "You are wearing the gown you bought Saturday?" he hedged, taking another step back so his gaze could take in her gown. Most of it was covered with a pelisse, the long, light coat hiding most of her gown.

"I am," she said as she turned slightly so he could help her remove the pelisse.

"You could wear nothing at all and be beautiful," he said before leaning over to buss her on the cheek. At her startled reaction, he blinked. "I meant that you could wear anything and be beautiful," he amended, his expression suggesting his original comment was made in innocence.

Diana had a suspicion he meant both.

"May I be allowed to say the same of you?" she whispered, aware her cheeks were bright pink from his words.

"As long as they're sincere."

"They are, of course," she replied with a nod. She took a deep breath, thinking perhaps she should tell him who her father was before they married. It wouldn't be fair to the man to discover the news afterwards, she supposed. "There's something I..." The sound of one of the front doors had her stepping back—taking several steps back, in fact—given they were standing far too close to one another. "I believe one of our witnesses has arrived," she murmured, dismayed that she didn't have a chance to finish her confession. She turned, expecting to see her aunt Elise or Lord Thorncastle come into the narthex. Instead, a blond-haired, blue-eyed man approached. He appeared to be around forty, his clothes impeccably cut and his top hat tucked into the crook of his arm.

From where he stood in shadow near the wall, Adam heard Diana's inhalation of breath and watched as she immediately dropped into a deep curtsy, her head bent in supplication.

"Your Grace," she whispered in shock. For there, just a few feet in front of her, stood James, Duke of Ariley.

Her father.

She hadn't even straightened before Ariley suddenly gathered her into his arms and dropped a kiss on the top of her head. "I could not stay away, Poppet," he murmured before he stepped back and held her at arm's length. "Not on a day where

I can pay witness to my youngest sister remarrying. You must be one of her witnesses," he commented lightly. "Rather sporting of her to invite you," he stated with a nod. "But then, you probably are her favorite niece. Have you had the chance to meet her groom?"

Diana nodded, surprised—and relieved—by the duke's words. "I have. Lord Thorncastle seems quite in love with her," she managed to get out, her heart beating so fast, she thought she might faint before she had a chance to say her vows. "And I do believe Lady Lancaster returns the favor."

Her father sobered suddenly. "My, how beautiful you look on this day. I'm reminded of how your mother looked the first time I spotted her at a house party," he managed to get out, a catch in his throat suggesting his bright eyes might be due to impending tears.

*House party?* Diana blinked as her head did a quick shake from side to side.

Her mother had said they had met at the theatre!

"You honor me, sir," Diana replied, finally daring a glance in the direction of Adam.

Ariley's eyes followed his daughter's and he straightened. "Breckinridge? Is that you? Why, what brings you to St. George's on this fine day?" he asked as he extended a hand.

Confusion apparent on his face—and perhaps a hint of annoyance, as well—Adam gave a bow before shaking the man's proffered hand. "A wedding, Your Grace," he replied. "And you?" The interloper had put his arms around Diana in far too familiar a manner. Why, if Ariley had been anything less than a duke, Adam thought he might challenge the man to a duel!

Ariley allowed a wide grin. "My youngest sister is finally marrying the man she should have married some..." His eyes rolled up, as if he were doing math in his head. "Eighteen years ago?" he finally guessed. He turned to Diana. "What were you back then? Five?"

"Seven," Diana replied, her head falling another fraction.

"My, but how the time flies," the duke commented.

"Lady Lancaster?" Adam guessed, a quick glance in Diana's direction showing her own eyes were downcast. She looked far too pale, as if she might faint. "I told Thorncastle I would be his witness," Adam added with a nod. "After he pays witness to my own nuptials."

This news certainly surprised the duke. "I didn't know you were about to be leg-shackled," Ariley countered, his manner rather jovial. "Got a child on some poor chit, did you?" he asked, *sotto voce*.

Offended—and rather incensed by the duke's implication—Adam frowned and shook his head. "I did no such thing, Your Grace," he stated firmly, a quick glance in Diana's direction revealing her rounded eyes before her head fell forward again. "Nor have I ever." He could swear he could see a teardrop about to fall from one of her eyes. He was about to move to console her, but he was still wondering why the Duke of Ariley had hugged her and kissed her as if she might be his mistress. His actions had been entirely inappropriate, especially in the narthex of a church! "And I would beseech you to keep your hands off my betrothed," Adam warned in a voice filled with menace.

Diana sucked in a breath at the same time her father's brows furrowed in confusion. When Ariley turned to regard her, Diana gave an audible sigh. "Please, do not find fault with him, Father," she said as she hurried to stand at Adam's side. "I haven't told him," she added, an eyetooth denting her plush lower lip.

"*Father?*" Adam repeated, his own brows furrowing with the revelation. He took a step back, which had his body nearly pressed against the wall.

"I apologize," Diana whispered hoarsely. "I was just about to tell you—"

"*Just about?*" Adam repeated, his shock still apparent. How could this be happening? How could he be betrothed to the daughter of a duke without... without *knowing* it?

*Because her name wasn't Burroughs!* Thorncastle had introduced her as Diana Albright. A teacher at Warwick's.

Not Diana Burroughs.

Adam's brows furrowed. *Is she a widow?* was his first thought.

*Or a bastard?*

Given the Duke of Ariley was her father and had married rather late in life, Adam realized it was more likely Diana was born on the wrong side of the blanket.

But that meant Ariley hadn't given her his name. She should have been Diana Burroughs. Instead, she was Diana Albright. And yet her father stood before her as if she were to the manor born.

*Damn it all to hell!* The embarrassment he felt just then rocked him to the core.

"You mean, you were going to tell me just now? Just before we were to be married?" Adam whispered hoarsely, his anger redirected on Diana. "Wot? Were you going to say something like, 'Oh, by the way, my father is the Duke of Ariley'?" He took a step closer to her, his voice lowering to a whisper. "You didn't consider that I might have wished to ask his permission to marry you?" he went on, feeling ever so much the fool just then.

His gaze left hers and was about to be turned onto the duke when the first tears left Diana's eyes. She had known this was coming. At some point, she knew she should have revealed the truth of her parentage, but at the same time, she never believed they would ever actually be standing in the narthex of St. George's church, with a special license in hand and an appointment with a bishop to marry them, Aunt Elise and Lord Thorncastle as their witnesses.

*Faith!* Why hadn't she mentioned this when they were

discussing her father at Gunter's? She hadn't even told him the truth about her mother!

Christ! What would he think then?

Suddenly embarrassed by his outburst, Adam gave a nod to the duke, murmured a, "Pardon me," and made his way out the front doors of the church. The bright sunlight blinded him before he could take the first step down toward the street.

Even so, he wouldn't have gotten far. Godfrey Thorncastle was taking the steps up two at a time, his countenance suggesting he was happier on this day than he had been on any other day in his entire life.

"Breckinridge!" Thorncastle called out as he closed the distance between them. "Not trying to run away now, are you?" he teased when he finally made it to the top step.

The younger viscount squeezed his eyes shut against the bright sun, the sparks of light that reflected from his waistcoat threatening to blind him even more. Jesus! *I'll blind myself before I blind any angels*, he thought in disgust.

*How could I have been so blind?* He met a beautiful woman on the street and thought only to marry her to fulfill his obligation to his best friend. Thoughts of her family or of proper parentage or even what might come after the wedding—a life together—hadn't been a consideration.

"I've just learned that the father of my betrothed is Ariley," Adam whispered hoarsely, as if he were afraid someone might overhear his words. "My baseborn betrothed." Or did everyone else already know the *on-dit* about Diana Albright?

*Am I the last to know?*

Who the hell was her mother? Certainly not the Duchess of Ariley! James Burroughs hadn't been married to Helen Harrington long enough to have a daughter Diana's age.

Godfrey Thorncastle winced at his words, but considered how to respond before allowing a loud sigh. "She is one of his illegitimate daughters," he admitted in a hoarse whisper, adding, "He had two with his long-time mistress, Lily Albright.

Elise told me about them last evening, when I asked why she referred to Miss Albright as her niece."

Adam regarded the older viscount for a moment, his manner calmer. At least Thorncastle didn't already know. Had the viscount admitted he did know, Adam was quite sure he would have put a fist into the man's face just then. "So, she claims she was about to tell me. Do you suppose she was thinking to marry me, and then tell me she was a bastard?" he asked, his brows forming one angry line above his eyes.

The other viscount jerked at hearing the comment, his look of disappointment suggesting he had an entirely different view of the matter. He gave a shrug. "Does it matter?" Thorncastle countered simply. "Be honest now," he warned, his chin rising so there was only one on display. "You merely thought her a commoner, did you not?"

"A commoner, yes, but... with a proper family," Adam allowed, his attempt at anger having come out sounding rather pathetic.

Godfrey gave him a pat on the shoulder. "I ask you once again. Does it matter? Christ, Breckinridge! She's a duke's daughter. Ariley has recognized her as such since the day she was born. Her sister as well. Why can't you?"

Lifting his head to regard the older viscount with a frown, Adam considered the words. "I should have asked Ariley's permission, dammit. And had Diana told me she was his daughter, I would have," he claimed in a louder voice. "I had the impression she and her father were estranged since his marriage!"

Marriage. Not *remarriage.* Adam blinked.

*He manages an estate,* he remembered her saying at Gunter's. Well, that was certainly true. The Ariley dukedom was definitely an estate.

*My mother died when I was fourteen.*

"Who was her mother?" Adam asked in a quiet voice. *The daughter of a baronet.*

The older viscount allowed a sigh. "Lily Albright. She was Sir Ronald's only daughter," he replied in a voice nearly as quiet as Adam's.

The younger viscount frowned, not familiar with a baronet of that name. "I don't suppose Sir Ronald was Sir Ronald Albright," he murmured, his expression growing more pained as he realized his betrothed's mother had been illegitimate as well.

"He was a Twickham," Godfrey acknowledged. "His mistress was a courtesan of some note, but Lily was their only child."

"And Lily? What was she?" Adam asked, his mind conjuring the worst possible scenario.

Godfrey shook his head. "Ariley's mistress. For nearly twenty years. He would have taken her as his wife, but she refused. Probably knew she would never be accepted in Society given her background as a courtesan," he explained. "And that is all I know on the subject." He paused a moment. "Elise has known her whole life. She has accepted Diana and her older sister as her nieces. Stayed close. Doesn't want to see either one of them hurt."

Adam lifted his gaze to meet Godfrey's, trying but failing to suppress the grimace he knew he still displayed.

*I don't have to marry.*

The thought gave him little comfort and only left him feeling dismayed.

Did it really matter?

Probably not. He still wanted to marry the duke's daughter —illegitimate or not—he decided, his stubborn nature overriding any practical considerations.

So, did it matter?

Well, it might to Ariley. After the duke's insinuation that he had to marry, Adam realized Ariley didn't have a very good opinion of him. Or perhaps the man simply believed the worst, no doubt because of his past behavior.

Well, he wasn't like that any longer. Not since he had taken a seat in Parliament.

The thought had him furrowing his brows, his father's words about reputation coming back to him. Well, he had a reputation to overcome. Perhaps this would be the best way to start.

# CHAPTER 26
# A VISCOUNT PROVIDES ADVICE

*A*s Godfrey Thorncastle watched Adam Comber come to some sort of decision, he realized something rather profound just then. *I am marrying a duke's daughter.*

A duke's sister.

As for asking permission, he was rather glad he had done so. He had asked Ariley's permission to marry Elise three times!

But why was Adam Comber, Viscount Breckinridge, so upset about *not* having asked permission?

"You might have asked her as to whom you needed to seek permission," Thorncastle suggested in a hoarse whisper, hoping the younger viscount would settle down a bit. "Certainly you discussed her family whilst you courted her—"

"Her mother is no longer of this earth," Adam interrupted, remembering Diana's comment over ice at Gunter's. He recalled a brief discussion about her father, but he had been left with the impression the man was out of her life since marrying his new wife. He'd certainly never had the impression the man was a member of the peerage, despite the comment about him managing an estate.

Thorncastle watched the younger viscount as he seemed to struggle with his thoughts. He was left wondering if Breckinridge was reacting to something entirely different. "Is this really about the young lady's father? You couldn't have been expecting a... settlement, or a dowry if you thought he didn't exist."

Adam regarded Godfrey for a full ten seconds, attempting to tamp down the sudden anger he felt at the insinuation. Of course he wasn't expecting a dowry! He thought he was marrying a commoner, a young lady who made her way in life from the little pay she earned teaching arithmetic and dancing at a finishing school. Just because he now knew she was the daughter of an aristocrat didn't change that expectation. Especially after the duke's comment.

*Got a child on some poor chit, did you?*

The ten seconds was enough time for Adam's emotions to even out, his reasoning to return to full capacity. "I was not, truth be told. Nor would I, even though I expect Ariley will now insist on some sort of settlement." He thought of Diana, of how the tears had begun dripping down her cheeks. His heart clenched a bit. Dammit. This was all her fault.

Wasn't it?

Or was it his? Jesus! They hadn't been properly introduced the entire time they had spent together on Thursday. He didn't even know her name! What right, then, did he have to know about her parentage—legitimate or otherwise?

He had half a mind to return to the narthex, but the thought of facing the duke, especially after the comments he had made to the man, had him deciding it would be best if he went for a walk.

"I believe I must take my leave of the situation," Adam said with a slight nod. "Ariley is in the church. He and his daughter will be your witnesses on this fine day." With those words, Adam Comber made his way down the steps of St. George's, completely ignoring the Aimsley coach parked at the curb.

# CHAPTER 27
# AN EXPLANATION IS IN ORDER

*eanwhile, back in the church*

Tears streamed down Diana's face, her watery gaze taking in her father's look of disappointment. Or was it concern? "I apologize, Father. I... I thought to pay you a visit. To inform you of Lord Breckenridge's intention to marry me, but I wasn't sure when your duchess would be in residence, and I didn't wish to embarrass her by—"

"She's well aware of you and your sister," Ariley countered in a quiet voice. "Looks forward to the day when she can make your acquaintance, in fact," he added with a sigh. *Or so she claims.* He never imagined that a gently bred lady of the *ton* would ever deign to be in the same room as her husband's illegitimate daughter.

Diana managed to stifle a sob at this bit of news. "She does?" she repeated, her eyes lifting to meet his in surprise.

"Indeed. Why, I would have been able to introduce you to her this instant except she decided she best stay home today. Both of our children are a bit under the weather—just head colds, is all—but she cannot bear to be separated from them when she fears for their health," he murmured. He turned his attention toward the front doors, wondering how far

Viscount Breckinridge might get before he could intercept him.

"He is not a rake," Diana stated then, tears still dripping from her cheeks. "I admit, I thought him a bounder at first," she got out between the hiccups of sobs, noting how her father's eyebrows seem to elevate at her proclamation. "I didn't think this..." She waved her hands to indicate the church. "Would really happen. But he's been nothing but sincere in everything he's said and done since the day I met him."

Ariley frowned. "And when was that?"

Diana gave a sideways glance. "Thursday last."

One of Ariley's eyebrows suddenly arched. "And *where* was that?"

"Outside of White's. I was on my way to Floris to buy a comb."

His eyebrows dancing even more at this bit of news, Ariley regarded his daughter for a few seconds before one of those eyebrows arched up even higher. "Did he say you were a 'ten'?" he asked, amusement apparent in his question.

Diana's eyes widened. She shook her head. "Not at first," she hedged. "Initially, he said he thought me a 'seven'."

It was Ariley's turn to widen his eyes, this time in alarm. "That's it, then. I shall challenge him to a duel in Wimbledon Common," he announced, his voice loud enough to be heard in the nave.

Blinking at his proclamation, Diana shook her head. "But you cannot," she argued. "He's done nothing wrong. He saved me, in fact, from making a fool of myself that day." She was half-tempted to tell him what she had done but thought better of it. "I fear I am to blame in all of this. I should have told him you were my father. I should have told him my mother was a—"

Her words were cut off when Ariley pressed a finger to her lips. "Do not ever refer to your mother as anything more than the devoted companion she was. I *loved* her," he stated, his voice urgent, his hoarse whisper more effective than his usual voice. "I would have taken her as my wife, had I that option," he vowed.

Diana stared at her father for several seconds, tears once again collecting in the corners of her eyes. "I always wondered," she whispered. "Still, I've gone and made a cake of this."

Angling his head to one side, James Burroughs regarded his daughter and finally allowed a wan smile. "I rather doubt that," he said on a soft sigh, pulling her into hug. He took another breath and dared a glance into the nave, sure he saw his youngest sister up at the front pew. Poor thing probably thought she was being left at the altar.

*Where the hell is Thorncastle?*

Ariley returned his attention to Diana. "I gave you my name for a reason, Poppet," he murmured, never having agreed with his daughters' insistence that they use their mother's name in their everyday lives. Although the Burroughs name would have given them cachet and a bit of clout, it would have made it both easier and harder in polite Society.

*I do not wish to gain a position in the Foreign Office just because I have your name,* Daisy had said to him, her defiance evident at an early age. Diana had heard the proclamation and realized she, too, wanted to gain a position because of her skills as a teacher—not because her father was the Duke of Ariley. They had their mother to thank for those beliefs, he knew, for Lily Albright would never trade her association with him for a high standing in Society. Nor would she allow her daughters to expect a comfortable life at the duke's expense. If they didn't earn their keep from employment in a respectable position, then she would instruct them in an alternative choice. One Lily knew the duke would not abide.

The one in which she engaged when she met the man. She was never again a courtesan after that day, though.

What could Ariley do but allow his daughters to live the

lives they thought best for their situation? Except, in this case, his name meant something more. Meant something rather important. Meant something to Society. To the peerage.

"It is times like these when you really *must* use my name. Your given name," Ariley stated firmly, his manner bordering on angst. "I do not require your permission to be your father."

At Diana's look of shock, he sighed and realized he was being rather harsh. "I am your father, Poppet. You can take comfort in it or not, but I am not about to give up my claim to you," he said in a voice that came out as a scold. He winced when he paid witness to her bright eyes, aware that more tears would be falling before long. "You love him, don't you?" he whispered, understanding creeping into his voice as he changed the subject. Diana wouldn't be crying if she didn't have feelings for the viscount. If she didn't think he was lost to her.

Her eyes hidden by wet lashes, Diana allowed a shrug. "Probably," she allowed before sniffling. "He was ever so insistent that we marry. I didn't believe him—I didn't think any of this would really happen, for if I did, I assure you, I would have told him about you and Mother. So that he could properly ask your permission—" So that he could decide if he really wanted to marry an illegitimate daughter of the *ton*.

"Hardly necessary given your age, Poppet," Ariley said, the endearment at odds with his comment. "I would never want your betrothed to be scared off by the idea of having a duke as a father-in-law," he added when he noticed her look of bewilderment. "Since it appeared you were about to marry the man, I do hope you planned to tell him sometime soon, though. What then? Did you believe his reaction would be any different?"

Diana dipped her head, her sniffles suggesting she hadn't intended any such thing. "I wanted to believe we would marry —he seemed so determined—but I didn't want to suffer the hurt if it was all just a ruse to get me to accompany him to Gunter's."

The duke blinked. "Gunter's?" Ariley repeated, his slight nod indicating he was impressed by the viscount's choice of an establishment to court his daughter. He removed a handkerchief from his waistcoat pocket and offered it to her. "I take it Gunter's wasn't a ruse, then?"

Diana shook her head. "Apparently not. But then I feared if he knew I was a duke's daughter, he might only be after my dowry," she reasoned. "I could not abide a marriage of… convenience."

Ariley regarded his daughter for a moment, his expression suggesting he understood her concerns. "If you've only met him last Thursday, then he must have a special license to wed."

Diana nodded. "He does," she acknowledged. "Even so, am I allowed to be in here? To be married in a church?" she whispered as another round of tears threatened.

Although he knew illegitimates weren't supposed to be allowed in church, he wasn't about to have his own daughter abide the rule. "You are. You have my name. I rather wish you would use it. And you're under my protection. Never think any less of yourself. Your mother, God rest her soul, never did. One of the reasons I loved her so," he murmured sadly.

Diana's eyes jerked up at his words, her wet lashes glistening in the dim light. He'd said them twice now, although she could never remember him doing so whilst her mother lived. "You did?"

The duke angled his head to one side. "As God is my witness, I did," he stated firmly. He swallowed. "Having said that, I must admit to loving my wife, as well. Despite knowing of my devotion to your mother, and to you and your sister, Helen does not deny me that part of my life. As a result, I adore her even more, and I am sure to remind her of my feelings for her every night before bed."

"And here I thought it was because she had born you an heir," Diana said between sniffles.

Ariley allowed a grin then. "And a daughter, whom I hope

you will meet sooner rather than later," he said as he gathered her into his arms. He felt a good deal of satisfaction in how she allowed him the hug.

Had the expectations of his life been different—had he not been a duke with a need for an heir—he would have kept his daughters close after the death of their mother. Duty called, though. A dukedom and people who relied on him. Parliament and King and country.

And now a different duty required his attention.

"Well, then. I suppose I shall go find your man and give him my permission to marry you," he stated before giving his daughter a slight bow and moving to the front doors of St. George's. He turned around suddenly. "Oh, and could you please see to your aunt? I do believe she's feeling a bit lonely up there at the front of the church."

With that, he took his leave of his daughter and the church.

## CHAPTER 28
## A FUTURE FATHER-IN-LAW
## STEPS UP

*N*ot too surprised to see his future son-in-law in a discussion with his future brother-in-law, the Duke of Airley waited a moment in the unusually bright sunshine outside the church. He was about to make his presence known to the two gentlemen when he heard Viscount Breckinridge's heartfelt words.

"I should have asked Ariley's permission. And had she told me she was Ariley's daughter, I would have," he said in a louder voice. "I had the impression she and her father were estranged since his marriage!"

"You could have asked her as to whom you needed to seek permission," Thorncastle countered in a hoarse whisper the duke barely overheard.

The older viscount went up a full notch in Ariley's estimation at that comment. Viscount Thorncastle had never particularly impressed him, but perhaps there was more to the man than he knew. His sister certainly seemed to think so.

Ariley jerked his attention back to the two viscounts when he heard Adam say, "I believe I must take my leave of the situation. Ariley is in the church. He and his daughter will be your witnesses on this fine day." Then he watched as Breckinridge made his way down the church steps. He half expected him to climb into the town coach bearing the Aimsley crest in bright gold paint, but instead, the viscount continued down the pavement to the left.

Ariley blinked. *The hell I will*, he thought, realizing he needed to pursue the younger viscount to convince him to marry his daughter.

"Your bride awaits, Thorncastle," Ariley stated as he passed the older viscount, his quick steps taking him down the flight of steps faster than Adam had taken them. He was abreast of the viscount just as the man passed his coach.

"My daughter was afraid you would react exactly as you did," Ariley stated from where he walked alongside Breckinridge. "Or worse, I suppose. Pray tell, what would you have done had you been in her shoes?"

Breckinridge whirled to regard Ariley, his open mouth almost comical on a man who should have been at the altar saying his vows just about then. Apparently, neither he nor Thorncastle knew that Elise Burroughs was at the front of the church waiting for her betrothed—and her two witnesses—to appear.

"She is my illegitimate daughter," Ariley said to Adam, as if he were daring the man to walk faster.

"That doesn't matter to me, sir," Adam replied. "I wanted her as my viscountess. My countess, when the time came," he said, his chin jutting out in defiance.

The unspoken 'but' hung in the air before Ariley frowned. "But?" he urged.

"For the wrong reasons, I have since realized. I had an obligation to Fennington— "

"Fennington?" Ariley repeated. "What the hell does Felix have to do with this?"

Adam winced at the duke's curse but kept his posture ramrod straight. "He's always been in need of funds. I agreed to marry by my thirtieth birthday so he could win a bet. Today is that day. He reminded me of it just a few moments before I spotted your daughter walking past White's." When he noticed how the duke angled his head with an unspoken question, he rolled his eyes. "I thought her a 'seven' at the time, Your Grace. A huge mistake I readily admit. I had half a mind to go after her, but then she suddenly stopped and made her way up the steps to the front door of White's."

The duke stopped and stared at Adam. "Wot?" he asked in disbelief.

"She knows what gentlemen in the bow window are doing whilst they watch the world go by—"

"You mean whilst they watch women walk by?"

Adam nodded, a roll of his eyes indicating his guilt at having participated in the act. "That, too," he agreed. "When the butler said she was asking for me, I had one of those epiphanies. It was fate, I was sure. I had been just about ready to go after her, but she came to me, so... " He gave a shrug.

The duke angled his head to one side. "So you decided to propose marriage? Based on only that bit of *coincidence?*" He was beginning to think it was better his daughter *not* marry the viscount.

"But, of course," Adam countered. "Don't you see? It was fate. And numbers. From her comments on the topic, I was sure she would have been satisfied to hear she was a 'five', but I had already thought her a 'seven'. So imagine my surprise—my very pleasant surprise—to discover she was neither." At the duke's arched eyebrow and expression of confusion, he added, "She was suitably doubtful about me. Once she learned I was a viscount, she might have dropped the skepticism. Might have decided I was a good catch and thrown herself at me with the same violence those doting mothers at Almack's do with their poor daughters. Instead, she remained guarded despite her... curiosity."

Ariley arched an eyebrow in understanding. "She made you work for her affection."

Adam's eyes widened at the comment before he dropped his gaze to the pavement. "She did," he admitted softly. "Although I wish to believe it was hers from the moment I first spotted her." After a moment, Adam resumed his stroll.

Ariley rejoined him as he considered the comment. He could do worse than Adam Comber, the future Earl of Aimsley, for a son-in-law. Much worse. As to whether he could do better, he would never know. He was quite sure Diana would not have been such a watering pot back at the church if she didn't feel some sort of affection for the viscount. If she was left at the altar, she might never deign to consider marriage again. As her father, he wanted her to have a protector—and he preferred that the man be her husband rather than a lover or an unscrupulous rake.

He often worried about Daisy, his eldest daughter, and why she never could divulge her whereabouts when she sent brief letters to him. If she had taken up her mother's profession, he certainly didn't know with whom, and he was sure he would know if she had. What could have Daisy called away from London for months at a time? He knew her bank account was flush with funds other than those he had bestowed on her when she had reached her majority. It was almost as if the girl was a spy for His Majesty's Home Office.

Ariley blinked.

Or the Foreign Office.

He made a mental note to broach the subject with Viscount Chamberlain when he was reminded of Elise. After what she had been through with Lord Lancaster—damn the cur—Ariley had never thought she would consider a second marriage. Thorncastle had held her in his heart for over eighteen years so that she might be his first and only wife.

His first wife, her second marriage, his daughter's first heartbreak on the viscount's thirtieth birthday and the eve of her twenty-fourth birthday. By a man who thought her a 'ten'. On the eleventh of May.

Jesus, it was true what the viscount had said.

It was all about the numbers.

The Duke of Ariley stopped suddenly, and after a few more steps, Adam finally did the same. He turned to regard the duke. "What is it?"

"What the hell are you doing out here? Walking as fast as you can away from St. George's?" Ariley countered as he pretended to regard one his fingernails. "My sister, Lady Lancaster, is up at the front of the church, by the way. Waiting to get married to the love of her life. She cannot do so without witnesses."

"I love her," Adam stated, straightening to his almost six-foot height. He blinked. "Your daughter, that is. Not your sister," he clarified.

Ariley regarded Adam for a moment, feeling relief at hearing the clarification and even more at the conviction in his declaration. His lips quirked at the expression the man displayed. An expression that suggested Adam Comber had at one time given up on love. On life in general. "I am not the one you have to convince," Ariley replied, his attention no longer on his fingers. "You have my permission to marry my daughter. I insist you do so, in fact. Now go get her," he ordered as he turned and realized that Adam Comber hadn't been walking away from the church, but merely around to the side of it. A nearby door apparently led into the front of the church.

Adam blinked. And blinked again as he halted his steps and regarded the duke. *My future father-in-law*, he thought before he allowed an almost audible gasp. "Aye, sir," he said with a quick bow. He was through the side door and halfway into the sanctuary before he realized Diana wasn't there.

At least, not at the altar. Or in the front pew.

And neither was Elise. But Lord Thorncastle sat in a front pew across the aisle with his hands clasped between his knees. His expression suggested he might faint at any moment.

"You look as if you're having second thoughts," Adam said *sotto voce*. "Are your feet cold?"

The older viscount gave him a glance, but not one of annoyance. "I have a confession to make," Thorncastle whispered.

Adam blinked. "Is the priest not available?"

Thorncastle frowned and shook his head. "I could never admit I'm still a... a virgin to a *priest*," he countered, his eyebrows nearly into his hairline.

The younger viscount was sure he heard wrong. Why, he could swear Lord Thorncastle had just claimed he was a virgin. The man had to be well past thirty—probably past five-and-thirty—how was such a condition possible for any man over the age of sixteen?

"You heard right, Breckinridge," Thorncastle continued sadly. "Now I must decide how I'm going to inform my new bride," he added with a roll of his eyes.

Adam could barely remember his life before he had been bedded by one of the housemaids at Aimsley Park, the summer retreat his father's earldom used as a hunting lodge and some-time-residence when he wasn't in London. How old had he been on that auspicious day? Fifteen? Sixteen?

What would he say to Diana should he find himself in the same condition as her? Why, it was doubtful they would know what to do! How to do it. What to put where. And when. How to move and how to stroke and caress and...

*Jesus! I am marrying a virgin*, he thought. He would have to be the one to teach Diana what went where and when. How to move, and how to stroke and caress and... well, she already knew how to kiss, thank the gods!

"You haven't yet told her?" Adam asked as he moved to join the older viscount.

Thorncastle shook his head. "No. I thought perhaps I could just—"

"Pretend you knew what you were doing? Christ, Thorncastle, she's a widow. She'll know you don't know what you're doing before you've doffed your robe!"

Frowning at the curse—they were in a church, for God's sake—Thorncastle rather wished he had kept his mouth shut. "I just wish to know what to *say*," he implored.

Wishing to find his bride so he could wed her and begin doing the very things he had just imagined, Adam allowed a sigh of frustration. "You tell her she has always been the most important woman in the world. The woman for whom you've been waiting to perform the most intimate act—besides kissing, of course. As a result, she needn't be concerned about contracting the French pox or some other god-awful disease," he murmured, thinking his response sounded rather simple, if not reasonable.

Thorncastle regarded Adam for a long moment. "You're a genius. That's exactly what I'm going to do. There is a good deal of truth to your words, I might add. I just have to make her believe me."

Relieved at how easy that was, Adam sobered. "I must take my leave of you and find my betrothed. I have an apology to make," he said as he got to his feet. "Courage," he murmured before he headed down the center aisle.

# CHAPTER 29
# VOWS BY THE NUMBERS

Emboldened by the duke's words and by Thorncastle's devotion to his bride-to-be, Adam Comber had a thought to call out Diana's name at the top of his lungs. He had a thought to follow it with, "I love you," just as loudly. But the quiet inside St. George's was almost deafening. As if any attempt at making a noise would simply be swallowed up, never to be heard by human ears.

Quite sure she hadn't left by way of the front doors, Adam hurried down the center aisle of the church, his gaze bouncing left and right in an attempt to discover any other exits from the church. He was halfway down one aisle and nearly out of the sanctuary when he overheard a slight sniffle.

Pausing, he whirled around to find Diana in a pew. Seated next to Elise, she appeared ever so sad, her head nestled into the older woman's shoulder, her expression completely at odds with how she had looked the moment before the Duke of Ariley had made his entrance just...

Had that only been a half-hour ago?

He gave Elise a beseeching look, which had the older woman giving Diana a quick hug and a kiss to her cheek. "I'll just be up in the front with Lord Thorncastle," he heard Lady Lancaster whisper.

As she passed Adam on her way, Elise gave him a testy glance, suggesting she was none too pleased with him.

Adam could hardly blame her. He wasn't too pleased with himself, either. Christ! He had fallen in love with a duke's daughter and nearly bungled his chance at a life with her!

Perhaps he had already bungled it!

Adam slipped into the pew and settled next to Diana. He had half a mind to kiss her on the cheek, much like Elise had just done, but instead he took one of her gloved hands in his and squeezed it gently. "Your father has given me permission to marry you," he murmured. "I am honored, of course..." He paused when he noticed her widened eyes.

"Honored?" she repeated, the word interrupted due to a sob.

"Indeed," Adam replied. "For I have done the math."

Diana blinked. "The math?" she repeated, wiping an eye with an enormous handkerchief.

"Yes. As I told you the day I met you, it's not my strong suit, but I can count," he said, his manner most serious. "Number one. As a duke's daughter and a teacher of young ladies, you will no doubt make an exceptional countess one day."

A sob and a sniffle were Diana's only response. He soldiered on. "Number two. Today is my birthday. I am thirty, the age at which I promised my best friend I would be wed. Based on that promise, he did a rather foolish thing and engaged in a bet from which he stands to gain a good deal of blunt should I be wed this day. If I do not wed, he may lose some money, although not so much as to send him to debtors prison. I do not wish to disappointment him." When he noticed Diana's frown, Adam realized he probably should have left out the bit about the bet.

"You're only marrying to win a bet?" she asked in dismay.

Adam blinked. "I gain nothing from the bet," he countered.

"Well, I hope to win you, I suppose," he amended wondering if she'd already forgotten point number one. He took a breath. "Number three. I have done the figures for how long I would last without you in my life."

This had her lifting her tear-filled eyes to his, although she didn't say a word in response to his odd comment.

"I believe I would die of a broken heart, you see," he went on. "I would last two, three days at most." He sighed rather dramatically. "Because, number four. I love you. Despite having only known you a few days, I cannot imagine spending the rest of my life without you." He paused and took both her hands in his. "My beautiful, sweet Diana. I apologize for my earlier outburst. I was so stunned that the duke would do what he did —in a church, no less—and call you by such an inappropriate endearment, I found my ire already stoked when you said your words." He allowed a sigh. "My reaction was unforgivable. I rather wish I could turn back time, so that we could do this all over again, for had I known you were Ariley's daughter, I would have sought his permission before even suggesting we marry." He frowned and swallowed. Hard. "That's not quite true," he stated. "I would have done the math and made it quite clear I intended to take you as my wife no matter what he said."

Diana regarded Adam for a long moment, a hiccup forcing her to sniffle again. "Even knowing I was born on the wrong side of the blanket?"

Adam allowed a wan smile. "Blankets don't matter, my sweeting," he said. He had a brief thought as to what his mother and father might think, but decided they would be more impressed he was marrying a duke's daughter than offended that she was baseborn. He could introduce her as Diana Burroughs, after all. Ariley had said she had his name.

At Diana's look of disbelief, he gave a shrug.

"But you were angry with me—"

"Because you didn't tell me you were a duke's daughter," he interrupted. "It was only fair you give me a chance to ask your father's permission to marry you. You had me believing your father was no longer part of your life." When he noted how her brows furrowed at his comment, he added, "When we were at Gunter's."

Diana nodded as she replayed parts of their conversation in her head, remembering she had been rather evasive when speaking about her parents. Deliberately so. But back then, she hadn't believed anything would come of the viscount's claim that he wished to marry her. "Truly, though. What would you have done differently if I had?" she asked in a whisper. "Am I to believe you wouldn't have taken your leave of me that very moment at Gunter's? Appalled at having learned you were in the company of an illegitimate daughter?" This last was said in a whisper, as if she thought her words would bring down a bolt of lightning from the church's ornate ceiling.

Adam allowed a wan smile followed by a grin that seemed to grow larger by the second. "I would not have, for it doesn't matter. In fact, had I known, I might have bought you the scent you thought inappropriate at Floris instead of the citrusy one I did..." He paused to sniff the air around her, his eyes closing as he breathed in the fresh scent. "... And a far better hairbrush than the one that matches the comb you acquired." At her widened eyes—he loved those blue-gray eyes!—he went on. "I would have purchased the naughty night dress I thought might suit you instead of the virginal night rail I caught you staring at in that one modiste's shop. And I would have had my father buy you a Thoroughbred instead of the Arabian that's being delivered to the mews behind my townhouse tomorrow afternoon," he continued, his hand gripping hers harder. "He wanted you to have it as a wedding gift."

Inhaling sharply at each of the items he listed, Diana stared at her betrothed for a long time before giving her head a shake. "But the hair brush is beautiful."

Adam blinked before holding up the fingers of his free

hand. He counted out each of the four items he had mentioned before countering with, "I am relieved you find it so."

"You're quite sure it wasn't for someone else?" she whispered in query.

Her betrothed's eyebrows furrowed in confusion. "Do you suppose I should have bought one for my mother?"

Her arms were around his neck before Adam knew quite what was happening. He felt her lips near his earlobe and heard her barely contained squeal of delight. Grinning at her before he wrapped his arms about her shoulders and pulled her into an entirely inappropriate kiss (given they were in the sanctuary of St.George's), Adam allowed a sigh. "Marry me, Diana. Marry me, and be my viscountess."

Diana giggled in delight. "I will, you bounder."

She was quite sure she had never thought to hear applause in a church, but Diana giggled when she did.

For Elise and her betrothed were clapping and cheering in delight from where they stood together at the front of the church.

"Shall we?" Adam asked as he released his hold on Diana.

"Yes," she agreed. They moved from the pew to the front of the church just as a bishop appeared from a side door. Apparently oblivious to what had been happening, the man waited until Diana and Adam joined them at the altar and then proceeded with the ceremony.

Given how pale Thorncastle appeared, Adam was sure the man would faint before the service was complete. But the older viscount survived his vows, and even seemed amused at the mention of 'forsaking all others'.

Before the clock struck noon, the two couples were joined in holy matrimony as James Burroughs watched from his seat in the third pew. His eyes wet with unshed tears, the duke made his own vow to stay in his daughter's life—and his sister's—despite his ducal responsibilities. Life was short, he knew, and he had no intention of losing the ones he loved.

# CHAPTER 30
# A POST-WEDDING CONVERSATION

*L*ater that day

"I must admit to a bit of nervousness," Godfrey said as he lifted Elise into his arms and carried her over the threshold, up the stairs, and into the mistress suite at Thorncastle House.

"As do I," Elise countered, her gaze taking in his obviously nervous demeanor. *Faith!* The man looked as if he might faint!

"You've been married before," he replied, the words coming out in a kind of complaint.

"True, but not to a man I..." She paused, wondering if she should admit her true feelings for her late husband, for the man had never declared his love for her because she was sure he had no capacity to feel such an emotion. She sighed in exasperation. "To a man for whom I have always felt affection."

The words were the most welcome Godfrey had heard in his entire life. "I adore you," he murmured in a whisper, setting her down next to the bed. He glanced around, as if he were seeing the mistress suite for the very first time.

*This is it, then.* This was the night he would finally bed a woman. The night he would give up the mantel of male virginity. The night he would make love to a woman who should have already been his wife for nearly twenty years.

He glanced at the door that connected the mistress suite to the master suite by way of a dressing room. He had certainly been in that room enough times in his life. "I'll... give you some time—"

"You'll do no such thing, my lord," Elise countered, her eyes dark and daring in how she regarded him. She was standing next to the bed, one of her hands pulling the counterpane down the bed so the quilt was exposed. She reached for the edge of the quilt and pulled it down as well, leaving only the bright, white bed linens to show. "My lady's maid has the evening off, if you'll recall." One of her eyebrows arched up as if Godfrey was to blame.

He stared at her in alarm. *Good God!* He had given her lady's maid the night off. As well as his valet. He imagined the two servants canoodling in their quarters on the floor above and felt an overwhelming sense of jealousy. At least they probably knew what they were doing when it came to making love.

"My valet does as well," Godfrey replied as he gave a glance toward the dressing room door. Perhaps if he said he was going to change into his robe—

"Which means I will have the honor of undressing you tonight."

Elise's words were as welcome as they were frightening. *Good God!* She would see him naked! No other woman could claim that except for his mother and his nurse.

But that meant he would be undressing Elise as well.

"And I have the honor of undressing you," he countered, his voice betraying his nervousness when a squeak erupted there at the end.

"Tit for tat?" she murmured as she stepped up to him and pulled the cravat pin from his neck cloth.

"Aye," he replied as he reached for the only visible pin he

could see in her coiffure. He plucked it out and stared at it a moment.

"You'll need to remove at least six more before anything will happen," Elise warned. She reached up and untied the fashionable knot at the front of his cravat.

Godfrey frowned as he studied her elaborate hairstyle. He wondered how long her maid had worked to create the masterpiece, feeling a hint of dismay at how he wanted nothing more than to ruin it. *Six more pins?* Well, this was a challenge that would keep his mind off of the inevitable.

He spotted another pin and pulled it out between his thumb and forefinger. As a result of his move, another revealed itself, and he pinched it, drawing it out from the chignon. "Is it like pick-up sticks? I pull out the one that holds it all together, and your hair suddenly comes tumbling down?"

Elise giggled, the musical sound surprising him. She angled her head and one lock of hair unwound itself and fell as if in slow motion to come to rest on her shoulder. "Something like that," she agreed.

"I've always wanted to play with your hair," Godfrey claimed as he removed another pin, and then another. Locks of her blonde hair unfurled in turn, each joining the one before it to come to rest on her shoulder or down her back.

"Indeed?" she countered, reaching up to unwrap the length of white silk from around his neck.

"Oh, yes. I lusted for your hair," Godfrey claimed, wondering what he should attempt to remove next. Not her necklace, certainly. He hoped she would wear it and nothing else for the rest of the night. The blue topaz and amethyst stones were exquisite against her pale, porcelain skin.

The earbobs could go, though. He thought of nibbling on her plump earlobes, and the earbobs would merely be in the way. He pulled first one and then the other from her ears, careful to place them on the nightstand where he hoped they wouldn't go missing on the morrow.

Even before he had returned to stand before her, Elise had her fingers on his topcoat buttons. "Just my hair?" she repeated as her lips formed the perfect pout.

Godfrey swallowed as he reached for another pin. "Well, not *just* your hair," he managed to get out without his voice sounding too strangled. He plucked another pin from her hair. *The straw that broke the camel's back*, he thought in delight as he watched her hair tumble down from its perch atop her head. The waves of ash blonde silk unwound and bounced and finally settled into a slightly curled mass that danced about just below her shoulders. He had a fleeting thought of what it would look like on bare shoulders and discovered he didn't have a reference from which to imagine such a sight. "I admit to some rather... scandalous thoughts about the rest of you," he admitted as one of his hands delved into her hair so that his fingers could comb through the silken strands. The tips of his fingers barely skimmed her scalp, sending a shiver of delight through Elise and desire through his loins. "All of you."

Elise allowed a wan smile, her fingers deftly undoing the buttons of his waistcoat. "Pray tell, when was this?" she asked in a seductive whisper.

Concentrating on trying to undo the buttons down the back of her gown while not actually standing behind her, Godfrey swallowed. *My whole life.* "Ever since I kissed you that first time," he murmured. Jesus! Why did his fingers tremble as if he were scared to death?

*Because I am scared to death.* Christ! He was finally going to bed a woman and his body was behaving like that of a boy brought to a brothel for the very first time!

Oblivious to what Elise had been doing, he slipped both the topcoat and waistcoat from his body. His cravat, already untied and unwound, was being pulled from around his neck by hands he had only imagined caressing his body.

The cravat's movement stopped. He looked down to find Elise staring up at him. "That was an awfully long time ago," she whispered on a breath that seemed rather difficult for her just then.

"Indeed. Sometimes it feels as if it were a thousand years ago, and other times it feels as if it was only yesterday," he replied on a sigh.

She seemed to give his words a great deal of thought. "Perhaps it's time we left the past in the past," Elise suggested, allowing her gown to slide down her body.

Godfrey regarded her for a moment, stunned to see her garbed in only a petticoat and corset. *Isn't there supposed to be something under the corset?* he wondered. *A chemise*, he remembered, if only because he had spied one in a modiste's window in New Bond Street. "Perhaps," he replied uncertainly. When Elise turned around and presented her back to him, he gulped. "What... what do I... ?"

Elise giggled as she turned her head and rested her chin on her shoulder. She gave him a sideways glance. "Just tug on the tie. I'm quite sure the laces will practically undo themselves," she claimed. "Merry pulled them far tighter than usual this morning. I've felt as if I were about to pop out of it all day."

An unintelligible sound gurgled from Godfrey's throat. The thought of Elise popping out of her corset was more than his manhood could handle—it was about to pop through the placket of his breeches. He inhaled slowly and girded his loins, deciding he could do this.

He could undress his wife.

Hesitating a moment more, Godfrey finally pulled on the most obvious tie, rather surprised when her petticoat suddenly made its way down over her hips and bared the back of her thighs to him.

Her bare thighs.

Her stockings, held just above her knees with blue satin ribbons, barely hid the rest of her legs. "Wrong tie," he whispered in dismay.

Elise giggled at the same time she wiggled her hips to help the petticoat make its way down to the carpet. "Now undo the tie at the bottom of my corset," she instructed. "I probably should have worn stays, but—"

"You could have worn nothing and I would have been quite fine with it," Godfrey commented in all seriousness.

Blinking, Elise gave a thought to turning around and admonishing him for such a thought, but she held her ground. She should be flattered by his comment, she realized.

Doing as he was told with respect to the corset tie and then blinking in alarm, Godfrey watched as the corset laces moved before his eyes, watched as the garment loosened from around her torso and threatened to remove itself from her body of its own accord. The thought of Elise practically nude—and her limbs on display despite the stockings—had Godfrey breathing far too fast. Far too much. Why, he would faint if he didn't remove himself from behind her this very instant.

"I... I think it's best I finish undressing in my bedchamber," he said through labored breaths. "And maybe shave," he added as he ran a hand over his cheek.

Elise turned and angled her head, wondering if he found her body lacking—or just the opposite. "What is it?" she whispered. She dared a glance down the front of her body. "Am I too fleshy?"

Godfrey's eyes rounded in alarm. "Oh, God, no," he replied with a shake of his head. "You're perfect, Elise. You've always been perfect," he added before giving her a bow. His quick move to the door that led to the dressing room had Elise blinking in shock. And blinking again as the door shut with a *thud* behind him.

Then the door opened a few inches. "I'll be back, of course. Give you time to do whatever it is women do before bed," he managed to get out between his labored breaths. The door shut again.

Her hands on her hips, Elise gave a shrug and went about getting ready for her wedding night. She rather hoped her husband wouldn't suffer a coronary before he returned.

If he returned.

# CHAPTER 31
# ANTICIPATION

*M*eanwhile, *in Adam Comber's bachelor quarters in Green Street*

Diana regarded her reflection in the mirror above the dressing table, wondering if the blush that colored her cheeks would always be there now that she was a married woman. Her new maid had her night rail spread out on the counterpane, the rows of lace making her realize why Adam found it so virginal. In only a few minutes, he would be joining her.

Adam had said something about hoping they might spend the entire night together in the bed. "I wish to wake up with my arms around you," he had whispered just before he disappeared into his bedchamber.

She took a breath, realizing she'd been holding it as she remembered his words. He had also reminded her about the pins in her hair. "Remember, I want the privilege of removing the pins."

Giving him a shy grin, she was aware of her face coloring up as she nodded. "I'll be sure my maid doesn't touch them."

*My maid.* Although she knew there would be several differences in her life now that she was a viscount's wife, there were two that would count the most. One was that she would no longer be living in one of the boarding houses at Warwick's Grammar and Finishing School. The other was she would no longer be sharing a maid.

The young woman who had been sent by the agency earlier that afternoon had assured Diana she could manage styling her hair (especially given the matching comb and brush set she immediately noticed on her mistress' dressing table). Susan was also somewhat educated, a surprise made evident when she announced all six pairs of Diana's shoes were accounted for in the dressing room, as were her five dinner gowns, two carriage gowns, and ten day gowns. Diana had been almost embarrassed by the count. The dinner gowns were only there because her mother had insisted she be properly outfitted should she be invited to a dinner party, or should the instructors at the finishing school decide to attend the theatre one night.

"*Ten* day gowns?" she repeated, just then remembering she did have a different one for each of the five days she taught school for a two-week period. It would have been the norm to wear only a few different gowns as an instructor, but she never thought it acceptable to have the well-to-do daughters of the *ton* think of her as a poor teacher. Not when she had the promise of a large inheritance someday.

"And one ball gown," Susan added, her appreciative gaze taking in the royal blue watered silk gown embellished with a gold sarcenet overskirt. "It looks as if it's never been worn."

Diana angled her head to one side as she reached up to pull off an ear bob. "That's because I haven't yet worn it. It just arrived this morning. It was a gift from my husband's mother," she explained with a slightly arched eyebrow.

Apparently the Countess of Aimsley thought she didn't have access to a suitable modiste in London. Which was true, to some extent. Her mother's modiste was no longer paying personal calls, but she still employed a team of seamstresses to create her elegant designs for her favorite clients if they visited her shop in Oxford Street. "The countess sent it with a suggestion that it be worn for the ball she and the earl are hosting in our honor," Diana explained as she pulled the other ear bob from an ear.

Diana couldn't imagine how the countess would have time to arrange a ball on top of everything else she had going on at the moment. The woman's own daughter, Emelia, had just accepted an offer of marriage from Felix, Earl of Fennington. Patience Comber would no doubt be in the midst of arranging a betrothal ball. In addition, there were rumors the woman was about to be engaged in some sort of trade, a situation that puzzled Adam but seemed to make his best friend, Fenn, rather happy. Although Diana hadn't yet met the man who was somewhat responsible for her marriage to Adam, she looked forward to the introduction.

And thinking of Adam, she wondered just where he might be, for he wasn't in her bedchamber.

# CHAPTER 32
# WEDDING NIGHT JITTERS

*M*eanwhile, *over at Lord Thorncastle's townhouse*

Her reflection staring back at her from the cheval mirror in the corner of the mistress suite, Elise angled her face first left, then right. She lifted her head and winced when her gaze went to her neck. *When did that happen?* she wondered as she leaned in closer and traced the fine lines with a fingertip. *Why doesn't my bridal ensemble include a length of silk I could wrap around my neck to hide the wrinkles?*

*Probably because I would hang myself with it.*

She dared a glance at the Rococo clock on the fireplace mantel. It had been at least an hour since Godfrey's odd departure. She imagined him sneaking off so he could head to his club. He had carried her over the threshold of Thorncastle House, up the stairs, and to the door of the mistress suite, over that threshold, and then deposited her next to the bed. He had helped undress her—although not as completely as she expected he would—and then he had taken his leave with a quick kiss to her cheek and a murmured comment about getting ready for bed in between labored gasps for air.

She had helped in that regard before he suddenly took his leave of her—sans topcoat and waistcoat—and hurried off to the dressing room that connected their two bedchambers.

*How long does it take him to undress and put on a dressing robe? And shave?*

Or had he experienced a coronary at having carried her up the stairs?

Her eyes widened in fright.

He had looked terribly pale upon their parting.

Pale and nervous. Breathing too quickly.

Although, why *he* would have any reason to be nervous was beyond her. This was probably something he did a couple of nights a week with whomever he had contracted as a mistress. Or perhaps he had been keeping a widow or two company. Everyone knew there were hundreds of lonely women whose husbands had died in the war against France.

Elise briefly wondered how many women had been the beneficiaries of his skills in bed. His name hadn't exactly been mentioned in that regard, though, nor had his initials been printed in *The Tattler* along with some salacious article claiming he had bedded Lady So-and-So until she screamed.

Or until she fainted.

Elise had half a mind to make her way to the master suite just to be sure he hadn't passed out from the exertion of carrying her up the stairs.

Or fallen asleep.

*Good Lord!*

The slight move to do so had her noticing the flowing chiffon of her blue nightgown. The fabric clung to her thighs but otherwise seemed to float around her, the bottom lacy edge allowing her peep-toe slippers to show beneath the hem when she walked. The matching transparent negligée barely covered her shoulders and did little to hide her arms from view. Completely open in the front—there didn't seem to be any sort of closure—the robe was obviously of French design. It didn't seem to serve any purpose except to flutter behind her when she moved. At least it was the same shade of blue as the gown. The blue enhanced her eyes and pale blonde hair, but it was the entirely inappropriate bodice of the gown—or the near lack of one—that had her purchasing not only this one, but another in peach, and still another in a rich purple.

One never knew what might be required in the way of seduction.

She considered a simple, white, virginal night rail, but quickly gave up on the idea. She was a widow, after all. She hadn't worn white in nearly twenty years! Once the idea of a night rail was forgotten, a trip to Jermyn Street was in order.

A short shopping trip in pursuit of the perfect wedding night ensemble had metamorphosed into a day-long sojourn involving no fewer than ten stores. She had returned to her townhouse in possession of a new, rather suggestive fragrance from Floris, corsets from Messrs. Shoolbred and Bradshaw, shoes from Carter, a book from Hatchard's, an especially large apple from Fortnum & Mason, female elixir from Bromstead's, and the naughty negligées from Madame Fumier's tiny shop. And because she could, she selected a mustard at La Maison Maille and arranged for a delivery of several cheeses from Paxton & Whitfield.

Having insisted she could walk to the coach, which was parked a few streets down in St. James Street, she had occasion to stroll past the bow window in the front of White's. Although she usually ignored the members who were seated in the bow window, on that day she couldn't help but notice a man holding up both his hands near the window's glass, all ten fingers splayed out and a huge grin displayed on his face.

And then she realized the hands belonged to Godfrey Thorncastle.

But whatever did the splayed fingers mean?

Perhaps it was some sort of fan speak. When a lady's fan was spread out to its full position and put on display for any man to pay witness, it meant *wait for me*.

But what did ten splayed fingers mean?

She gave him a wink and a grin and made a mental note to ask Godfrey whenever they might have a moment between wedding-night activities. In the meantime, she took another turn in front of the cheval mirror and allowed a wan smile as she watched her gown and negligée swirl about her legs.

Elise stopped and regarded her reflection in the mirror again, her attention on her bosom. Although she could never claim to possess a pair of full moons *a la* Adeline Morganfield, Elise could at least lay claim to a couple of perfectly proportioned and rather pert peaches, the two of which were mostly on display due to the scandalous bodice of her gown.

She wondered why she had thought it necessary to wear such a gown on her wedding night. Or any night, for that matter. She already knew Godfrey found her appealing. He had told her so many times—as had another part of him—so she had no reason to doubt his claim. Stifling a grin at how he had failed to hide his reaction to her late-night visit behind an almost empty tumbler, Elise felt a frisson shoot through her body. Why, she rather thought a large beer stein wouldn't have been able to hide his arousal just then.

She had been tempted to suggest a visit to his bedchamber, if for no other reason than to put the man out of his misery. But he had been drinking, and she really didn't want to experience her first night with her husband-to-be when his breath was sour and his brain was in an inebriated state.

But the fact that his inebriated state found her as attractive as his sober side was rather satisfying. That his manhood would deign to stand at attention in her presence was even more satisfying.

Lancaster had never been able to perform when he was inebriated.

Thank the gods.

Another frisson shot through her body, reminding her exactly what that particular erect rod of anatomy was designed to do. At least, she hoped it would. Not having had a very good lover for her first husband, Elise was rather looking forward to being bedded by a man who had experience pleasing a bedmate. Providing pleasure before he saw to his own.

The pleasant sensation of another frisson had her inhaling sharply, which had her peaches nearly escaping from the lacy bodice of her diaphanous gown. Then they nearly did again when she realized Godfrey was watching her from the dressing room door.

Elise stilled her movements and regarded him for a moment. Garbed in a dressing gown of deep blue, he looked every inch the viscount he was. He also looked a bit pale. As pale as he had appeared when he had first set her down after carrying her to the bedchamber.

"How do," she murmured, embarrassed when she realized he might have been watching her the entire time she had been twirling about in front of the cheval mirror. She hurried over to him, hoping the gown and negligée were doing their duty in floating behind her. "You look ..." She paused when she realized he looked even more pale and nervous than he had when he had dropped her next to her bed. "Like a newlywed," she managed to get out.

Having already taken in her gown and negligée, Godfrey managed a nod. "My compliments to your modiste," he whispered hoarsely. "Jesus, Elise. You look like some sort of Greek goddess," he murmured. "One of the naughtier ones."

Her inhalation of breath loud in her ears, Elise took another step closer to her husband. "Truly? I thought perhaps... it might be a bit much. Or not enough?" she added as one of her eyebrows arched up, daring him to make some sort of suggestive comment. She allowed the sentence to trail off, though, when she realized he hadn't yet moved from where he stood, nor did he grin at her attempt at humor. "Are you... feeling well? I apologize if I was such a burden when you carried me..."

She couldn't complete the thought when Godfrey's lips were suddenly covering hers. Covering hers with a kiss that was exactly like the first one they had shared. *Faith!* That had been when they were but nineteen and sixteen years of age. Betrothed in spirit, but not in fact. Committed to one another, but destined to live apart. Live lives that didn't meet their expectations.

When Godfrey finally pulled away to regard her, Elise opened her eyes and stared up at him. Still pale and still looking as if he might faint at any moment, his gaze managed to speak volumes. Elise furrowed her brows. "Whatever is wrong?" she asked in a hoarse whisper.

Godfrey finally allowed a long sigh, his solemn manner completely unexpected. "I have something I need to tell you, my sweet," he murmured. "And..." He paused to take in the bright, white linens that were exposed on the bed before allowing another long sigh. "I can put it off no longer."

At least, that's what he imagined he should say to his new wife. He wasn't quite sure what he said just then.

# CHAPTER 33
# CONTEMPLATING A BEST FRIEND

*M*eanwhile, *back at Breckinridge's quarters in Green Street*

Adam dismissed his valet and thought of Diana. She was in the hastily made up mistress suite just on the other side of the dressing room. He knew her maid was with her for he could hear the chit hanging up clothes through the door that connected the bedchambers.

Tamping down the bit of nervousness he felt, Adam forced himself to take a seat at his writing desk. He considered penning a congratulatory note to his best friend. Fenn was about to be a rich man, for not only did the earl win a rather lucrative bet at White's—Adam's marriage to Diana had accomplished that feat—Fenn claimed in a short note that he had sold something of immense value for a good deal of blunt. On top of that, he would be gaining a dowry from marrying a well-respected daughter of the *ton*.

*My sister.*

Adam rather doubted it would be as large a dowry as what James Burroughs, Duke of Ariley, had settled on him. Quite unexpectedly and without a verbal word, a liveried footman had delivered the short note late that afternoon. *The Right Hon.*

*The Viscount Breckinridge* was printed on the outside in a hand obviously owned by a fastidious secretary or clerk. Inside the paper was a cheque for the amount of fifty-thousand pounds and a short missive.

*Dear Lord Breckinridge,*

*Now that you've gone and made my daughter your viscountess, I know you'll strive to make her a happy woman and, eventually, a proud countess. May I suggest you use the enclosed cheque toward the purchase of a larger townhouse? At least fourteen rooms, I should think. I suspect there is no nursery in your humble abode, and I expect you'll make me a grandfather within the year. In fact, I am counting on it (as is my duchess). You'll need an heir, after all. Do take care of my daughter, won't you? After our discussion this morning before you said your vows, I have every reason to believe she feels affection for you, so I would be disappointed to learn her feelings have changed because you've gone and done something unforgivable.*

*Very disappointed.*

The missive was signed and sealed with the ducal insignia, although a postscriptum was also written in smaller script, as if the secretary had penned the main letter and the duke himself had written the rest.

*When you meet my eldest daughter, Daisy, do encourage her to pay me a visit. We have been estranged these past eight years, although I cannot figure why. I thought we had parted on amiable terms when she left our care. Perhaps an encouraging word from you will have her paying me a visit.*

*Ariley.*

Adam blinked after reading the postscript, and blinked again at the signature.

*Ariley?*

He sat down hard on his bed and reread the missive. Well, he had every intention of pleasing Diana. He had every intention of getting a child on her, if not tonight, then in the next day or so. Or week, if that's what it took. Having used French letters for his other encounters with women who had long since given up their virtue, he had no experience in the matter of bedding a virgin.

He rather hoped his wife didn't have any experience whatsoever, and then they would be on equal footing. So to speak.

# CHAPTER 34
# A VISCOUNT MAKES HIS CONFESSION

*M*eanwhile, *back in the mistress suite at Thorncastle House*

Godfrey Thorncastle peeked through the opening he had created when he pushed on the door that connected his dressing room to the mistress bedchamber. He watched as Elise Thorncastle twirled about, her scandalously translucent gown leaving absolutely nothing to the imagination when it came to her arms, her breasts, her body, and her toes. Why, he could have stood there all night and simply reveled in the fact that she was doing such a thing in the mistress suite of his townhouse. Her twirling about suggested she was happy to be his wife. Happy to be the Viscountess Thorncastle.

*My viscountess.*

*My wife,* he reminded himself as he felt his member respond. Well, at least it could respond. He had feared his body would betray him on such an auspicious occasion.

The most important night of his entire life.

The fact that he could pull her into a kiss probably surprised him more than it did her. At least part of his brain was working. When his lips finally let go of hers, he remembered her comment and realized he hadn't yet responded.

"You were not, nor shall you ever be, a burden, my lady," he managed to get out as he felt the dressing room door close behind him. *That would be because I'm leaning against it*, he reasoned. Using it for support. *Goodness, but when had Elise managed to get so close?* he wondered as he realized she was giving him an expression of expectation. An expression that suggested she was far more ready for what was to take place in her bed than he was.

Elise regarded him with a wan smile. "Thank you for saying so, Godfrey," she whispered. "I can call you 'Godfrey', I hope?" she half-asked. "Or Thorncastle, should you prefer, but—"

The viscount blinked. "Whenever you wish," he acknowledged with a nod. "And may I call you 'Elise'?"

Elise blinked. Had the man ever called her anything else? "But, of course," she replied with a quick nod of her head.

He nodded in turn. "Your gown is... bewitching," he managed to get out, his gaze traveling down the front of her body and back up until their eyes locked. "You look like a goddess."

"I have others like it," Elise murmured, immediately regretting the comment. She had intended to use them on nights when she needed to curry favor with her husband. No need to forewarn him they existed.

"Then I shall be under your spell for the rest of my life, I expect," he countered quietly.

Elise allowed a sigh of contentment. "Thank you for waiting for me. I truly thought you would find another to take as your wife. To make your viscountess when my brother interfered with our plans," she managed as she leaned into his solid body, the front of her body molding into his as if they had been made to embrace. "I wouldn't have blamed you if you had. Not one bit." She took heart in how his arms encompassed her body and pulled her hard against his chest. Goodness, but his heart was beating fast. Beating hard.

"There has never been another, Elise," he whispered, his voice sounding urgent.

Elise leaned her head back and regarded him for a moment. "And what of your mistress?" she asked, thinking he must have employed one for the past ten or so years. Perhaps he had even fathered a child or two. The man was in his mid-thirties, after all. "What nights do you share with her?"

Godfrey blinked before allowing a frown. "I don't," he replied. "In fact, I've never employed a mistress."

It was Elise's turn to blink. "Oh," she replied in surprise. *Dammit.* That meant the man simply took his pleasure with whatever lady of the evening might be available on any given night. Were they delivered to his back door? Or did he visit a brothel...?

Watching Elise work out the more obvious conclusions had Godfrey wondering at how much he should admit just then. He wanted to tell her there had been no others, but to do so meant he wouldn't have the opportunity to simply try making love to his wife without the benefit of any experience in the matter.

*What wife would be accepting of a husband who had never bedded another woman?* Elise was probably expecting an experienced lover. A man who could see to her pleasure before taking his own. And do so several times in one night.

*Oh, God*, he thought in dismay. *Not me.*

"Is there a particular night you pay a visit to a...?" Elise started to ask.

"No," Godfrey replied quickly. He managed a rather loud sigh. "If you recall, my father died on the eve of my sixteenth birthday," he said as his forehead moved to rest on hers.

Elise felt the weight of his head fall onto her forehead. She had to tamp down the thrill she experienced at realizing her husband no longer took pleasure in the arms of a mistress or a prostitute. "You honor me, husband," she whispered with a sigh. Her eyes widened before she pulled away from him.

"I *always* have, my lady," Godfrey replied, one brow arching up in the hopes she would take his meaning.

Godfrey was rather stunned when Elise planted her lips against his, the firm pillows taking purchase in an urgent, hard and completely unrelenting kiss that had him so surprised, he forgot his immediate concern and concentrated on returning the kiss.

They had never kissed like this, not when they were younger, and certainly not since his proposal. He rather hoped they would do this often, embrace one another and simply get lost in a kiss.

When Godfrey finally pulled away, determined to catch his breath and to determine just what had her behaving so, he allowed a wan smile. "I've worried for years you wouldn't be satisfied with a virgin for a husband," he added with a sigh of relief.

Elise stared at her husband for a good ten seconds, wondering if perhaps she should respond or accuse him of being a bounder. "*Virgin?*" she repeated in shock.

Godfrey realized too late that Elise hadn't understood his earlier words. She hadn't made the connection when he made his claim that she had always been the only one. Hadn't known of his devotion to her from afar.

When it was evident he could no longer keep secret his monk-like life from the lady, he sighed. "I couldn't bed another," he said. "Another woman would never have meant anything... " He stopped when he realized Elise was staring at him, the look of shock still on her face.

"You've never bedded a woman?" she whispered, a hint of dismay coloring her voice. And then Godfrey watched as her head seemed to sway and bobble before her eyes suddenly rolled up and her body went limp.

Given his arms were still around her body, Godfrey was quick to keep her from falling to the floor. In fact, he was able to scoop her up into his arms and place her onto the bed, his murmured, "No, no, no, no," rising in volume as he did so. "I thought *I* was the one who was going to faint," he said, despite knowing Elise probably couldn't hear him at that moment.

He had certainly felt as if he would, the way his breathing was so labored, his heart racing too fast. With his concern now for his wife, he found his thoughts completely on her, his worry for her rather than on his impending performance—or lack thereof.

Once he had her on the bed, he frowned as he worried about how he might revive her. With the translucent fabric of her gown hugging her every curve, and the robe that barely covered anything, and her blonde hair splayed out across the pillows, she looked as angelic as she did devilish. As much a goddess as a seductress.

He rather liked the thought of her seducing him for the rest of his life. Rather liked the thought that she might spend her nights in his arms—in his bed or in hers—as he slumbered.

His member certainly had no intention of slumbering just then, he realized. *Good God!* He was as hard as ever, aroused beyond his normal morning tumescence.

Placing a hand along the side of her face, he lowered his lips to hers and gave her a quick kiss. "Sweeting, wake up now," he whispered. He rubbed her cheek with his palm, his thumb tracing the curve of her lip. When her hand covered his, she opened her eyes.

Godfrey allowed a sigh of relief. "I cannot believe you would faint on me on our wedding night," he accused with a teasing grin. He brought her hand to his lips and kissed it.

Elise took a deep breath, the motion causing the barely-there bodice of her gown to expose far more than it had when she was standing. Godfrey dared a quick glance down before returning his attention to her eyes, aware his manhood had taken notice as well.

"And here I thought *you* were about to faint," she countered with a wan smile.

"I was," he admitted, leaning down to give her another kiss. When he pulled away, he angled his head and sat down on the edge of the bed. "Are you disappointed?"

Elise reached out with a hand to wrap it around his elbow. She gave it a tug, an invitation of sorts for him to join her. When he didn't move to do so, she said, "Lie down, won't you? So that I may tell you how honored I feel at this moment."

Godfrey's double-take had his brows furrowing. "You're not disappointed?" he asked again as he settled onto the bed next to her. When Elise rolled against him, he lifted his arm to wrap it about her shoulder, hesitant in his moves. When she rested her head into the small of his shoulder, he finally relaxed a bit. "Or feeling a bit deceived, perhaps?"

Allowing a titter in response, Elise slid her hand beneath the opening of his robe and reveled in how he sucked in a breath at her touch. "I am not disappointed. Not exactly," she whispered, deciding not to admit that she was looking forward to an experienced lover. "As for feeling deceived, I suppose it's my own fault. Like you, I assumed something that wasn't true."

"Because there was gossip about me?" he asked. Although he didn't read *The Tattler*, he occasionally overheard the *on-dit* at White's. He'd never heard anything said about him.

The pads of her fingers found one of his nipples and barely skimmed over it, eliciting another gasp from him before she replied, "I don't recall. In fact, I don't believe I've ever seen or heard anything about you in that regard," she admitted, lifting her head to regard him directly. "I suppose an apology is in order."

Godfrey allowed a wan smile, rather liking how her soft curves had molded to the side of his body, and how the curtain of her blonde hair nearly hid one of her eyes. "Let's just say we're even and leave it at that," he suggested, pulling her down so he could kiss her again. He groaned when her questing hand found a particular spot beneath one rib, causing a shiver to pass through his entire torso. "How did you know how to do that?" he whispered in query, tamping down the flash of jealousy he felt at thinking Lancaster might have been the beneficiary of her touches in the past.

"I didn't," she replied in a matching whisper, her hand moving to another rib and then to the soft flesh above his curlies. She delighted in how he jerked and emitted a low growl when she circled a finger there.

"You minx!" he accused.

Elise giggled, the musical sound bringing a grin to his lips. "Do you mind? I find I'm rather enjoying this opportunity to get to know you better." She didn't wait for his response but moved her fingers lower.

Godfrey sucked in another breath. "This isn't fair, I tell you," he said in a strangled whisper, especially when her forefinger trailed the vein down the back of his erection. He was sure she could feel how he throbbed, how at any moment, her touch would set off a release he would have no hope of stopping.

"Fair?" she countered with an arched eyebrow.

Sputtering a bit, Godfrey finally sighed. "What am I allowed to do?" he managed to get out just before her finger made a circle over the tip of his manhood. He sucked in a breath and concentrated on controlling himself.

"What do you want to do?"

Godfrey blinked, not sure how to answer the simple question. "I wish to make love to you. To make you feel these same sensations. To bring you to ecstasy and ensure you'll never want to share a bed with another man for the rest of your life," he murmured, his words tumbling out as he lifted his body from the bed and pushed hers back down onto the mattress so she was flat on her back.

Elise felt a rush of excitement when he traded places, but realized he wasn't about to do anything more without some sort of direction.

Permission.

"I will admit, I was rather looking forward to marital relations with a man of some... experience—"

"Teach me," Godfrey begged as he supported his torso on his free elbow and gazed down at her. "Teach me how to make love to you. How you like it. Tell me what to do to bring you to ecstasy."

Her warm hand still pressed against his chest, its heat increasing so he felt as if she were slowly branding him, Elise shook her head. "I'm afraid I wouldn't know," she whispered. "I've never found sexual relations very... pleasant."

Godfrey stared down at his wife, her words a mix of surprise and—dare he think it?—relief. At least he had the benefit of having read some books on the subject.

Well, not *read* so much as studied the illustrations.

He knew what went where, of course, but there was so much more to sexual relations, wasn't there? Seduction. Touching. Kissing. Providing pleasure. "Then we shall have to learn from one another," he murmured before settling his lips over hers.

Before she could begin to return the kiss, Elise felt a tremble of excitement—or perhaps it was merely anticipation—pass through her body. His lips barely touched hers, as if he feared bruising them.

Moving one hand to the back of his neck, Elise pulled him down closer, an invitation he accepted in how his lips opened and deepened the kiss. It was some time before he finally pulled away and regarded her with a look of worry.

"Are you cold?" he whispered, his lips hovering over hers as if he were trying to decide what to kiss next.

*Cold?* Her addled brain wondered why he could think such a thing, but then she realized her entire body seemed to vibrate beneath him. "No," she breathed before she reached up with her lips and captured his again.

He moved his lips from hers, trailing the soft kisses down her cheek, along her jaw, and down to her earlobe, where he pulled the soft flesh between his teeth and gently nibbled. Spurred on by her almost soundless gasps, he continued the kisses down her neck. Soft kisses, as if flutterby wings were flitting over her soft flesh.

*This is easy*, he thought with some satisfaction. *Perhaps I can just do this all night.*

Of course he would have to do more, but for now, kisses were enough.

# CHAPTER 35
# WEDDING NIGHT WONDERS AND WONDERINGS

*M*eanwhile, back in the mistress suite in Breckinridge's bachelor quarters

Wearing a robe loosely tied about his middle, Adam Comber, Viscount Breckinridge and future Earl of Aimsley, entered the mistress bedchamber of his small townhouse in Green Street by way of the dressing room. He gave a nod to his new wife's maid, who quickly curtsied and took her leave of the room as if she were scared to death of him.

"I didn't mean to frighten her," Adam murmured as he turned to regard his wife's reflection in the mirror above the dressing table. He took note of the white night rail on the counterpane and then realized Diana wore only a dressing gown as she sat at the dressing table.

He had to tamp down the sudden arousal he felt when he realized she was naked beneath the dressing gown.

She allowed a grin. "I take it you two haven't been introduced," she teased. At his quick head shake, she added, "Susan didn't know we were newlyweds until I forbid her from taking the pins from my hair."

Adam moved to stand behind her and considered where to start. "Do you know how many pins there are?" he asked as he plucked first one and then another out. When nothing happened—her hair remained in its loose bun atop her head —Adam leaned forward and stared down, unaware of Diana's look of amusement as she watched his reflection in the mirror.

"I apologize. I was so nervous when I was inserting them early this morning, I didn't keep count," she said as he found another and pulled it out from the base of the bun.

"You pinned up your own hair? Today?" The question suggested he was shocked.

"Someone had to. I haven't had the benefit of my own maid since I lived with my parents," she replied with a shrug.

The movement caused her dressing gown to slide down one shoulder just a bit, and from his vantage, Adam was glancing down a deep, dark crevice. When his arousal threatened to send his cock peeking out from between the robe's opening, he returned his attention to her hair and the pins therein. He yanked out another. When not a single lock of hair fell, he stepped back.

"Is there some trick to this?" he asked, obviously perplexed by her coiffure.

Diana shook her head and a lock of hair dislodged itself from the rest, falling down so it ended at the top of one of her collar bones. From his question, she realized he had never done this before when she'd had the impression he had done it for all the women he had ever bedded.

"It's long then, is it?" he whispered, his voice holding a good deal of appreciation. Awe, even.

"Somewhat," Diana agreed. The feel of his fingers barely touching her scalp had a shiver of anticipation racing down her spine. "So... you've not done this before?" she ventured as she continued to watch his reflection in the mirror.

"Played lady's maid?" he replied quickly. "I have not." He paused a moment. "Unless you count the time I braided my sister's hair. Made a cake of it, but she didn't seem to mind. I think she was three or four at the time. Sick maid, or some such."

Her eyes widening in surprise, Diana turned around to regard him. "Lady Emelia? Is that right?"

Nodding and rather happy to have a new vantage of his wife's décolletage—and her bun—Adam pulled several more pins from her hair. "She has recently returned from finishing school in Geneva. She's..." He paused a moment to figure how old she was. "Seventeen. Eighteen, perhaps?"

This information had Diana's brows furrowing. "Could she have been one of my students a few years ago?" she asked. She remembered his comment about Emelia Comber attending finishing school in Switzerland, but she wasn't sure she had taught Emelia Comber during her first year at Warwick's.

"Doubtful," Adam replied as he searched for another pin. "She was in Geneva these past three years. Living with a family friend—Lord Andrew, the youngest son of..." He paused, realizing his wife was related to Andrew. In fact, the man was her uncle! "The youngest son of your grandfather—and attending finishing school with his daughter, Lady Sophia."

Diana considered this bit of news. "Why Switzerland, do you suppose?"

Adam brightened. "My mother attended that particular finishing school in Geneva," he explained proudly. "And I think there may have been a hint of scandal associated with one of the instructors at Warwick's during Emelia's time there. Had her quite unhappy, so Mother saw to it she was sent off to the Continent."

Although she hadn't yet been hired when that 'bit of scandal' had occurred, Diana had been hired as a result of it. She replaced the teacher that had caused the trouble. "I'm so sorry for what happened to her," she murmured.

Adam considered her apology. "There's no need for you to apologize, my lady. It happened before you were hired there, I should think. Besides, I am of the opinion it did Emelia some good to be away from London for a time." He screwed up his face a bit. "I still can't believe she's only been back in England for... what? Eight weeks? And she's already betrothed."

Diana's eyes widened as she turned to give him a glance. "Don't you suppose she's saying the same thing about you?"

Adam blinked and then grinned when he remembered they had only known each other for five days. "Touché," he murmured. "I still find it hard to believe she's betrothed to Felix. Are you quite sure?"

Giving him a shrug, Diana nodded. "I'm quite sure."

He resumed his search for pins as if he were on some sort of prized hunt. Then his hands stopped in their quest and he glanced at her reflection in the mirror above the dressing table. "Emelia? Betrothed to Fenn?" he questioned again with an arched brow. He let out a bark of laughter. "I rather doubt my father would agree to such a match." He paused a moment as he pulled two more pins from her bun. "Mother wouldn't mind a bit. She loves the bloke more than she does me," he murmured as he slid several fingers back into the now-messy bun, continuing his search for hairpins. He took great delight when the mass finally unwound on its own and fell down past her shoulders.

Watching her reflection in the mirror, Adam speared his fingers through the dark mass, combing it as he watched the charcoal black waves settle onto her satin dressing gown. When he finished, he regarded her as his eyes darkened. "I had no idea it was so silky," he murmured. "You may find my face pressed into it on the pillow when you awaken in the morning."

Diana couldn't help the flare of color that pinked her face just then. She turned around on the dressing chair so she could gaze up at him directly. "I do hope you don't regret this," she whispered. "Marrying a... bastard, I mean."

Frowning, Adam leaned down and kissed her forehead. "Never," he murmured. "You are every bit the lady as any of those who can claim relations to an aristocrat."

She sighed. "Whatever will we tell the earl and his countess when they ask as to how we met? Your mother has been so gracious. She sent me a ball gown today! I cannot help but think they'll believe I'm some sort of opportunist—"

One of Adam's fingers landed on her lips, effectively silencing her. "I wrote to them both this morning to let them know I would be marrying this day," he whispered. He reached into a pocket in his robe and pulled out a folded piece of vellum. "Here's the note from my mother. It was delivered whilst we were saying our vows." He handed it to Diana.

Her eyes wide, Diana realized how it was the countess had known where to send the blue watered silk gown. She slowly unfolded the elegant vellum to reveal a short note written in an even, feminine script.

*My dearest son,*

*Thanks to your visit a few days ago, your happy news hasn't caught us by surprise. It is good news to me, for I have oft worried you might never settle. We so look forward to the day when you'll introduce us to your viscountess. Although I am not familiar with her name, and therefore not with her, I trust you have chosen a woman with whom you will have a happy life, the ton be damned. (Yes, I have just written a curse, and no, I will not apologize for it.)*

*As your life changes, so does mine. Your father has gifted me with the means to pursue an unusual avocation, but one for which I am well suited. Although you cannot speak of it to anyone, I will divulge that I am the new owner and editor of The Tattler. My first issue will release this Thursday. I promise that anything I include about you and your new bride shall be nothing but complimentary. She who controls the news is able to protect her own, after all.*

*Do have a wonderful honeymoon, and please know that the earl and I wish you all the happy in the world.*

*Yours very truly,*
*Mother.*

Rather stunned by how amenable the Countess of Aimsley seemed when it came to her oldest son's marriage, Diana was even more surprised at the news about the countess taking on the duties of owner and editor of *The Tattler*. Why, Diana had feared for the past few days that news of her afternoon in the company of Viscount Breckinridge—without the benefit of a companion or a maid—might land her on the front page of the gossip rag. Now she had assurances she might never be mentioned.

Although she wouldn't mind being mentioned as the new wife of Adam Comber, Viscount Breckinridge.

*L*ater that night

A sudden chill had Diana opening her eyes. She stared up at the unfamiliar tufting of her bed's canopy, the royal blue satin appearing almost gray in the dim light from the room's only window. She glanced in that direction and realized almost immediately why she felt cold. Adam had left the bed. Silhouetted in the window, he stood staring out, his arms crossed over his chest, his erect cock poking out from its nest of brown curls, and a frown firmly in place on his lips.

Diana slipped from the bed, pulling a bed linen with her to wrap about her torso as she did so. Moving to join him, she glanced out the window in an effort to determine what had his attention. When she saw nothing of note, she turned to gaze up at him, but before she could even put voice to a question, his arm wrapped about her back and pulled her close.

"I didn't mean to wake you, my sweeting," he whispered before kissing the top of her head.

"The bed grew cold without you in it," she countered, her voice clearly pitched to tease. When she noted how he still appeared too serious in the dim light, she felt a bit of panic. This was exactly what she had feared in agreeing to marry the viscount after such a short courtship. "You're having second thoughts, aren't you?" she whispered, a sense of melancholy settling over her. After such a wonderful wedding night, she had thought her initial fears unfounded.

Adam pulled her into a hard hug, his hardened manhood pressing into the linen that covered her soft belly. He allowed a groan before kissing her hair, the side of her face and finally her lips. When he pulled away, he left his forehead pressed against hers. "Not in the least," he murmured in reply. "However, I am bemoaning my promise to my mother."

Diana frowned. He hadn't made mention of any promises. And what might the Countess of Aimsley have made her son promise on the occasion of his marriage? "What promise was that?"

Adam straightened and cleared his throat. "She warned me that I shouldn't be too greedy on my wedding night, or my bride would not welcome me back into her bed. Perhaps for several nights," he whispered in what sounded like despair.

Blinking, Diana moved a hand up to his face and cupped his cheek. *Greedy?* She realized right away to what the countess must have meant. She did feel a hint of soreness at the apex of her thighs—a sort of delicious discomfort that would be replaced with heavenly pleasure should they renew their earlier explorations of one another. Besides, the desire she felt for her husband's attentions more than countered it. "And what if your bride demands that you return to her bed? To continue what you were doing earlier?" She punctuated her questions by sliding the palms of her hands up the front of his body, the pads of her fingers brushing over his nipples so he suddenly hissed.

He took one of those hands in his and brought it to his lips. "Are you sure?" he asked, his voice hoarse with desire. "I don't want to hurt you."

A shiver passed through Diana, punctuating the excitement she experienced at the thought he might do to her again what he had done earlier. "Of course, I'm sure," she replied, gripping the hand that held hers and moving toward the bed.

Adam had her lifted into his arms before she had a chance to climb onto the bed, her shriek of surprise followed by a giggle as he settled her down onto the mattress. He covered her body with his. Although he was aware of her legs wrapping around his lower back, he didn't immediately impale her, choosing instead to use his lips to caress her heated skin from her collarbones to her breasts and then to her nipples.

Diana mewled as he worshipped her with his lips, sucked in a breath when his teeth took purchase on a nipple and gently bit it before his lips suckled it. It wasn't until she begged for him that he finally impaled her, his own breath briefly robbed as he thrust himself into her wet haven and her chest rose up in response. "Jesus, Diana. If I didn't know better, I would swear you were born to be an enchantress," he managed to get out.

Thrilled at his words, Diana smoothed her hands up the sides of his body, her thumbs brushing over his nipples as he pulled out of her. His groan was followed by another thrust, her counter thrust meeting his this time.

Although her mother had never arranged for her to bed a man in order to learn what to do in a marriage bed—Lily preferred her daughters remain virgins in the event they could arrange advantageous marriages based on their ties to their father—Diana was quite sure her mother would have seen to a suitable bedmate if she had requested one. Instead, Lily had described in great detail what happened in a marriage bed, told of the nuances of lovemaking, explained how simple touches and tugs and squeezing could send a man into ecstasy.

Her mother's instructions suddenly at the forefront of her brain, Diana took delight as she put each one into practice.

Diana reveled in hearing Adam's breath hitch when she drew a finger down the vein at the back of his engorged cock, grinned when her questing fingertips stroking through his dark curlies had him groaning, and almost laughed as his entire body shivered when her lips took purchase on one of his nipples. She would have continued her exploration of his body, her lips moving to the inside of his elbow to suckle the soft skin there, but Adam had her on her back, his deep growls a warning she was about to be impaled by the very manhood she had stroked only the moment before.

The first time he entered her, Diana expected a pinch of pain. Adam's fingers had seen to enhancing her arousal, their tentative exploration and entry into her tight, wet haven slowly stretching her in preparation for his manhood.

When he finally did enter her, it was slowly, carefully, so that, although she felt full and stretched to her limit, she didn't feel pain. She sensed his thrusts weren't as hard as he would have liked, but she didn't know what to do to encourage him. She didn't know the language necessary to communicate her thoughts, so she used her hands to hold on and countered his thrusts with those of her own when she could.

His lips captured hers for just a moment, his quick kiss ending just as she pulled him back into her body, her hips lifting from the bed when his manhood was as deep as it would go. "You minx," he murmured, his head lifting from hers.

Diana watched in wonder as his entire body seemed to seize and freeze in place, the tendons of his neck straining, the muscles in his upper arms flexed.

She felt the heat of his release as his seed spilled into her, the bloom of warmth spreading through her abdomen. And she heard his growl next to her ear when his body seemed to suddenly collapse atop hers.

She delighted in how he covered her, in how the warmth from his heated skin permeated her own and left her feeling satiated and happy. But most of all, she reveled in how he stayed right where he was, boneless and breathless and hers to hold for a long time.

# CHAPTER 36

# A WOMAN AWAKENED, A
# MAN EMBOLDENED

*eanwhile, in the mistress suite at Thorncastle's townhouse*

Elise thought she had never felt anything quite so exquisite against her skin. Even the chiffon of her nightgown wasn't as soft as how Godfrey's lips barely caressed her. Coupled with his warm, soft breaths, the light touches had her wondering if she should be doing something in return. And then her thoughts flew from her head when one of his fingers drew a line along the edge of the bodice of the gown.

"May I?" he whispered, his head lifting as he waited for her to respond.

Elise blinked, her last breath held in anticipation and her brain having a difficult time understanding what he was asking.

*Permission?*

"Please do," she managed on the exhalation of breath.

His finger traced where one breast was barely contained by the bodice of her gown, its heat seeming to leave a scorching trail as he gently pushed aside the fabric. When her engorged nipple was exposed, he immediately covered it with his mouth, his tongue tracing the shape of it as he gently suckled.

"Oh!" Elise managed, sounding ever so breathless as shivers of delight possessed her entire body.

Suppressing the urge to chuckle—he actually felt more relief than humor at her response—Godfrey moved his attention to her other breast. Using his chin, he pushed aside the strip of fabric that had already crept down her arm, the bit of sleeve that would have held the gown up if she'd been standing. As if she understood his intent, Elise pulled her arm out of it and moved her hand beneath his robe to grip his back just under his shoulder blade.

The invitation had him kissing the newly exposed upper arm, the small of her shoulder, the edge of her collarbone, before he covered her breast with his mouth and worshipped it with his teeth and tongue.

Elise's reaction was nearly violent as her chest rose from the bed and her fingers gripped him, waves of pleasure cresting so she found herself almost unable to breathe.

Concerned he might have hurt her, Godfrey quickly moved from atop her, sat up against the cushion of the headboard, and pulled her into his arms. "I apologize. I didn't mean to—"

"Oh, but you did nothing wrong," Elise managed between labored breaths, her head settling onto his chest as he managed to pull the bed linens and a quilt over most of her body. Her entire body trembled despite his hold on her.

"You're cold. You're—"

"I'm rather warm, actually. Blissfully so," she murmured as her breathing returned to normal. She lifted her head from his chest and regarded him with an arched brow, her look of contentment suddenly changing to suspicion. "I thought you said you'd never done this before."

Godfrey allowed a chuckle. "I have only imagined it a thousand times. Probably ten-thousand times," he amended with a sigh. He kissed her hair before rolling her off of his body so that he could move farther down the bed.

With her torso elevated on the mound of pillows at the

head of the bed, Elise relaxed and considered what he might do next. The space at the top of her thighs seemed to throb with need, the dark blonde curls damp.

"May I... taste you?" he whispered as one of his hands smoothed over the side of her body until it reached a thigh. His fingers gathered the chiffon of her gown into his fist until one of her legs was left completely bare.

Elise held her breath at hearing the question, and then inhaled sharply at the sensation of his questing fingers against the soft flesh of her thigh. She gasped again as first the tip of one, then another finger trailed along the top of her leg and through her curlies, the caresses much like she had done to him only moments before.

*Taste me?* she thought, a shiver of anticipation gripping her. She had a thought to put voice to a protest, but his fingers were suddenly between her legs, their tips gently nudging her thighs apart. When she was aware of his body shifting even lower on the bed, she gave in and allowed her knees to fall apart. She shuddered as his hands moved to smooth themselves first around her hips, then beneath her thighs, and to finally hold the globes of her bottom. When he lifted them, she nearly screamed when the tip of his tongue made contact with her moist, feminine folds.

Elise had a thought to pull her knees together, to prevent him from pursuing whatever he sought to do next. But she was boneless, breathless, and unable to do anything but grip the counterpane.

But when his tongue touched her throbbing womanhood, her torso lifted from the pillows beneath her. She had half a thought as to what she must look like, what with her breasts fully exposed, her gown in disarray, her knees spread open, a man pleasuring her betwixt them. A wanton, no doubt, although the image didn't scandalize her as much as it once might have. Not knowing that it was Godfrey who pleasured her—he was the only one who would ever see her like this.

She couldn't help the mewling sounds she realized were coming from her throat, nor could she stop the scream when his tongue set off an intense spasm she had never before experienced.

This... this is what her sisters had intimated with their comments about marital relations. This was what had been missing from her marriage to Lancaster. But she couldn't think of that right now. She couldn't think of anything but how positively exquisite her entire body felt just then. She was still experiencing a wave of pleasure punctuated with darts of delight when she realized Godfrey had ceased whatever he had been doing with his tongue and lips.

Elise dared a breath and stilled herself, wondering what was to come next.

At the sound of her scream, Godfrey's ministrations stopped, his head bobbing up from betwixt her legs to regard her with a look of concern. "Did I do that wrong?" he asked in a hoarse whisper. He lifted himself to his elbows and slid a hand up the front of her body.

Elise had to suppress the urge to giggle at the same time his hand set off another series of delightful shivers beneath her skin. *Will his simple touch always do this?* "I rather doubt it," she managed between attempts to breathe. She dared a glance down the front of her body and allowed a self-conscious grin when she found him regarding her with a wry smile.

Elise considered how she must look to him at that moment, her robe splayed open, her gown rucked up to her hips, the lace bodice no longer hiding her breasts from view. "You must think me a wanton."

Godfrey arched an eyebrow. He wasn't exactly sure what he thought just then, other than he was feeling a great deal of relief. Pride, too, in realizing he had accomplished part of what he set out to do that evening. His wife seemed happy. Pleased. And, god, but she was lovely. Like a woman out of a painting created by a Master with only sexual gratification on his mind. "I only wanted to please you," he murmured.

Lifting her torso so she was supported on her elbows, Elise angled her head to one side. "Then you have succeeded most assuredly, my darling," she murmured. She rather liked the look of relief that seemed to come over his expression, as if his entire reason for living had been validated. A naughty thought had one eyebrow arching up. "May I attempt to return the favor?"

Marital relations with Lancaster had never been like this. He had never made love to her—never pleasured her or prepared her for the assault of his manhood into her body. A few minutes of thrusting, a few grunts, and he took his leave of her body and of her bed.

There was a time she thought to learn what she might do to change their quick couplings—more to keep him from pursuing pleasure outside of their marital bed—but Lancaster had made it clear he already had others who could sate his baser urges. *I can hardly tie up my viscountess to a bedpost, now can I?* he had asked that night.

Elise remembered the shiver of fear that passed through her, remembered how evil Lancaster's eyes had seemed that moment, as if he dared her to demand fidelity.

Her overtures unwelcome, she simply learned she was to be nothing more than an occasional tumble on the few nights a month he was reminded he needed an heir. She didn't remind him, of course, but she was quite sure his friends did.

Godfrey felt a thrill in hearing her endearment. *My darling.* He hadn't given any thought to what he might be called in private, but 'darling' suited him just fine. As for her offer to provide him pleasure—he could imagine any number of things she might do in that respect—but he also realized he wouldn't last much longer. His cock was throbbing, and if she so much as touched it, he was sure he would be spent before he had a chance to bury himself into her soft body.

"On any other night, my sweeting, I would welcome the favor, but I fear I will not last long. I cannot abide the thought of spending another day as a..." He allowed the sentence to trail off and lifted one of her hands to his lips. He kissed the palm, then kissed the tips of her fingers, finally pulling one into his mouth to suckle it.

Elise inhaled sharply before pulling her hand from his grasp. She moved it to the back of his shoulder and did the same with the other, her gentle tug an indication he should come atop her.

Godfrey dipped his head to the space between her breasts as he moved up her body, the edges of his robe forming a curtain around her. He placed a gentle kiss there, aware of how her legs lifted from the bed, of how her thighs wrapped about his hips, and how her hands moved down the sides of his body. One reached between his legs and guided his manhood to her entrance, the touch setting off a groan from deep within him. The warm, wet tip hovered there for a moment before Elise lifted her hips until she was half-impaled, her hands moving to his buttocks to grip and guide him.

Godfrey dared a thrust, well aware it was what his body wanted—what it demanded. When he saw how Elise's chest rose and her head fell back in the pillows, desire for her nearly overwhelmed his senses.

He knew exactly what to do.

Or perhaps his body just knew, for he pulled out of her about halfway and then thrust into her again, this time more completely. Supporting himself on his elbows, he repeated the motion and nearly cursed. He knew he wouldn't last but one more thrust, and yet he wanted nothing more than to experience the pure heaven of making love to Elise for as long as possible.

How long could he stave off the inevitable?

.   .   .

$\mathcal{E}$lise marveled at how careful Godfrey made his moves, at how hesitant he seemed, as if he feared hurting her. But once he had thrust himself into her twice, a sort of excitement gripped her. Anticipation. She knew he wouldn't last much longer—he had warned her he was on the verge of whatever it was that men experienced just before they spilled their seed. Just before their bodies froze in a sort of agony, suspended, until the intense spasm of pleasure wracked their bodies and left them boneless and breathless.

"I love you, Elise."

The unexpected words had Elise pausing in an attempt to pull him back into her body, her hands still splayed over his buttocks. "I know, my darling." She pulled hard at the same time he moved to thrust into her, the perfectly-timed motion setting off a tickle deep in her body. Once he was inside as deep as he could go, she heard the growl she knew was the beginning of his release at the same time the anticipation that had increased in her seemed to give way. Warmth flooded her lower body as a wave of pleasure curled through her. She clenched on him in response, which set off another growl from deep within him.

A moment later, and Godfrey seemed to collapse onto her, his head landing next to hers, his labored breaths loud in her ears.

Moving her hands to the middle of his back, Elise sighed her contentment and waited for Godfrey's return to the here and now.

Although, if he merely stayed where he was, she wouldn't mind, she decided. Not one bit.

# CHAPTER 37
# WEDDING NIGHT WONDERS

*L*ater that night

At her look of bewilderment, Godfrey allowed a grin. "Just because I've never bedded a woman doesn't mean I don't know the mechanics," he assured her. "I own several rather salacious books on the matter. Illustrated tomes, in fact."

"French, no doubt," Elise said with a twinkle, her head settling back onto his shoulder.

His brief look up and slight nod to one side suggested she might be right. "However, they are sorely lacking in what comes before all the..." He paused to take her lips again, this time sliding his tongue between her lips to separate them and then giving her tongue a quick touch with his own. When he pulled away, he continued as if nothing had happened. "Thrusting and deep breathing and mewling and groaning."

"You've paid witness to it," Elise accused, her eyes wide. "In a brothel? Or a—"

"My father's bedchamber," he interrupted, not wanting her to imagine the worst. "Whilst he made love to my mother. Not a sight a boy of ten should see, I assure you," he said with an arched brow. "Or hear, either. I was about to admonish my father—"

"You didn't!" Elise whispered in shock, her eyes wide.

"I didn't," he agreed. "Not when I heard her speak the word 'yes' almost exactly the way you did a few moments ago. A rather welcome word to hear, by the way."

As if she couldn't feel any more heated, a blush colored her face. "I couldn't help myself."

Godfrey brushed his lips over her forehead and wrapped his arm tighter around her shoulders, pulling her closer. "My mother let out a scream I thought would raise the dead."

"I would never," Elise said with a shake of her head.

Godfrey blinked. "Well, I do not believe it was a scream of terror or pain," he countered. "I had the impression she was quite... satisfied, in fact."

Elise sighed even as her exposed skin seemed to glow with a deeper shade of pink. "I have heard..." She stopped, unable to say the word that almost came to her lips.

"Heard?" Godfrey prompted. He dipped his head to her collarbone and traced its silhouette with the tip of his tongue.

"Orgasms can be rather... enjoyable," she whispered, inhaling sharply as his tongue delved into the hollow of her throat.

"I have heard the same," Godfrey agreed, his lips skimming over her skin until they once again reached the edge of the barely-there bodice. With Elise's body left boneless and angled on several pillows against the headboard, he openly admired her state of dishabille. With the negligée and the tiny lace sleeve of her gown completely off one arm, she looked like the very naughtiest Greek goddess. "My compliments to your modiste," he murmured as he used his chin to once again push the lacy fabric over an erect nipple so that he might suckle it again.

"Madame Fiére," she managed before she inhaled sharply.

"I do believe 'fire' is an appropriate word for how hot your skin is at the moment," he murmured before giving her nipple a gentle bite. When she inhaled again and let out a sound of shock, far louder than she had when she was beneath him, Godfrey decided to repeat what he had done with the other.

He rather enjoyed how her bodice gave way to the slightest nudge so that her breasts were entirely exposed for his teeth and tongue. He was reminded of ripe, juicy peaches, slightly blushed red from the sun and warm and sweet. Urged on by her slight gasps and then even more when the fingers of one of her hands speared his hair, Godfrey dared to move one of his hands down her torso until he could gather up the filmy fabric of her gown.

Once the apex of her thighs was exposed, he slid the same hand down through her tuft of dark blonde curls. His middle finger parted her folds just as her body stiffened and he heard what might have been a sound of protest. He dipped his head to kiss one of her nipples again before asking, "Am I doing this right?" Elise wasn't putting voice to any protests, but then, she wasn't exactly saying anything to urge him on, either.

Elise inhaled sharply, about to admonish him for pausing in his ministrations. "I think so," she managed to get out, just before his finger brushed over the part of her body that seemed to throb with need. The spasm of pleasure caught her off-guard, forcing her to inhale again.

"No fainting on me," Godfrey warned as he kissed her nipple again, giving it a gentle tug with his lips just as he brushed over her swollen womanhood again with his finger.

The way her body suddenly arched against his touch had Godfrey pausing a moment. He slipped an arm beneath her waist, aware of how her body was at once boneless and yet tensed as if in anticipation of... something.

Her almost silent plea of, "Please, hurry," had him wondering just what he was supposed to hurry.

His movements?

His kisses?

Quickening the movement of his middle finger, he watched in delight as her chest rose from the pillows and her breasts seemed to swell before his eyes. Although he tried, he couldn't take one entirely into his mouth, but the combination of his attempt to do so along with how his finger was brushing over her womanhood faster and faster had her mewling a most welcome refrain. He replaced his finger with his thumb and pressed against her womanhood a bit harder. A bit faster.

The sound she made was nearly that of what his mother had emitted all those years ago. Not a scream, exactly, but close enough so he was sure she was in the throes of an orgasm.

Copying what he remembered his father doing, Godfrey quickly shed his robe and lifted himself over her body, positioning himself between her legs and lifting them so her knees were bent on either side of his torso. Although he didn't know exactly where he was supposed to press his manhood, she obviously knew, for one of her hands was guiding his throbbing manhood into her wet cocoon.

Godfrey couldn't help the groan of relief and pleasure he emitted just then. Nor could he stop the spasm that had begun even before he buried himself deep into her body, his seed spilling forth before he could even manage another kiss or an attempt at another thrust. The blinding light and stars reminded him of a night at Vauxhall Gardens, when fireworks lit the sky, their exploding bright lights dazzling him. But the accompanying pleasure was unlike anything he had ever experienced, different because Elise's arms were wrapped around his back, her fingernails gripping his skin so she left behind half-moon indentations that were both painful and pleasurable.

When her body arched into his and he heard her whispered, "Yes!", Godfrey gave up his attempt to hold himself up and over her, and collapsed onto her soft curves in submission.

"Oh, I do so love you, Elise," he managed before his vision went black.

. . .

*E*lise sighed as Godfrey's body fell onto hers. She supposed she should feel alarm at his sudden stillness, but from the feel of his pounding heart against her chest, she knew he was merely napping. He was still breathing, although his breaths were no longer so labored. No longer the gasps of a man in ecstasy.

*In my arms*, she thought with a hint of satisfaction. He didn't simply remove himself from the bed and hurry off to his own bedchamber as she expected, but rather lay nestled atop her body, his body bent so he didn't squish her into the mattress too much.

She remembered how she had slid her hands down the sides of his body, reveling in how his breath seemed to catch, as if he'd never been touched by a woman before.

*He hasn't been*, she had remembered thinking then, a grin of satisfaction displayed on her lips. *I am his first.*

*And only.*

*For the rest of our lives.*

When her hands had reached his buttocks, she had splayed her fingers, smoothing them over the surprisingly hard mounds and pulling them until she felt the tip of his manhood at her entrance. She heard as much as felt his breath catch again, almost amused at how hesitant he seemed.

"Make me yours, Godfrey," she had whispered, her lips nearly touching his ear. And then she had pulled with one hand while guiding his engorged manhood with her other. Her pull on him had been so hard, he had entered her all at once. Buried himself in a single thrust that had stretched her and filled her completely.

Although she'd been prepared for a bit of discomfort—sexual relations with Lancaster had never been a comforting experience—she was quite surprised to feel a tickle of pleasure race up her spine. That and a rather primal sensation course through her lower body as his sac collided with her quim. "Oh, yes," she had whispered, her body suddenly robbed of breath. She lifted her knees slightly—or perhaps he had pulled them up—pinning them at the sides of his torso—and she inhaled sharply when it felt as if he'd impaled her completely in one thrust. The tickle raced up her spine again and exploded in a spasm of delight that had her nearly robbed of breath. After that, shock waves of pleasure coursed through her lower body.

Sleep took her just then, leaving behind a slight smile on her lips and a soft sigh of breath.

*G*odfrey's return to consciousness was slow and filled with images and sensations. *I never want to leave this bed*, he thought as he considered what had just happened.

Stunned at how easily he had slid into Elise's body, Godfrey had half a mind to kiss her senseless over how she had simply seen to their coupling with a quick tug on his bottom. Even now, he was well aware of her fingers, of where they were and what they were doing.

Which was just as well given he didn't quite know what to do next.

He would have to see to those fingers later, he thought absently. Pull each and every one into his mouth, one after the other, and kiss and suckle them in gratitude. And then do it all over again every night for the rest of their lives.

He didn't want to move, though.

*This is heaven*, he remembered thinking, being buried so deeply into Elise Burroughs. "My love," he managed to get out on his next breath. And then the words he never thought to put voice to followed. "Although I've... I've never done this before, I do believe I shall do so as often as possible." His elbows pushed into the mattress on either side of her torso, caging her in place as he considered what he was supposed to do next.

Aware of how her nipples barely grazed the dark, curled hair on his chest, tickling him where they touched, he moved his chest ever so slightly. Her sudden gasp had his lips coming down to kiss a hardened nipple, and when her entire body seemed to arch up in response, he kissed the other.

He delighted in watching how her heavy-lidded eyes watched him, in how her lips, slightly parted, seemed to invite him to kiss her. So he did that, too. When he finally pulled away from the languorous kiss, he murmured, "I don't want to move. I want to stay like this for the rest of our lives."

When he realized her hands had moved up to his hips, he was reminded that he had to move. Needed to move. To pull out and push in, if he wanted to repeat what had happened a few moments—or was that a few hours—ago?

Besides having watched his parents for that brief moment when he was but ten years of age, he had paid witness to the act of sexual intercourse one other time—again, unintentionally. That's what had happened when he entered Lord Weatherstone's library without first knocking. Although he didn't suppose the knock would have been heard above the labored breathing and mewling and growling that had emanated from the leather divan.

He pushed his hips forward before he pulled out a bit, eliciting a gasp of surprise from Elise at the same time her torso seemed to meet his once again. Such exquisite torture, to have her beautiful soft body pressed into his, her nipples ripe and red in invitation. He nipped one again, rather relieved to hear her mewl of appreciation. He nipped the other as he became aware of the flats of her hands skimming the sides of his body, her thumbs reaching out to brush against his nipples.

The unexpected sensation beneath his skin had his body giving a start. And then it was if his body knew exactly what to do next. Thrust and retreat. Thrust and retreat. He likened it to a military campaign at first. Order the troops forward in a mass surge, and then retreat to regroup and do it again. After the first two or three thrusts, the analogy was so ridiculous, he nearly chuckled. He managed to stifle it by closing his lips over Elise's, kissing her until he found he couldn't because he needed to breathe. He could barely manage to inhale, though, as his entire body seemed to seize up, his insides contracting and robbing him of breath and any sense of the here and now. Lights danced before his eyes as an intense pleasure gripped his entire body—even down to his very toes.

A moment passed, and it was if his body had turned to gelatin. His arms seemed incapable of holding him up, his hips no longer able to move. He was quite sure he was crushing Elise into the mattress, but he had no energy to push himself off of her, nor did he want to. His head finally settled onto the pillow next to her head, and sleep deprived him of further thought.

Reaching out for a bed linen, Elise finally found the edge of the quilt and pulled it atop their intertwined bodies. Although she was blissfully warm—she was nearly completely covered by Godfrey's body—she feared his bare back and buttocks and thighs would grow cold and have him seeking his own bed should he wake up. She had no intention of allowing him to leave her bed on this night.

Elise allowed her knees to slide down his body until her feet touched the mattress while her arms wrapped around his back. The slight movement didn't seem to disturb his slumber in the least, but given how her body seemed to thrum, she rather doubted she would be joining him in dreamland anytime soon.

*What the hell had just happened?*

The intense sensations that had coursed through her body had been entirely unexpected. Altogether exquisite. Completely consuming.

Lovemaking with Lancaster had never felt like this. But

then, Lancaster had never truly made love to her, had he? He merely tumbled her, or bent her over the bed, claiming he preferred the padding of her bottom over the more intimate alternative.

Godfrey had just made love to her. Twice. Kissed her, caressed her, worshipped her before even making an attempt to claim her. Even then, she had been the one to make the move so they joined together, merged into one being, melded at the point where time seemed to stop. The only sensation besides the pure pleasure that seemed to consume her was that of a wash of warmth filling her lower body. That was the moment Godfrey seemed to lose himself, she remembered, when his entire body froze, suspended over her, the tendons in his neck straining, his chest broad, the muscles in his arms bulging.

The mere memory of it had her insides contracting once again, the now-familiar wave of pleasure a mere fraction of what it had been only moments before but still such a surprise, she nearly gasped.

The pads of her fingers traced the blades of his shoulders and trailed over the bumps of his spine.

What had he said just before she pulled him into her?

*I've never done this before.*

She was quite sure for just a fleeting moment that he wasn't going to come into her of his own accord. Or that he didn't quite know what to do. Or how to do it.

She certainly hadn't expected him to behave in such a *hesitant* manner. He was a grown man. Five-and-thirty, wasn't he?

*No. Six-and-thirty*, she remembered. His birthday had been just a few days ago. The day he had sent the letter with his proposal of marriage.

She had been so sure he had bedded women before. Courtesans, if not a mistress or two or three. Even prostitutes, although he never struck her as a man who would bed just any woman.

Still, she expected him to... to *take* her. To *possess* her. Strip her of all her night clothes, which he hadn't begun to accomplish given she still had most of her diaphanous gown around her body. Even the negligée was still on one arm even though it didn't cover any of her body.

She had expected him to simply impale her with his hardened manhood in a move that would leave her feeling, well, rather disappointed. She was his, after all. His property.

But he hadn't.

He had probably always thought she was his—and she had thought the same of him—given his promises from when they were mere teenagers. From when they believed their innocent love would conquer all.

And then he had said those words.

*I've never done this before.*

She nearly giggled at the thought before she suddenly sobered. Godfrey Thorncastle had never been in the company of a mistress—at least, not in public. Nor had there been a hint of gossip about his conquests in the bedchamber in *The Tattler*.

So, it was true what he had said. That he was a... a *virgin*. *Had* been a virgin, at least, up until just a few moments ago.

Elise nearly giggled. How ridiculous to think a man of his age and his rank wouldn't have bedded a woman or two in his lifetime. *No*, she thought, nearly shaking her head in the pillow. *It cannot be*. But it was.

*I've never done this before.*

The words echoed in her head. She remembered the look on his face. How unsure he had seemed. How... *hesitant* he had been.

Sobering, Elise stilled her fingertips. He hadn't bedded a woman before. Hadn't because he was saving himself for someone special.

Saving himself for...

Elise's eyes widened when she remembered his words.

*He was saving himself for me.*

The man who lay pressed upon nearly all of her body, and

whose manhood was still quite stiff inside her, had saved himself for her and her alone. Had she never become a widow —perish the thought!—he might have died a virgin, a man better suited to a life dedicated to the church.

Instead, he had saved his worship for her. Every movement, every kiss, every touch, every glance had been as if he had held it in wait for her. "Oh, Godfrey," she whispered, one of her hands sliding up his back and over his shoulder to rest on the side of his face. "Why didn't you tell me before tonight?"

But, then, he had, in his own way. In everything he did. In the things he had said. Of course, he had imagined the worst of her, but despite his imaginings, he still cared for her, still loved her.

Still worshiped her.

*After all these years*, she thought in dismay. To not take comfort in the arms of another when he could have had any beautiful mistress, any gorgeous courtesan. He had instead waited for her.

Elise turned her head slightly to kiss him, her lips meeting the corner of his mouth. She sighed a rather sad sigh, and then followed it with a happy one, for she found his one visible eye open and watching her. "I adore you," she whispered before giving him a kiss again.

G odfrey's eye closed as he allowed the simple words to permeate his addled brain. *Good God!* No wonder men seemed to want to have sexual relations all the time! Why, if he'd had any idea just how...

He stifled the thought before he had a chance to complete it.

*No.*

He would not have engaged just any woman for such an intimate act. Would not have spilled his seed into any other woman than the one on which his body was so comfortably resting. Would not have allowed another to see him naked and aroused. He would not have allowed another woman besides Elise to hold him like this, to kiss him so sweetly and murmur words he'd been waiting to hear for so long.

No. He was where he belonged this very moment.

He rather hoped Elise wasn't about to send him to his own bed. He was rather comfortable right where he was. Warm, and satiated, and cast in a golden red glow given off by the few embers still lit in the fireplace. Well, not all of him, he realized. Somehow she had managed to cover him with some bed linens, the sweetheart.

Knowing she still watched him, Godfrey lifted his head from the pillow and opened his eyes. "I do hope I'm not squishing you into the bed too much," he murmured. He managed to get an elbow beneath him so he could rest his head in one hand.

Elise grinned. "Not at all. In fact, you're not allowed to move. At least, not from this bed," she amended, deciding she wouldn't mind a bit should he decide that twice of what they had done was not enough on this night.

Godfrey leaned over then, his lips coming down onto hers in a slow, deep kiss. When he finally pulled away, he sighed. "I do hope you weren't too terribly scandalized by what I said."

One of her fingertips moved to his lips. "As I said earlier, I was honored, actually," she said quietly. She allowed a wan smile to touch her lips. "It's true then, what you said?"

"Hmm." The quiet murmur was accompanied by an expression that suggested he was disappointed. Or sad, perhaps. "If you don't count how many times I've *imagined* us making love," he whispered on a sigh. "Then, yes, it's true."

Elise grinned at that. "Pray tell, how many times do you suppose?"

It was Godfrey's turn to grin. "Nearly every night since the day we first kissed," he replied. "Which means we have quite the task in front of us if we're ever to outnumber the number of times we've made love in my imagination."

Her grin widening, Elise gave him a quick kiss. "I am ready whenever you are," she challenged.

Godfrey's eyes darkened as he gazed at her. "As I will be again rather soon, my sweeting."

Elise arched an eyebrow. "I believe you already are."

**CHAPTER 38**
**NINE**

*M*eanwhile, in Lord Breckinridge's townhouse

"By the way, I thought you a 'nine' at the time."

The sound of Adam's voice had Diana slowly opening her eyes. Warmth permeated her entire body, especially where he had pulled her against the side of his. "A nine?" she repeated, unsure of what he meant.

"A huge mistake on my part, I must admit," he murmured as a finger drew light circles on her bare arm. "I'm rather glad I didn't mention it when you asked." When Diana didn't respond, he allowed a grin. "You did ask how I rated you," he reminded her, his finger trailing down to her breast. It circled her nipple, eliciting a gasp from her before his lips followed it and gently nipped.

"I remember," Diana managed, wondering in which direction his mistake had landed on the rating scale. It was hard to concentrate when Adam seemed so intent on making love to her.

Again.

And then she remembered hearing something about a 'seven'. She lifted her head from his shoulder, a lock of hair falling in front of one of her eyes.

Adam thought she looked positively wanton by the dim light of the candle lamp on the nightstand, and he was about to suggest a course of action when Diana's eyebrows furrowed.

"A 'seven', wasn't it?" she replied, her brain having a hard time reconciling his comments about the number nine.

"Why, you're a 'ten', sweeting. Once I was close enough to see you clearly, I quickly revised my rating of you."

Diana allowed a huge grin before she kissed him on the lips. In mid-kiss, though, she frowned again. "Is a 'ten' the highest or the lowest on the scale?"

Surprised by the question, Adam allowed a chuckle. "Why, 'ten' is the highest, of course." He sobered as he continued to gaze at her. "But you must know, you're also a 'one'."

Blinking, Diana inhaled sharply. "In what way?" she asked in dismay.

"In my heart, sweeting. Number one in my heart." He inhaled deeply. "And that shall be the extent of my use of numbers on this day, my dear," he added. "I've warned you before. I don't have the head for mathematics."

Amused and a bit relieved at his comment, Diana settled her head into the small of his shoulder and sighed, rather relieved that at least she could do the numbers for the both of them.

# CHAPTER 39
# TEN

*Meanwhile, in the mistress suite at Thorncastle House*
"How do you suppose Breckinridge is getting along with his new bride?" Godfrey asked from where he had landed on the mattress just a few moments ago, his once-labored breathing finally settling into a more regular pattern. He lay staring up at the canopy above Elise's bed, rather mesmerized by the pattern of tufting that seemed to hide a good deal of the yards and yards of satin that must have gone into its creation.

He would have turned to lay on his side, but he found he had no energy to move. Even if the bedchamber was on fire, he didn't think he would be able to make it out of the bed.

He was rather gratified when Elise made the move to join him then, rolling over so the front of her naked body molded against the side of his. He did manage to move an arm so it wrapped about her shoulders, his fingertips lightly brushing her upper arm. His murmured, "Thank you," was barely audible.

Elise didn't admit she had been wondering the same thing, although her thoughts were more on Diana. The poor girl was a virgin and probably finding the marriage bed a bit uncomfortable on this evening. "Her mother was a courtesan," she replied, not addressing his query.

Godfrey's brows furrowed. "Is that supposed to imply anything in particular?" he asked, his voice betraying his confusion. Perhaps Breckinridge had just discovered his bride wasn't a virgin.

Sighing, Elise gave her head a shake where it rested on his chest. "I suppose not, but I can't help but think Lily provided her daughters with some education when it came to pleasing a man in bed."

Considering her comment for a moment, Godfrey thought Elise might be jealous of her niece. "I rather imagine Breckinridge will appreciate having all the help he can get. I know I do."

Elise blinked before lifting her head from his chest. "What are you implying?" she asked in alarm.

The viscount yawned. "Although Breckinridge has a reputation as a troublemaker—he was nearly expelled from Eton and apparently failed philosophy at Oxford—he's only ever been a prankster. He's never been caught in a compromising position with another man's wife, nor has he ruined any young ladies. And the man hasn't exactly had a string of mistresses."

Rather surprised to hear Adam Comber wasn't the rake she had imagined him to be, Elise still wasn't convinced Diana was in good hands. "Does he favor brothels instead?" she asked, concerned her niece might be contracting a rather awful disease this very moment.

Godfrey shook his head. "Doubt it. He loathes the idea of sharing a woman. And of contracting an awful disease," he added as his head finally turned so he could see his wife directly. He grinned. "God, but you're beautiful," he said as if he were seeing Elise for the very first time.

Elise couldn't help the blush that colored her face. Drowsy and still satiated from their early morning coupling, thoughts of Diana were replaced with her memories of what she and

Godfrey had been doing all night. She loved the sound of his growl and how his arm had wrapped around her shoulders to pull her closer. She sighed when she felt his lips place a kiss atop her head.

"Thank you for marrying me," Godfrey whispered, the backs of the fingers of his free hand once again stroking her bare arm.

"Thank you for asking." She smoothed a hand over his chest, her fingers separating the graying curls until her palm rested on his stomach. "I wouldn't have had the nerve to do so."

Godfrey gave a chuckle, his chest rumbling with amusement. "I rather wish you had. We might have been married long ago had you done so."

Elise didn't have the heart to tell him it was unlikely she would have offered—or accepted—an offer of marriage any earlier than when his arrived. Sometimes, the timing just didn't work quite right in life. "Would you have been ready to be leg-shackled any earlier than this day?"

Inhaling, Godfrey considered the question. "If I'd known then what I know now, then yes, of course," he replied, managing to lift his head to regard her.

"Now you sound like a bounder," Elise accused, a hint of a grin touching the corner of her mouth.

"Never," he replied as he settled his head back into the pillow. It was several moments before he said, "I don't wish to move." His words sounded every bit as drowsy as she felt.

"Please don't," she managed.

"I don't think I could if I wanted to," he whispered. "I wasn't aware a man could... " He allowed the sentence to trail off as the fingers of his free hand seemed to form a varying number of numbers. He dropped his hand to cover hers, deciding it was better if he didn't admit his ignorance as to how often a man could make love in a single night.

Although he'd heard the young bucks at the club claim they could perform three or four times in one night, he never believed them. Now they would never believe what he had managed—at his age—in one night

Elise allowed a giggle. "Three? Or four?" Although she felt a hint of soreness at the apex of her thighs, she was quite sure she would accept him into her body once more should he be so inclined. The sensations he had created in her were far more delightful than a bit of discomfort could counter.

The formation of his fingers into the number 'five' had her head bobbing up from his shoulder. "By the way, what does this mean?" she asked as she lifted both hands over his chest, her fingers splayed out. "Is it some sort of fan speak? You were doing it when I spotted you in the bow window at White's."

Godfrey angled his head in an attempt to make out what she was doing. He managed a chuckle as one of his hands took hers and brought it to his lips. He kissed a knuckle. "That's a ten, my sweeting."

Elise blinked. "A ten?"

Godfrey grunted an affirmation as he settled his head back into the pillow.

"But what does it mean?" she asked, hoping he wasn't already asleep. He had a tendency to nod off after they made love.

His eyes were closed but his lips widened into a huge grin. "You're a ten, Elise." There was a long pause, as if he had drifted off to sleep in mid-thought. "You've always been a ten."

Elise considered his words for a moment. "Ten is... good?" she ventured, hoping he wouldn't go to sleep and leave her wondering for another hour or two.

The beginnings of a chuckle rumbled beneath her head and finally exploded into laughter. "The best," he replied. "The very best."

Settling her head back into the small of his shoulder, Elise allowed a satisfied grin. "Five," she sighed.

A moment passed before Godfre lifted his head from the pillow and regarded her. "Five?" he repeated.

Elise nodded, her expression a rather happy one. "We get to make love five more times before leaving this bed."

Godfrey blinked, deciding he wasn't about to sort the math she was employing.

Five sounded good to him.

After another minute, though, he shook his head. "Only if someone brings us breakfast," he murmured. "Otherwise, I'll only be good for one or two more."

Her own stomach growling, Elise found she couldn't agree more. "I don't suppose this is the time to remind you the servants have the day off."

Godfrey allowed a happy sigh. "Not the cook. I made sure there would be food," he countered in a hoarse whisper.

Elise grinned and settled back onto his shoulder. "Five it is, then."

# CHAPTER 40
# TWO?

*The following night*

"A week ago, I didn't even know you. And now... now I can't imagine living a single day of my life without you," Adam said as he climbed into Diana's bed.

He had woken that morning to find her standing in the window, her face lit by the early morning sun and bearing an expression of contentment. She was wearing the night rail she had never had a chance to don the night before, looking ever so angelic despite the devilish things she had done to him in the middle of the night. She might have been a virgin, but she was certainly knowledgeable about lovemaking, he realized. The mere thought—and the fact that it was morning—had his cock ramrod straight and tenting the bed linens. When he asked if he could rejoin her in the bed later that night, she had been most willing.

Bless her heart.

They had spent that afternoon with an agent, touring available properties in several terraces and streets adjacent to Hyde Park. Their final viewing proved perfect, at least according to Diana. The townhouse had enough rooms and bedchambers to support several children, and it was close to the park. As for the cheque his father had given him, it proved unnecessary when it came to paying for the property, for the dowry the Duke of Ariley had sent the day before was enough to cover the entire purchase and then some.

Adam figured the *then some* would include bride clothes for Diana and a phaeton they could use when riding in the park during the fashionable hour. He was sure his mother would have more suggestions as to what he would require to complete his married life, but until then, he was content to believe they had what they needed.

Although he would agree to another go at shopping. He rather enjoyed spending time in shops with Diana.

After a quiet dinner and an evening spent discussing the move—Diana's furnishings were still at Warwick's and would be transported in dray carts to the new townhouse—they had retired to their bedchambers.

"Will you still be staying with me tonight?" Diana asked rather sheepishly.

Adam blinked. "May I? I feared I might have overstayed my welcome last night."

Her face blooming with color, Diana gave her head a shake. "Not at all."

Now that he had finally joined her in her bed and made slow, passionate love to her, and then had made his rather profound announcement, Diana opened her eyes to find him reclining on an elbow, his bare chest just inches from where she lay. She stared at him in awe, his words more welcome than any he had said before. "This is good news, husband, since you're now stuck with me," she said as the corners of her lips lifted in a teasing grin.

"As are the both of you with me," he murmured, pulling her so her back was pressed against the front of his body. One of his hands moved to her belly and caressed it lightly, sending shivers of delight beneath her skin. Satisfied when he heard the sudden catch in her breath—the thought of how easy it was to provide her pleasure had him rather proud just then—Adam closed his eyes as he kissed the top of her head. He settled back down into the mattress, his arm still holding her body against the front of his. He was almost asleep before he heard her delayed response.

"Both?"

Adam allowed a chuckle, which had the entire bed vibrating. "Yes, my sweeting. That bit of math I can do."

# EPILOGUE — A MARCHIONESS WONDERS

"I have the most glorious gossip," Adeline, Marchioness of Morganfield, said in a whisper. Her fingers were caressing her husbands ribs in an attempt to rouse him from the slumber he had fallen into once he had completed his latest round of lovemaking. There were nights he seemed almost insatiable.

Or perhaps it was she who wanted him more than once.

David Morganfield opened one eye. "Do share," he whispered hoarsely, clearing his throat when his first attempt came out rather garbled. His brain always seemed a bit behind after his wife had her way with him. He knew there was an ostrich feather somewhere near the end of the bed that she would wield if he didn't at least pretend to pay attention.

Or there might still be ice in the bucket next to the bed. He rather hoped it had all melted during their first coupling. Although he sometimes welcomed the combination of ice and mint, he found it would be beyond his appreciation at the moment.

He was exhausted.

"Lady Lancaster married Lord Thorncastle yesterday," Adeline whispered in his ear.

Both of Morganfield's eyes opened. "Indeed?" Was all he could manage.

"As did Lord Breckinridge, although no one seems to know much about his bride," she added, her voice pitched as if she hoped her husband could provide more information on the matter.

"Breckinridge?" he repeated. He managed a frown. "I hadn't heard he was even in the market for a wife." The thought of a particular bet in the books at White's had him stiffening a bit.

Adeline managed a sigh of frustration. "You're no help," she accused. "I was hoping you knew something about his wife."

Morganfield sighed. "Do you have a name, perhaps?" If it was true that Breckinridge had married, then he stood to lose a bit of blunt over it. *Damn that Fennington*, he thought in annoyance.

Adeline smoothed her hand over his chest and wondered if there was any ice left in the bucket. "Diana Albright was the name on the order for dance slippers at Carter's," she said, as if that bit of information was useful.

Familiar with the name, Morganfield settled back into the pillow. "Diana Burroughs, actually. She's the Duke of Ariley's daughter," he whispered, hoping he would be allowed to sleep now that he had provided her the information she sought. He had no idea how shoes at Carter's mattered, but he wasn't about to ask.

Adeline blinked several times. "Do you suppose Aimsley knows?" she asked in awe. She was really wondering if Aimsley's *countess* knew the identity of her new daughter-in-law. The woman was the queen of gossip. Could probably write her own gossip rag should she be so inclined.

Remembering Aimsley's comments about having to increase his son's allowance, Morganfield just then realized why that might be. "He knows," Morganfield replied, his voice barely audible. And since Aimsley's countess had the earl wrapped about her pinky—both of them, in fact—it was a sure bet she was well aware of the marriage. "She knows, too," he added with a grin, remembering that any money he had lost to Fennington would be gained from Thorncastle's marriage.

Some bets were sure bets, no matter the numbers.

"Oh," Adeline replied in a voice filled with disappointment. "I was hoping to share the news during tea tomorrow."

Morganfield pulled her down onto his chest and ran his fingers through her raven hair. "Well, you can tell everyone that Lord Breckinridge is married to Lord Thorncastle's new niece," he offered, thinking few would figure out that particular relationship.

Adeline's eyes widened. "Oh, do you suppose *he* knows?" she asked in awe.

Closing his eyes, Morganfield decided to feign sleep instead of saying, "He knows."

Sometimes Adeline needed to do her own math.

# EXCERPT



"Where do you suppose they are?" Adele asked for at least the tenth time since she and the earl had arrived at Torrington Park. Although Graves, their driver, admitted to some trouble in negotiating the snow-covered road, he had the coach-and-four arriving in the late afternoon. The servants' coach—the coach that held their valet and maid as well as their trunks—was to leave a bit later, if only because one of Adele's trunks still hadn't been loaded by the porter when they departed *The George.*

Glancing out the same window Adele stood in front of, Milton allowed a sigh. "I told Haversham to get to the nearest coaching inn if he had the least bit of trouble. His coach is far heavier than the one we rode in," he reminded her.

"And if they got stuck?" Adele's voice was filled with worry.

"Now, now. There's no need to fash yourself. They won't get stuck, and even if they do... " The earl paused, not having given that possibility a thought. There was that fairly deep snow drift just outside of Darlington. "My valet is a clever man, and Haversham has been a driver for me for years. He knows the way, as does Higgins, for that matter. Banks knows all the coaching inns. Higgins is a crack shot, so I rather doubt a highwayman will give them trouble. They're fine, my sweeting."

He hoped his voice sounded more sure than he was. Truth be told, he was more worried than he had been before Adele put voice to her concern. Perhaps he shouldn't have ordered Banks to spend an extra day or two in Darlington. But just to make sure the valet followed his orders, he had given Haversham a sovereign and told him to be sure they stayed in the town at least two nights.

Besides, the extra days would allow a few more horses and lighter coaches to pack down the snow. The mail coach from Edinburgh would also help establish a track they could follow. Until then, it would be nearly impossible to get a heavier coach through.

In the meantime, he and Adele would manage without the servants. He knew he could.

He merely had to convince his countess she could, too.

# ABOUT THE AUTHOR

A self-described nerd and lover of science, Linda Rae spent many years as a published technical writer specializing in 3D graphics workstations, software and 3D animation (her movie credits include SHREK and SHREK 2). An interest in genealogy led to years of research on the Regency era and a desire to write fiction based in that time.

A fan of action-adventure movies, she can frequently be found at the local cinema. Although she no longer has any tropical fish, she does follow the San Jose Sharks. A member of Novelists, Inc. and frequent speaker at book conventions, she makes her home in Cody, Wyoming.

*For more information:*
www.lindaraesande.com
Sign up for Linda Rae's newsletter:
Regency Romance with a Twist

www.ingramcontent.com/pod-product-compliance
Lightning Source LLC
Chambersburg PA
CBHW030609170726
48283CB00002B/528